Donald Barr Chidsey

THE

WICKEDEST

PILGRIM

WILDSIDE PRESS

To Mary Ann Chidsey

WITH ADMIRATION

All Biblical quotations in this story are from the Geneva—the so-called "Breeches"—translation. The Authorized (King James) Version had been published at that time, but it was still expensive, and the Pilgrim Fathers all used the older version.

The Wickedest Pilgrim

Chapter One

Sal Boyd was drunk. He slithered on a cobble, and in falling heeled with one hand a horse apple. He belched indignantly. *"God verdomme,"* he muttered; for though as a seafaring man he could curse in five languages, Dutch seemed the most appropriate here.

It was dark, and there was nobody about. A drizzle filmed the air like fog. The mud between paving stones was as stubborn as glue. Sal rose lumbrously, for he was a large man, and when he struggled on down to the quay it was as though he forced his way through hip-deep water. He panted. With a leather sleeve he wiped sweat from his face.

There was a cock, only one, the boatman asleep. Sal all but capsized it when he dropped in, rocking a series of wavelets across the Catwater.

"That one, over there."

Unsteadily he lowered himself to a sitting position in the sternsheets. He was fighting sleep.

The cockman started to row; but he seemed puzzled by Sal's choice. There might have been thirty vessels at anchor in the Catwater, the inner bay of Plymouth, this night of September 5, 1620.

"Matey, I'll take you there, sure. I'd take you to the gates of Hell for a pennypiece. But are you—"

"Don't want to go to Hell, yet," Sal muttered. "Time enough when I die."

"—sure you've got the right one?"

"Beefwit," Sal said wearily, "don't you think I know my own vessel?"

It was midnight or even later, and the city was still, as was the Sound, no church bells tolling in one, no ship's bells in the other. When the boatman ceased to row and there was no longer the creak of tholes, the only sound was a sad susurrance at the prow, and even this faded as they were gulped by the shadow of a ship. Softly, apologetically, they nudged the larboard side, at the waist. Grasping the thwarts, Sal Boyd rose. More by instinct than by sight or feel, his hands and then his feet found a ladder. He caught a deep breath, shaking his head. He dropped a coin to the bottom of the cock.

"Look, matey, could it be that you're off of—"

"*Baissez mon cul,*" whispered Sal, as he climbed aboard.

The deck was deserted. The usual clutter of gear was there, as at all times but especially before a sailing—pinrails, cleats, ringbolts, chocks. With this Sal had no truck, for he was concerned only with powder and ball, with pinstocks, lanyards, match tubs, and the brass and iron pieces themselves, all below just now.

He decided not to risk the long trip to the forecastle. It stank. So, no doubt, did Sal; but he would be less aware of his own odor out here in the open. Unlike so many mariners he knew, he had never been afraid of fresh air. And the rain had ceased.

It took him a long while to get to the mainmast, though it was only ten feet away. He was wary. Drunk, it was harder to walk a deck that was still than to walk one that rolled; he fairly *sneaked* to that mast.

Somebody took his arm. Sober, he might have been startled, for he had heard no step. As it was, concentrating on the mast, he shook himself impatiently, not turning, like a dog that has just emerged from water.

"Brother, can I help you?"

"You can take your bloody hands away, that's what you can do."

"Brother, if you'd only let me—"

"Aw, bing a waste, ye son of a punk!"

He whirled, and punched the man full in the face. Then he teetered, windmilling his arms in order to regain his balance. As soon as he dared, he grasped his dagger, ready to draw, since he assumed that the other would return an attack. Nothing of the sort happened. The man turned away, sobbing, slubbering, and lurched into the shadow of the aftercastle.

There was no other sound, and no shadow stirred.

Sal shrugged. Very carefully he returned to his task, and in time he made the mainmast. He allowed himself to slither down this, his hands flat, until he sat on deck. This was foreward of the mast, not aft, where the knight was, so that he had an un-obstructed space in which to stretch his legs. He sighed and rested his head against the mast. It was hard; but Sal was accus-tomed to hard things.

Sleep swept over him with a black, roaring rush.

Chapter Two

When he woke he was at once conscious of the motion of the ship. This did not fubble him. Their vessel victualed and watered, for several days they had been itching to up-anchor. Plymouth was not for such as them. The authorities had bombarded them with writs and stay orders, but in matters such as this the skipper was as slippery as any eel. No doubt he had abruptly found himself in the free and had given an order to sail, even though it was night, fearful that some crafty lawyer might concoct yet another obstruction. That was the way it was in this line of business. You got used to swift departures.

The sounds too were familiar. Without having opened his eyes, Sal recognized the querulous squeal of timbers, the rattle of sheaves, footsteps thudding the deck as mariners dropped from above, a wind that moaned through the shrouds . . . All was well. They didn't need him now, and they'd leave him alone as long as they could. Time enough for the guns to be run out when they were off soundings and could start looking about for a prize. Meanwhile he'd go back to sleep.

Then there was another sound, a nearer one, and it jolted him, for it was the sound of children's voices.

> "Sally go round the sun,
> Sally go round the moon,

Sally go round the chimney pots
On a Saturday afternoon."

Was he dying? Was his past life streaking through his consciousness? He hadn't heard that air since he was a tot in London.

"Eeny, weeny, winey, wo,
Where do all the Frenchmen go?
To the east and to the west
And into the old crow's nest."

Now, *those* words he never had known, though the melody
was old enough. So it wasn't memory. Frightened, he opened
his eyes.

There were nine or ten of the children, all neatly dressed, and
they were holding hands and circling Sal—and the mast—very
slowly, solemnly, doggedly, while they continued to sing.

"Itzey, mitzey, titzey, tool,
Ira, dira, domin-*oo!*
Oker, poker, dominocker,
Out goes *you!*"

They all stopped, and pointed their fingers at him.

It was disconcerting. Sal's eyes throbbed, and no doubt were
red. He would have liked to close them for an instant, but he
was afraid to. He tongued his lips—tentatively, as though not
sure whether they were still there.

"Hello," he said at last.

Mariners scurried by, paying no heed to the children or to
Sal. Back on the poop an officer shouted.

The children regarded Sal.

"Who are you?" one asked.

"Well, my name's Salathiel Boyd, and I'm a master gunner."

"Will you shoot off some guns for us?"

"Say, not just now, eh? I got a headache."

"You were drunk."

"Well, you might call it that. But—who are *you?*"

A boy said: "My name's Wrestling."

"Are you sure?"

"That's right. My father is Elder Brewster, but he's at prayer."

"I see."

"And this is my brother, Love Brewster."

"How d'ye do, Love," Sal said.

There were no further introductions, for the children had tired of Sal, and they joined hands and began again to go around the mast, singing a different song.

> "Ipsey wipsey spider
> Climbing up the spout—
> Down came the rain
> And washed the spider out."

At this point the officer who had shouted from the poop came down into the waist, and with arms akimbo, staring over the heads of the bobbing, revolving children, regarded Sal Boyd.

Sal had never seen him before, and didn't like him.

"Now, who are *you?*" this officer asked. "You ain't one of these saints?"

"I'm no saint, no. What're you talking about?"

"And I know you're not a member of the crew."

"Then you know too much. I happen to be the master gunner of this vessel."

"Master gunner my arse!"

"Who wants it, apple-squire?"

"We've got a gunner. Joe Webster."

"Never heard of him. When did he sign on the Meermin?"

"The—the—the Meermin! Well, I'll be a Dutchman!"

"If you was a Dutchman, that would make sense," Sal pointed out. "All Captain Oosterlinck's officers are Dutch. Naturally."

"Ah, ah, you're one of Oosterlinck's men, eh? I thought you looked like gallow's meat."

Sal surged to his feet. Though his brain was clobbered, he had an inkling of what he had done. But no matter where he was, on no matter what vessel, he wasn't taking talk like that.

"Lookee, if it's a fight you want—"

"This ain't the Meermin, my fine pirate! This is the May-flower!"

"Which Mayflower?"

"And you're going to see the skipper, right now!"

Sal, shaking a groggy head, pushed through the children, who paid him no mind.

"You can bet your ballocks I am," he cried.

The children closed their ring, and continued to circle the mast.

> "Out came the sunshine
> And dried up all the rain—
> Ipsey wipsey spider
> Climbing up again."

Chapter Three

Christopher Jones was a man of middle age, thick, flinty, each eye a purple squirt of vinegar.

Sal, who had always believed in the offensive, pounded the table.

"You got to put back! Just because I picked a henheaded boatman—"

"You were drunk."

"And is there any law against that? Just because I get aboard of the wrong vessel on a dark night, that doesn't mean I have to go all the way to—to— Well, where *is* this ark headed for?"

"America."

"America!"

"Aye. The northern part of Virginia Land, near the mouth of Hudson's River."

"I won't go!"

Captain Jones hawked, and spat.

"You'll walk back, then?"

"No, you'll *take* me back!"

This was in the poop house, a low-ceiled chamber about sixteen feet deep and as wide as that at the forward end but narrowing in the stern. However, it seemed much smaller by reason of a temporary partition, a series of screens, on the other side of which, Sal gathered, extra passengers were quartered. The ship swarmed with passengers, rather dowdy ones, men and women alike, besides the children.

"See here, we've been cooped up for weeks, and supplies running low. D'ye think that now we've got a wind at last I am going to put back to deliver one lousy Sallee pirate to his fellow cutthroats? Because if you do, you've got another think coming."

Sal got taut, and the mate, right behind him, took a firmer grip on the cudgel he held. There wasn't much room for a swing, but no doubt the mate was expert with this weapon.

"We're not pirates! We're privateers!"

The Hollanders and Zealanders had lately patched up a peace with Spain, after many years of war, and the Beggars of the Sea, those formidable freebooters, were out of work: they lacked legitimate pickings. Many—Simon de Danser of Amsterdam, Jan Jansz of Haarlem, who had "taken the turban" and was known among the Islamites as Murad Reis, Mathys van Bostal, Sal's own Captain Oosterlinck—never had known any other life. To be plunged into peace was too much for them; and they had taken service under the obliging Emperor of Morocco, a potentate of whom King James was, on paper at least, an ally—though the King of Spain wasn't.

Christopher Jones shrugged.

"Call it what you like. Anyway, we're not putting back. Nor will I heave to for a transfer, if we should meet anybody. That might mean losing this wind, and I've got every bonnet cracked on. I guess you're coming with us."

"I guess I am," miserably.

"I don't know where you'll sleep. There ain't an inch left in the forecastle, or anywhere else."

"Say, there's the truth, Captain. I never saw so many passengers anywhere. How many've you got?"

"A hundred and two. And now you."

"I'm no passenger. I'm a gunner."

"We don't need a gunner. Webster's plenty, with only four falconets. I don't know what you'll do, Boyd. Just keep out of the way, I guess."

"What about food? You can't let me starve."

"What makes you think I can't? Lookee, Sallee, you're not having any of the crew's rations—not unless some of 'em're willing to split with you, which I don't think they will. The passengers—oh, that's up to them. They carry their own food and beer. They're a highly holy pack, though, and maybe if you do enough psalm-singing they'll toss you a crust. Or maybe not. Anyway, I want them to have a look at you."

He addressed the mate.

"Fetch Elder Brewster and also Master Martin. I'll take care of our 'privateer' here. He won't get frisky."

"Why two?" Sal asked, when the mate had gone.

He was a sailing man, and he took what came. There would be no sense in getting sore. Also, despite himself, he couldn't help sympathizing with Captain Jones, a much put-upon man.

"Because one's a saint and one's a stranger. The saints are separatists. Come from Leyden, most of 'em. The others are very religious too, but they don't belong to the same church—whatever that is, some sort of crazy Brownist congregation, as far as I can make out. So I want both sides represented in everything I do. To keep the peace. This is going to be a long voyage, Boyd."

"Why do they want to go to America?"

"To settle."

"To *settle?* Why, it's all swamps and wild shrieking savages, from what I hear. Never been there myself."

"I've never been there either. And for the life of me I can't see why anybody'd want to go. But then, I'm not a Brownist."

Martin was a red-faced, square-faced man, pugnacious, positive. He glowered at Sal.

"Never saw him before. And let me tell you right now, he's

not going to be eating food that was paid for by the adventurers. Not as long as I am responsible for those accounts."

Elder Brewster was otherwise. He was smallish, and mild of manner; and though most of the passengers, from what Sal had seen of them, were young, and the children were many, "elder" suited this one, who must have been fifty. He grinned at Sal, a greeting that could have caused him pain, for his nose and upper lip were blue with bruise.

"I'm sorry about that punch, sir," Sal blurted.

"My fault," said Brewster. "I should have given you more warning."

"Why didn't you smash me back? Half a sneeze would've knocked me over."

"It might have been better if I had turned the other cheek."

"I didn't hit you in the cheek, sir."

"You didn't seem in a mood to listen. No, Captain, I can't say that I have never seen this man before. It was only once, early this morning. But we can't let him starve."

"He'll not eat out of company rations," Martin stormed.

Sal started: "Why don't you go out in a cow pasture and pull your head over a—"

He paused. Captain Jones snickered, but Elder Brewster leaned forward politely.

"Yes?" asked Elder Brewster.

"Never mind—sir."

"Well, we'll try to arrange something," Elder Brewster said.

An embarrassed silence followed. On each side of this cabin was a window, and through these Sal could see that already they were well out—past Mount Edgecombe—and bowling along. He saw no other sail. Nor was any likely to be putting in, with the wind, as it was now, straight from the south.

"Those kids I met in the waist, Love and Wrestling," Sal said. "They're yours, sir?"

Brewster beamed. When he did this he had wrinkles that

jumped across his face as though to greet the person he addressed.

"Aye."

"They're dink, I'll say that for 'em. But—why'd you ever call the boy Wrestling?"

"Wrestling-with-the-Devil is his real name. We just call him Wrestling for short."

"I see."

Captain Jones stacked papers, harrumphing. He put a toothpicker into his mouth.

"So that's settled. Master Clarke, this is a prisoner-at-large. As long as he behaves himself, let him alone. But if he causes any trouble—any trouble at all, you understand?—"

"Aye, aye, sir."

"—then hit him on the head. Hard."

"Aye, aye. Come along, you."

Blinking in the rowdy-dowdy sunlight of the deck, Sal Boyd looked around once again. He exhaled, easily resigned. An orphan, he was tough, ingenious, amiable except when drunk, and willing to meet the worst. Like a cat, he could land on his feet.

"If you haven't anything else to do," Elder Brewster offered, "perhaps you would care to join us in some prayers?"

"I thought your son said you were praying only a little while ago?"

"We pray much of the time, having so much to give thanks to the Lord for. Also, we sing."

"Oh? Well, it's clever of you to ask me, and I'd admire to join you most times, but I think that right now I'd best finish my sleep. Because my head feels like an anvil."

"Ah, poor boy!"

"And my mouth tastes like the blacksmith's bib. So, if you'll excuse me—"

The children were still going around the mainmast.

> "To market, to market,
> To buy a fat pig.
> Home again, home again,
> Jiggety-jig."

Sal implored their forgiveness for breaking the ring, though momentarily. They paid him no attention, and by the time he had resumed his previous position they were circling the mast once more, their determined voices raised.

> "To market, to market,
> To buy a fat hog.
> Home again, home again,
> Jiggety-jog."

Sal smiled, the sunlight upon his face. He closed his eyes, and went back to sleep.

Chapter Four

Mayflower might have been 170 or 180 tons, which was a lot
of ship; but she was stocked with a pinnace, an assortment of
settlers' supplies, wood for a long journey, and many hundreds
of barrels of salt pork, water, beer; and she carried more than a
hundred persons besides a crew of thirty. This made for elbow-
bumping.

Sal was used to short and rancid rations, a hard bunk, dirt,
disease; for these were the ordinary conditions of life at sea.
Especially was he accustomed to overcrowding. Every ship was
overcrowded when she sailed, to make allowance for the deaths
by scurvy, but your pirate vessel was the most uncomfortably
crammed of all. There were several reasons for this. Pirates were
not sure how often or where they might put in for supplies,
there being many port authorities who looked with disfavor
upon the profession, and so they stocked ships that might have
to hold the high seas for a long while. A pirate was even more
susceptible than a merchanter to manpower losses, there being,
besides sickness, battle. Guns too were growing bigger, and
called for more men to work them, to handle the matches, the
swabs, powder, ball. It was all very well for this floating con-
venticle to set forth with a single gunner, the man Webster, and
four falconets; but any corsair who hoped to strike fear into the

hearts of his victims needed an artillery park ten times that size. In addition to the gunners, a great many men on deck, men who yelled fiercely, making a show of their weapons, could be useful in causing the vessel overhauled to strike without a fight. No pirate cared for fighting if he could get out of it. Finally, when a prize was taken and stripped, that called for more storage space below. Or, if the prize was thought worth keeping, a squad large enough to sail her, at the same time holding the regular crew in subjugation, had to be transferred; and this meant still more men.

Oh, Sal was no stranger to close quarters! But he never had seen anything like Mayflower.

"Growl ye may but go ye must" was an old saying among seamen, and the mariners who handled this vessel were no exceptions. Dour of visage, sarcastic of voice, underfed, underpaid, overworked, most appallingly did they curse the conditions; yet they got their jobs done, as seamen will; and in a few days, Sal knew, they would settle down to the routine resigned disagreeableness of the forecastle, blasphemous only as a matter of habit, complaining only because complaint was expected of them. It was in no wise unusual for mariners to be queasy, even sick, the first day out. They had swamped their stomachs with the rich food of landsmen, laced, of course, with wine, ale, geneva. They had spent all their money. The first few days at sea, then, made up a time for bellyaching.

But—the passengers! *They* were the ones who should have howled their woes, like a dog baying the moon. *They* should have trumpeted their grievances. Yet they were silent. They permitted themselves to be pushed about, and even apologized for getting in the seamen's way. Without games or any means of amusement, they occupied themselves in the waist, the only place topside where they were permitted, by preaching to one another, reading from the Bible, and intoning psalms. They did not sit for these sessions, and neither did they kneel, but simply stood with their hats on, their hands clasped before them like those of schoolchildren about to recite. They were not austere of aspect, nor did they, save on Sunday, dress in black, as Sal had supposed that all separatists did. They smiled often, if distantly and somewhat dutifully; and their clothes, though not flamboyant, being the clothes of poor persons, featured a great deal of scarlet and blue, with a bluish bright French gray trimmed with pewter buttons as their favorite.

Clarke, the first mate, was fond of breaking up those gatherings in the waist, using as his excuse that the space was needed. Sal Boyd, who knew this to be nothing but meanness, always refused to go below. He might be a prisoner-at-large, he pointed out, but he wasn't taking orders from any *pudendo pendejo*.

"Now I don't know what that means, but you—"

"Why don't you try to guess?"

"—might remember what the Captain said. I could clap you into the darbies."

"Aye, you could. But you wouldn't have many teeth left by the time you got me there."

"Listen, if you—"

"Want to try?"

The saints and strangers, though they must have sensed persecution, obeyed. Meekly they went below, meekly (when permitted to) returning.

They were the sufferingest lot Sal ever had seen, determinedly martyrs. They never moaned, no matter what the pressure. The sickness among them all but caused Sal's own guts to wamble. Though the weather day after day went on being bland, the wind steady from the northwest, Mayflower moving with little roll, while they took over no green water so that the gunports could be kept open, and though surely these peaked, pale women and men were unaccustomed to rich food, nor had any of them ever known the pangs of hangover, below as in the poop cabin the smell of vomit was stifling. Half of the passengers, themselves

twisted in pain, emptied pails for the other half. Even on deck
the wretches spent most of their time lining the gunwale on the
leeward side, so that there was not always room for all of them,
and on occasion the very scuppers ran with sour-smelling stuff.
They always cleaned up afterward. And they would always
smile, if wanly, and wash their mouths and dab their faces with
water, being careful not to waste any.

"Won't you join us?" was what Sal heard most often in the
waist. It meant: wouldn't he participate in a prayer meeting
or listen to a preachment? For they'd assemble for worship, these
curious travelers, at the drop of a hat. They didn't need church,
chapel, meetinghouse; the very sight of an altar would have scan-
dalized them; and they numbered in their midst no clergyman,
only Elder Brewster, a man of God, surely, but not an ordained
priest; yet they were forever holding assemblies.

Sal, when sober, was an amiable man. He strove to please. The
mate he couldn't abide, and from the beginning he and the
husky young cooper were at daggers-drawn, but for the most
part he liked these mild, earnest passengers, even though he'd be
hanged if he ever got to comprehend them. It was instinctive
with him to make friends, ingratiate himself. He didn't really
mind the services, though the singing was nasal, monotonous;
but it graveled him to stand while at prayer.

For these separatists did not approve of kneeling. "Roman,"
they would cry. "Pagan."

"Millions of people do it," Sal would plead.

"Pagan!"

"Everybody *I* ever knew has always done it."

"You can search for your soul," he was told.

"I've got something more substantial to search for," he might
have answered just at first; but he never did, for he didn't want
to hurt their feelings.

There were a couple of mariners who were not members of
the crew but had been hired by the saints to serve them for a

year in the New World, and these, one named English, one Allerton, Sal found standoffish: they distrusted him professionally, as a pirate. Webster the gunner was a glum suspicious man with whom it was impossible to spin yarn. Nor did Sal hanker after the other members of the crew, who, like Allerton and English, eyed him askance. He thought them too gruff with the passengers. Sal had, however, gone out of his way to make up to the cook, a saturnine scarecrow called Harris, and from the galley he gleaned many bits of food—and of information.

Soon it would be cold. Sal had been sleeping on deck, as though this was the tropics. He had thought to try the hold, which held, largely, barrels; but the cooper, who had some sort of special authority there, or thought he had, put a stop to this. The cooper hated Sal.

The answer to this problem came unexpectedly from a Mrs. Bradford, a woman who had no children aboard—though she had left a five-year-old boy at home—and who perhaps for that reason took a special interest in Sal Boyd. Surreptitiously, almost as though she was doing a shameful thing, she lent him a long woolen cloak. It was warm in the poop cabin where she and her husband and eighteen or twenty others, besides the officers, had their quarters: so she told him. She would not need the cloak, she said. Wrapped in it nights, seated on a soft pine deck, his back against a mast, Salathiel Boyd was as snug as a bug in a rug. Weather never had meant much to him, who had led an unsheltered life, and only in the worst of rains would he consent to crawl under the longboat lashed on the larboard side of the hatch. For the rest, he kept to the open, his natural habitat.

Though certainly they were psalm-singers, these passengers were not what men called hot-gospellers. That is, they did not rant or snivel; they didn't thump their chest and roll their eyes, purporting to see the Devil behind every snubbing post. They disapproved of many things, and constantly were reading or

having read to them the Book, yet "thou shalt not" were words
Sal never heard cross their lips.

The attitude of Mrs. Bradford was typical. Soon others too
were offering him articles of clothing, but doing this secretly so
that he needn't feel silly to accept. He never did accept. The
cloak was all he needed.

It was the same with food. Sal gathered from what he overheard that these were poor folks, who had struggled to get the
money to make this trip, and their accumulated provisions must
last them not only for the crossing but, since they would land in
America in winter, for many a month more. Yet Sal never was
permitted to go hungry. The irascible Master Martin represented only the financial interests behind the strangers; he did
not represent their temperament.

Just at first it was difficult for Sal. For this there were two
reasons: most of the passengers were unaware of his status, if he
could be said to have a status, and all of them were so sick that
the very mention of food, even for somebody else, was a stab of
pain. But after a few days, as soon as word got around that this
genial if hairy ruffian was aboard the vessel by mistake, and was
penniless, offers to share food poured in upon him.

The saints would not make these offers in such a way as to
embarrass him, treating him like a dog that prowls around a
table. They did it quietly, with no smirk. And they did it again
and again.

Sal began to fear that his only worry would be to keep from
gaining weight. He began to think that perhaps this wouldn't
be such a bad voyage after all.

Then too, there was the Mullins girl.

Chapter Five

It was not until the third day that he saw her, his first sight being of her buttocks as she bent over the gunwale, a fact that was to trouble him, since it seemed indecent, even slightly sacrilegious. She must have been confined to the cabin all that while. He assumed that she had taken to her bunk at the first freshening of the wind, to remain there until the afternoon of the third day out, when Land's End long since had been dropped astern. He was sure that she had not been in sight when he awoke to see those tots song-stepping around him. Befuddled though he was when he rose then, he would have noticed her.

To Sal Boyd all women were hags or whores. He was no misogynist, and still less was he a cynic. He was aware that there were other kinds of women, but he never had known occasion to meet these. He couldn't remember his own mother, and if he had any sisters he could not remember them either. He had never walked out with a maid.

A sailor takes his fun where he finds it, which is usually near the shore, for what with his outlandish garb, his rolling gait, his vocabulary, so complicated and technical that it calls for an interpreter, he looks ridiculous when he gets a few miles from his own element; and he knows this. Among themselves seafaring men like to tell the story of a salt who came ashore at the end of a long voyage and announced, to the snickers of his companions, that he was shut of the sea. He had his pay, a pocketful of coins, but he did not spend this on the quay. Instead he put an oar over his shoulder and started to walk inland; and he said he didn't know where he was going, but the first time somebody asked him what was that thing over his shoulder, *that* was the place where he'd stop and settle down. Yes, they tell this tale, but it is to be doubted that many of them believe it. The truth is, the mariner gets nervous, edgy, uneasy, when he can no longer hear the slap of waves; and, as all the world knows, women along the waterfront are not invariably of high moral character.

Sal, then, when he saw a shapely backside outlined under a gown, never hesitated to admire it. He admired this one, whistling in amazement.

The women of the Mayflower, all married, most of them mothers, were admirable no doubt; as Sal knew, they were kind; but undeniably they were plain. Their angular walk, their stringy necks, and flat, unmammillary fronts held no charm for Mijnheer Oosterlinck's strayed gunner, who preferred his women, as he did his gin, raw.

This one was not like the others. Maybe she was not really a woman at all, but surely she was no child. The children, anyway, the dogged, indefatigable, undiscouraged children, were on the forecastle deck, where they were not supposed to be, only a few yards from where Sal had come to a stop, his mouth making an "O" as he whistled. The children were playing some kind of interminable patty-cake game.

> "Round about the rosebush,
> Three steps,
> Four steps.
> All the little girls and boys
> Are sitting
> On the doorsteps."

She who leaned over the gunwale jerked and shivered a little, so that the buttocks did a joggle, very pleasant to see. She couldn't have been wearing much about her middle, underneath that petticoat, was Sal's thought. What was she doing? Pulling in a fish?

It is another trait of the average mariner that when he approaches a woman at all he does so directly, for indeed he seldom has time to be circuitous, even if he knew how. Sal Boyd stepped to the gunwale, and he swept off his hat and held it across his heart.

"Can I be of any help?"

She straightened, wiping her mouth with a kerchief, and her eyes, when she swiveled them upon Sal Boyd, were hollows of pain, the cheek beneath them tinged with green. Yet she took the kerchief away, and even as she fought nausea she managed a grin.

"Thank you, I—I think I'm a little better now."

He could have kicked himself. A fish! He had been watching this happen for three days, and yet the sight of a pert and pretty behind had so unsettled him that he broke in upon its owner at the worst possible moment. Yet, again, he was glad that he had. It was good to look right at her. He too grinned.

"So God help me, ma'am, I didn't know. I thought maybe you was fishing."

He swallowed, his Adam's apple corking up and down. He laughed, and it sounded as though he had his head inside a barrel as he did so. He did not replace his hat, for he had forgotten it.

"It's all right," she whispered.

She was wearing the French gray so many of them affected. Bodice and petticoat alike were made of a new material from the farther Indies, expensive yet not showy, called calicut. They were somewhat loose: she'd fill them better once she got her sea legs. She wore no jewelry, not even the simplest ornament. Her head was bare, the hair wind-tossed, and this together with a skirt that Sal found shockingly short, for it showed her feet, lent her a somewhat hoydenish air—an air no longer noticed by one who looked into the seriousness and pain of her face.

It was a pretty face, for all its present pallor, for all the greenish shadows under the eyes, and the pinched nostrils, pale lips. No woman who has just been throwing up her breakfast should be expected to look lovely. Feed this one properly, and she'd be a beauty. Even now when she smiled the effect was dazzling.

It was a round face, yet not phlegmatic, not Dutch. The cheekbones were high, the mouth long. The eyes, though not really large, looked large because of their vivid coloration, a fine, rich, dark blue, almost like Parma violets, and in sharp contrast to the flat, straight, unexciting hair. The nose was small, slightly upturned, and there was a faint wash of freckles—they wouldn't have shown save in the sunlight—across its bridge.

"You'd better go back to your bunk," he said earnestly.

"Yes, I suppose so. I thought maybe a little air—"

"You'll be all right in a few days. It gets everybody, at first."

"Yes."

She paused. She swallowed, wincing. She might have been seventeen, as Sal estimated, but her sense of social responsibility was well developed. Putting aside her private misery, she sought words of politeness.

"You—you aren't one of us?"

"Not a saint, no. I guess I'm a stranger, ma'am. *Really* a stranger. I got aboard of this vessel by mistake."

That she hadn't heard Sal's story testified to the extent of her sickness.

"And so now I'm going to Virginia Land with you," he finished.

"I hope you're enjoying the trip more than I am," she said, and smiled again.

It was no wan smile of self-pity, such as might have been expected, but a full-blooded sunny expression that spread all over her face.

"Oh, I'm all right," he said. "I'm used to it. And you'll get to be, soon."

"I doubt that. But I'll try."

"You'll be all right in a little while," he assured her. "But right now, I think you'd better get back to your bunk."

"I'm sure you're right. Thank you."

"Can I help you, ma'am?"

"No, I can walk all right. Thank you again."

"It was a pleasure," muttered Salathiel Boyd, standing there like a great, gawky lout, still holding his hat over his heart, as he watched her make for the poop.

It was then that the cooper confronted him, disengaging him from his dream.

This cooper was a tall, heavy-set young man from Southampton, a port at which Mayflower had put in on her way from Holland to Plymouth, and where she had victualed. He was not a saint, and as far as Sal knew not a notably religious man, if he belonged to any church at all. He had been taken on at the last minute when the separatists learned that because of a new shipping regulation designed to protect stave timber they would be obliged to hire a cooper for this voyage. He had all the arrogance of youth and great strength, and from the beginning Sal had disliked him; but since the cooper was conscientious and spent most of his time tapping and otherwise inspecting the barrels stored below, the two had not often come into contact.

Now the cooper, using it like a maul, hammered a thick forefinger against Sal's chest, while Sal sheepishly replaced his hat.

"Listen, I want to talk to you—below."

"Now?"

"Now."

Normally Sal would have told the lad to go to Hell, but at this time Sal still had hopes of establishing a haven in the hold, a place to retreat to when the going got really rough in mid-Atlantic; and so he held his temper, nodding.

"All right."

It was dingy down there, and dark. All Sal could see was barrels, in serried rows, lashed against dislodgment. The ceiling was low. It would be no place for a fight, especially a fight between two such big men. But at least it was clean. And it was orderly. The cooper knew his business.

He didn't know Sal's.

"You stay away from Miss Mullins."

"Your daughter, no doubt?"

The cooper ignored this. He shook an angry head.

"You stay away from her. She don't want any Sallee rover pawing her with his dirty hands."

This was language Sal Boyd could understand. For a moment he was silent, and when he did speak it was with considered syllables.

"Listen, you Allobrogensian bastard. These hands are mine, and they always have been, and I'll put them wherever I want to put them, and if I should ever put them on you it'll be to yank both your arms off and beat your head with them. Bear that in mind."

He felt better as he turned and climbed the ladder. This voyage got more interesting every day.

Chapter Six

The separatists, though they did not wallow in disapproval, had one phrase that tickled Sal Boyd's ear. When they wished to caution a friend whom they deemed rash they'd admonish him "to preserve better walking."

Sal decided to preserve better walking in the case of the cooper. The burly young Alden had enjoyed a month of companionship with Priscilla before Sal came aboard, and if he considered her as good as his fiancée this was because he had known no competition. Not that he took Sal to be such! Sal was a scrap of garbage from the murky nether world of London, against whom Priscilla must be protected; and John Alden, who stood high in the estimation of her parents—he had taken pains to insure this—as a matter of course had appointed himself the protector.

This could lead to trouble, especially in a place where there wasn't much room to move about. Sal, though piqued, told himself, and sternly, that in the presence of this proprietorial young giant he would not give an inch; but neither would he go out of his way to seek a fight. To Sal, brought up in the streets of London, streets he had roamed like a wild beast, aggressiveness was a shield for the unarmored, the safest defense a vulnerable man could devise. Ever since he could remember, since baby-

hood, Sal had kept himself ready to do battle at any time and
with any weapons or with none. Fighting was essentially dirty,
and he saw no romance in it, no glitter. Not for him the punc-
tilio of the duel! Giving the other man an equal chance struck
Sal as stupid. His motto—he would not have been alive had it
been otherwise—was "hit before you get hit."

Among the separatists it was different. Sal sensed, aboard Mayflower, an unspoken scorn for his type of truculence. These soft-
spoken men had muskets and swords, not on their persons but
stored below, and Sal had been told, though he couldn't persuade Webster to show him, that they had four field pieces in
the hold. This was natural enough, since they were heading for
a wilderness inhabited by savages who from all accounts were
fiends, ferocious, bloodthirsty. The Mayflower passengers not infrequently squabbled among themselves, pale and passionate,
their eyes aglow; though whether these spats were concerned
with matters theological or only with money Sal had not learned.
But no fists were raised, or even voices. They tried to settle
things without fuss. Sal's own considerable talent for butting,
scratching, punching, kicking, gouging was wasted aboard of
this vessel. It would be regarded not with awe, but in a stunned
shocked silence. He knew this. He felt it. So it was that he
eschewed the company of the cooper.

Christopher Jones, Captain, had classed his passengers as
saints and strangers, and this was as far as Sal went for some
time. The saints had come from Leyden, where for many years
they had worked and worshiped away from their original homes
in England. They had left the Low Countries, Sal gathered, not
because of any persecution but in part because their children
were speaking only Dutch, forgetful of an English they had perhaps never properly learned, and in part because the lack of
decorum and even the frivolity with which the Dutch treated
the Lord's Day reflected an attitude too painful for the saints to

endure. These did not seem good reasons to Sal Boyd; but he said nothing.

A mild, sweet-smiling old man named Carver was the leader of the saints, as far as Sal could make out, though the one Sal had slogged that first night on deck, Elder Brewster, was also a personage of importance among them, as was William Bradford, a tall, deadly serious, much younger man, husband of Sal's cloak-benefactress.

Sal made note that the members of the Leyden group never did call themselves saints, though they called the others, about half of the passengers, strangers. Whenever the word "saint" was used it was used sarcastically. Whenever the word "stranger" was used it was used in pity.

The strangers, led by the loud-mouthed Martin, were a more heterogeneous lot. They were not separatists. Most of them belonged to the Puritan wing of the Church of England, being in favor of some reform, but reform from within. Others were indifferent, and only a few showed any inclination to listen when the saints preached.

Among these last was William Mullins, a pudgy, harassed man with light blue eyes and a distracted manner, a man who continually muttered to himself as though doing sums in his head. He might have been forty, or even older. He had sold his shop in Dorking, a draper's shop, and was one of the adventurers in this enterprise: that is, he had invested money in it, as had Mr. Martin.

It would have been hard to imagine a more *un*adventurous man, as far as appearance went, than Mr. Mullins, whom Sal Boyd at first regarded simply as the father of Priscilla. Yet in so crowded a place, and as day crawled after slow day, Sal began to ponder the mystery that was William Mullins.

Why should this pursy, absent-minded person, this man of paunch, sell his snug business to transport himself and his family—for besides Priscilla there was a Mrs. Mullins, a wan slight female of indeterminate complexion; Joseph, a much younger brother; and two servants, the Rigdales—to the wilds of North Virginia? Was he inwardly restless as outwardly he twitched? Did he yearn for the sight of lands, lakes, and forests never before seen by such as him? He hardly looked that way. Had he always longed to travel? Then why not take a trip on the Continent, which would be cheaper, safer, and less uncomfortable?

Money? Did he look upon this venture as a possible way to swell his beginning-of-a-fortune? Was he *that* greedy? It did not seem possible. Sal Boyd, who never had had cash for more than a few hours, had been told that the more you owned the more you wanted, the more you got to love the stuff; but he never had been able to bring himself to believe this. True, there were many stories calculated to prove the depths to which men had sunk in their scramble for gold. It was true too that the glazed eyes and ever-moving lips could be taken to indicate a miser; but William Mullins, though scarcely bright, did not look that mean. A capitalist about to sidle into a new world for the sake of fattening his moneybag would not take his family along.

There was another possible explanation. Mullins might be in search of his own soul.

Sal wobbled here, in his thoughts. He was not sure of his ground.

Mullins wasn't one of the Leyden group. He had never before been out of England. He wasn't a separatist. But though he was listed as a stranger, he might think of becoming a saint. So Sal decided, watching him, gauging him. Mullins attended virtually all of the meetings on the waist deck, and he prayed and responded with a fervor that was not just for show. He was devout. He wasn't forever quoting the Bible, and he did not thump his chest, but he was thinking about his Creator, and conceivably he had come upon this voyage for that sole purpose. Would he join the separatist group formally? Perhaps he had already done so, had stepped over the line, if there was a line to *be* stepped over. Sal couldn't know. But he watched William Mullins.

He watched Mullins' daughter even more assiduously. Priscilla was a delight. Once she had steadied her step and the color had come back into her cheeks, he was able to see a great deal of her. There was sewing to be done, but her mother was a brilliant seamstress, as was also Mrs. Rigdale, so that there was not much left for the girl. Sometimes she was assigned to keep an eye on her little brother, Joseph, but there were a great many children —more than thirty, and it could seem like three hundred—and they played well together under the eyes of sundry parents. Priscilla was too old to play with them, as she was too young to converse in an edifying fashion with the adults. There were two other maids aboard Mayflower, servants, but they were stolid, stupid, and poor company for Priscilla. There were eleven strapping young male servants, but these were unimaginative louts. There was another strapping young man, the strongest of them all, and independent, his own master and signed on only for one year—the cooper, John Alden. But he too, though thick-thewed, was thin of wit. He bored Priscilla, who preferred Sal, especially after the fifth day out when Sal, having succeeded in borrowing a razor, shaved.

They talked of a great many things, most of them inconsequential.

Priscilla was dismayed when he told her that he'd been drunk the night he boarded Mayflower.

"Don't you know," she asked with a primness not usual in her, "that strong waters are bad for you?"

"Wouldn't be any fun drinking 'em if they weren't."

"Don't you know that Bacchus has drowned more men than Neptune?"

"Well, sure. But the ones he finished off had more fun than the poor devils that got wrecked and then woke up with sand in their ears. Besides," Sal added, "I don't reckon I'll ever have money enough to drink myself to death on."

Countering, he reproached her for the shortness of her skirt. She colored at this. She explained that she had been growing fast and that her father said he couldn't afford to be buying new clothes all the time, so she'd been letting them out, a bit by a bit. She conceded, however, that this particular petticoat, which had no hem left at the bottom, already had gone as far as decency would allow.

"You'd better stop growing."

"Oh, I think I have. I mean—up."

He reprimanded her, too, though in the gentlest manner imaginable, about her habit of going around bareheaded. She said she saw nothing shameful in this. He said not shameful, no, but foolish. He pointed out that they were on the open sea, with heaps of wind; and what would her hair look like after a few weeks of that? It was straight enough already. Even if she had a gaffering iron—

"Oh, my father wouldn't let me use one!"

"You'll wish you could, if you don't keep covered up."

She could follow such reasoning. Next day and every day thereafter she wore a bonnet.

Her upbringing had taught her to take as sacred the fourth Commandment. This, as Sal long ago had noted, was a sign of the true Puritan. You might steal, murder, commit adultery, you might covet your neighbor's ox or his ass, or bow down to graven images, but still if you expressed repentence and prayed earnestly enough you could be forgiven, you might yet hope to see Heaven. But if you took a walk or kissed your wife or read a sonnet on the Lord's Day, you were doomed.

They always called it that—the Lord's Day. "Sunday" they esteemed pagan, idolatrous, whereas "Sabbath" was Hebraic.

When on the second Lord's Day at sea she came out of the cabin and saw all hands working, she was dismayed.

"It's an old rule," Sal assured her.

"I must speak to Captain Jones."

"I wouldn't. Half the grown-ups did that, the first time. You was still in your bunk then. And he didn't like it. In fact, he blew up like a volcano. This is his vessel and he'll run it the way he wants, he said. Only he said it stronger than that."

"But we can't stand by and—"

"It's an old rule," he told her again. " 'No Sundays off soundings.' The men even got a little rhyme about it:

"Six days shalt thou labor and do all thou art able,
And on the seventh holystone the deck and scrape the cable."

She giggled. She couldn't help it. And he shook a reproving head, grasped her arm, and started to lead her away from there.

"The first service is getting under way. May I escort you, ma'am?"

Chapter Seven

Sal crawled out from under the boat of a brisk October morning, and he felt very good indeed, expansive. He flexed his shoulders, then windmilled his arms, grinning as he felt the blood pound. It was good to be alive. It always astonished him.

They were booming along—six knots maybe. They must have been halfway over, the middle of the ocean. It was cold, but it was clear and bright, and the acrid odor of vomit was gone, for nobody was sick any more.

Soon Priscilla would come out of the cabin. He wished that he could greet her with something more substantial than a smile, with some gift suitable for a pert young miss aboard ship, even if it was just a piece of ribbon. He sighed, his shortcomings as a swain oppressing him. Though he had been all beams a moment before, now despite the weather's glint he felt sad, sorry for himself.

"All right, pirate, now I'm going to rip your guts out!"

Sal whirled, stepping backward, in a crouch; and his hand grabbed the hilt of his knife.

The man who faced him was tall, slab-sided, young, pale, gaunt, with dark hollows for eyes and hair the color of moldy hay. He had lately been sick, as his complexion testified; yet there was sarcasm, there was mockery, a challenge, in his mouth and in the way he held himself, swaying against the motion of the ship, his feet spread wide, fists on hips.

"Touchy, eh? But quick. Just like old times, eh, Sal?"

"Sawn Matthews! What the Devil are you doing here? I thought you was shut of the sea?"

The other shrugged, his earrings swinging.

"A man's got to live. If you could call this living. But what are *you* doing here, with this gaggle of psalm-singers? You leave Oosterlinck? Or did he throw you out, the way he did me?"

"It was an accident. I got drunk."

"It was never an accident before, when you got drunk. You always meant for it to happen that way."

"I woke up on this vessel. Different, eh?"

Matthews laughed as though it hurt his mouth, but his eyes shone still with mockery.

"Aye, a good bit different. Remember that place we careened in—Bahia Verde or something like that? Remember them bousing bouts? And the palm trees? And how you used to go swimming every afternoon? Damnedest thing I ever saw—a seaman that can swim! And then at night we'd have six, seven, eight of them native girls come aboard, for a couple of beads apiece, only we never could get 'em to go below with us, so instead we'd use the space forward of the anchor coil, which was pretty bumpy, but as Spitch Mitchell used to say even a bumpy ride is better'n no ride at all. Remember that, Sal?"

"You're, uh, you're crew here?" Sal asked.

"Do I look as if they'd made me sailing master?"

Sal nodded. The mariners of the Mayflower were only beginning to appear in their entirety. The first few days, even the first week, a good half of them would be laid up in the forecastle, too sick to work, hacking at their pluck, and weak. That was usual in merchant ships. It was not so in privateering craft like the Meermin. Captain Oosterlinck had made it clear that he wouldn't tolerate such inefficiency. He simply couldn't afford to. A man in that business had to be ready for anything at any time. This was the reason why Sawn Matthews here had lost his post: he was an honest man not because of his heart but because of the wambling of his guts perforce.

You never could advise mariners of that sort. If you asked them why they suffered so, voyage after voyage, and why didn't they stay on land, they just didn't know what you meant.

Mayflower, it would seem, had somewhat more than her share of these unfortunate seamen; and this meant that at first the able-bodieds, the ones who could get around, were seriously overworked. No doubt this was why Sal Boyd had not seen Sawn earlier.

"Saw you day before yesterday. Yes, and yesterday too," Sawn reported. "But I didn't get a chance to say hello. They're drivers, these mates. Buggering drivers, I tell you."

"Sh-sh!" said Sal, for some of the saints were passing, and Sawn Matthew's voice was a loud one.

"Why? Who're you sh-shing, Sal Boyd? Why, of all the bloody God-damn'—"

"Now, wait a minute!"

"Are you getting like them, for Christ's sake? What's come over you? Getting whittled and boarding the wrong ship, that's one thing. That's funny. Something to tell the boys about, over a bottle. But yesterday I looked down and what did I see but you singing with these bloody Brownists. *Singing!* Right as though they was real people!"

"They are real people," Sal said swiftly.

He startled himself, and was abashed by what he had said.

"I—I mean," he stuttered, "that they aren't half as upsy-Frieze as you might suppose, Sawn. Really."

"Oh?"

Matthews, fists still on hips, looked slowly around. The waist was filling with passengers who stumbled up, blinking, thick with yawns, from below. Sawn's mouth was magnificently curled.

"They look to me," he said at last, "as if they spit marble and piss vinegar. Do they?"

Sal had seen Priscilla Mullins come from the poop cabin. He touched Sawn Matthews's forearm.

"Well, it's been good to see you. We must get together again some time, eh?—and talk about the old days at Bahia Verde."

"You haven't answered my question yet, Sal. Do they?"

"But just now, well, excuse me."

Sawn stood there for some time, teetering on the balls of his feet, even though Clarke was bellowing for him aft. He shook a sad head.

"Poor Sal," he muttered. "It just don't seem possible."

Chapter Eight

Peace was not for the likes of them, though they were peace-loving and would have worked for it. With what a sudden savagery, with what a barbarous abruptness, did the change come! It was as though the Lord sought to scatter them with a whirlwind such as took Elijah into Heaven. At one moment all was serene, but the next was chaos, it was Pandemonium.

It started in the middle of the night, catching them when they were weakest, least prepared. Sal, who as was his wont was wedged between the mainmast and one of the knights just aft of it, Dorothy Bradford's cloak wrapped around him, was popped out of that place like a cork from a bottle, and went skittering across the waist, a starfish, all legs and arms. He was slammed into the scuppers on the larboard side, and there he lay stunned, gasping, so that the great sea that came tearing across the waist reared over a prostrate man. Sal saw it. He might have screamed: he did not know. He couldn't have heard himself anyway, what with the howl of the wind and the crack of canvas as sails were being whipped away. He really thought that that moment was his last.

The weight of water smothered him—it all but cracked his bones—and it knocked out of him what little wind had been left. He felt himself rise on that sea, back away from the gunwale a bit, and then he was propelled right toward it. He couldn't struggle. There was no question of resistance. The next instant he was over the side.

The water was so cold that it burned. It hissed around him like steam. A touch of Hell beforehand? A hint of what would come?

Something struck his cheek a stinging blow. He grabbed it and found that he had hold of a rope.

It was as though somebody had seen him being washed over and had thrown him this line. That couldn't, of course, be. The only other persons topside when the blow hit were an officer on the half deck and a lookout in the crow's nest, and those two, even if they knew of Sal's presence, and cared, would be having all they could do to hold on.

A halyard? That must have been it. A mainmast halyard that had somehow been torn loose when the canvas was carried away.

And if it was a halyard, and if it had not been torn entirely free, then it might hold him.

He couldn't know, just at first. He wasn't sure which way was up and which down, or even in which direction was the May-flower. All he knew was that he gripped a rope in both his hands and hoped to God it would tighten.

It did. He was not sure of this for a little while, so turbulent was the water. Then he began to feel it, unmistakably, in his elbows and shoulders. He was being pulled. He was being towed behind the ship.

For some time he could do nothing more than hang on, fighting to get back his wind. At last he took a deep breath, and started to haul himself in.

Two seamen who had just tumbled out of the forecastle and who did what they could to help Sal clamber and slither back over the gunwale said afterward that his lips were working all the while. They assumed that he was saying his prayers; but in fact he was cursing.

There was nothing superstitious, any more than there was anything lubberly about Salathiel Boyd. He did not believe that God was smiting the saints and strangers of the Mayflower as through Joshua He had smitten the Amalekites at Rephidim. He did not suppose for an instant that these seas had been brought about by the sword of the Lord and of Gideon. He knew what it was. Mayflower had met the westerlies, the equinoctial storms, head on. That was to be expected at this time of year in this part of the ocean. The strangers and saints had thought to sail from England much earlier, but a series of leaks and sprung masts on a smaller vessel that was to have accompanied them, Speedwell, brought about repeated delays. They should not have sailed at all, in September. But they could not afford to wait until the spring. This was one of the reasons why, when Sal's presence among them became known, the Captain positively refused to put back again, even if it meant losing only half a day.

All of this Sal understood. What he didn't understand—and what caused him to curse so frightfully as he hauled himself in —was why the blow had come so suddenly, without warning. That was tropical behavior, that barbaric abruptness. Weather in the North Atlantic was supposed to be dirty practically all the time.

He was badly bruised, his ribs hurting him so that he could scarcely breathe. Nobody paid any attention to him, not even the mariners who had helped to haul him in, and he stayed on hands and knees for some time, his chest heaving.

Less water was sluicing across the waist, now that so many of the sails had been struck or had been torn away, but even so, it sometimes creamed half as high as his elbows.

He would not be needed. All hands had been called up, and they knew their duties. The passengers would remain below. Besides, if anybody did want Sal they knew where they could find him.

Slowly, painfully he crawled to the longboat and wriggled underneath it.

The boat was maybe 20 to 25 feet long, 7 feet wide at its beamiest. Double-ended, upside down, mounted on chocks, and lashed to ringbolts in the deck, it formed a sort of bell, a shell, a whispering gallery in which all the sounds from outside—the squeal of lines through sheaves, the slap of canvas, shouts of officers, spitting spume, tumbling seas—were echoed and re-echoed, multiplied many times as they banged back and forth. Being under that boat was like being inside of an enormous but otherwise empty hogshead.

Sal didn't mind. He had been there before. He squirmed up to the under part—which because the boat was inverted was now the upper part—of one of the seats amidships, and there he curled up in his cloak, shivering. It was narrower than the deck, but no harder. It would do very well. Sal had no complaints; he was too glad to be alive. Soon he slept.

Chapter Nine

The ones Sal was most sorry for were those belowdecks. Except for the two individualists—John Alden, who slept upon his barrels, and Sal himself, who went on using the longboat—those aboard Mayflower were divided, slumberwise, into three categories. There was the forecastle, a crowded place but comparatively high, in which a mariner might be tossed about but could stay dry. There was the poop cabin, split by a row of screens between the ship's officers and certain married couples: the Mullins family, for instance, also John and Dorothy Bradford, and the Carvers. A majority of the passengers, some seventy in number, were cooped in the main cabin amidships.

Mayflower was known as a "sweet" vessel. Before she was chartered by the merchant adventurers of London who were backing this venture she had been in the Mediterranean wine trade, and wine traditionally cleanses the air of a hold. True, before that Mayflower had been used to fetch sundry malodorous cargos, such as turpentine, tar, and fish, from Norway; but the subsequent wine had done its work well; and when at last she sailed from Plymouth, though she had been overcrowded through several months of delay, as ships went she was fragrant. Before they were fairly out to sea it had been thought advisable to bolt the gun ports, two on each side, and this made the main

cabin stuffy. Even then it had been possible, except in times of
rain, to keep open the hatch to the main deck; but this no longer
was the case. The forecastle was well ventilated, with six feet of
head room, two doors to the prow deck, two doors to the waist.
Those in the poop house had a door that opened directly upon
the half deck, in addition to ports that from time to time—for
they rode well above the waterline—could be opened a little, on
the leeward side, for the letting in of air, the dumping out of
slops. In the main cabin for days on end they could not venture
forth to empty their buckets; so that the smell, which had been
merely disgusting, became revolting, a shock to the most stolid.
It could be doubted that there was a prison in all England more
noisome. Just to pass through that dim wretched place brought
tears to the eyes, so acrid was the air, and the stomachs of the
hardiest would give a giddy lurch.

Yet Sal never heard a whimper; and prayers and the reading
of the Bible, even when it was impossible to stand save by everybody clinging to his neighbor, went on and on.

Sal had sailed since boyhood, but he never had known anything like this. It was not a simple storm they met: it was a
condition.

"Maybe your friends don't sing loud enough, maybe that's the
trouble?" Sawn Matthews snarled at Sal once in passing.

There was no lull. The lowering sky seemed a madman filled
with rage, intent upon lashing this ship. The seas marched past
mast-high, foam flying from their crests like snow from the ridge
of a roof. They rocked, crazily, drunkenly, sometimes colliding
like blind insensate beasts; and now and then, for all the efforts
of the helmsmen below and the officer at the shout-slot, one of
them would fall like thunder upon Mayflower. That she was
not swamped was a miracle. There were moments when she
coasted on her beam-ends, when she was cat's eyes under. But
she would right herself somehow, water cascading from a hun-

dred places, while her timbers shrieked. She was a well-found ship, was Mayflower.

As far as Sal could see, she leaked very little. She had carried a second suit of sails and perhaps even a third, and after the wild confusion that followed the onset of the storm the mariners were able to hold a certain amount of canvas on her—not the spritsail or any topsails, but a reefed square or two—so that by dint of constant alertness and with two helmsmen at all times working the whipjack it was possible to keep her headed into the blow, headed still, they hoped, for America.

She might have sprung her sticks a bit, but if so it was nothing that a handful of strong men armed with mauls and wedges couldn't have repaired—if ever they were given a chance.

The greatest damage was topside, amidships. The waist was a shambles from the beginning, as was only to be expected. The main hatch had been carried away, and the jury hatch was hardly waterproof. Most of the gunwale on the starboard side, and part of that on the larboard side as well, had been smashed to splinters. Footing there was treacherous, and for the use of the mariners—passengers were forbidden to set foot on deck all this while—lines were rigged between forecastle and half deck.

Worst of all, from the point of view of the occupants of the main cabin, the pounding of the seas had opened seams all around the cannonports and also on the main deck itself, so that, in addition to what slipped in around the sides of the ill-fitting hatch, water seeped through the walls upon them, and dripped from cracks in the ceiling.

In the forecastle it was sometimes possible to have hot food. In the cabin, never. Hard tack and cold salt-horse were their portions; and the beer was going bad.

They were wet all the time. Their clothes were wet, their bunks, their blankets. It had become much colder.

Sal hand-over-handed his way to the poop house, where he tried to return her cloak to Mrs. Bradford, who must need it.

She refused to take it back; but she refused so sweetly, her gaunt face streaked with the dryings of tears—for she had been thinking about her only child, left in England—that Sal did not insist.

No doubt because the visit gave them heart and was a change, they made much of him in the poop house. Priscilla, though she was sick again, smiled persistently and pluckily from her corner. Elder Brewster gave him some cold peas, a treat. Mrs. Carver, who feared that he might catch cold, gave him a muffler she had knitted. Indeed, Sal might have stayed there much longer had not the mate, Clarke, grumpy after being on watch for a long time, peremptorily ordered him out.

"The waist's good enough for a Sallee man. You might even get washed overboard."

"I was, the night we ran into this blow. A couple of your salts helped to haul me back inboard."

"Tell me who they are, and I'll see that they never sail with me again."

The shelter of the longboat, in truth, was becoming uncomfortable. There was no place for him in the forecastle, and certainly not in the poop house, where the officers were in control; and though the long-suffering passengers in the main cabin would have found room on the floor for him somehow, Sal did not find the heart thus to inconvenience them, for he knew how much every inch counted.

The best place for him was the lower hold. Though the stink of bilge would be bad, it could hardly be worse than the main cabin. The hold would be cold, but Sal could endure cold. However, he'd be hanged if he would ask that cocky young cooper for refuge. So he stayed out of doors.

He saw Alden only once during the storm, sometime in the middle of the second week. With a crack like that of a cannon a main deck beam had buckled, terrifying even the veteran mariners. There was talk of putting back. They had propped the broken beam by means of a great screw, and the skipper decided to take a thorough look at his vessel, aloft and alow, before he decided whether to fly back to England with the wind or to keep his dogged course.

The findings of this survey were a secret while it was in progress, but at one time, the second afternoon, they called on Salathiel Boyd for advice.

Besides the Mayflower's pieces, the colonists had some cannons of their own, stored far below, and it was the thought of Captain Jones that if there was any chance those pieces might work loose from their lashing and slam back and forth, it would be best to haul them up on deck and dump them overboard. He did not consult with the owners of the cannons about this, but he did consult, naturally, with his gunner, Webster, and by way of afterthought called Sal in as a secondary expert.

Sal could fire such weapons well enough, but he was no engineer, and neither was he a military man, so he knew nothing about moving them. He accepted the invitation to have a look for several reasons. It was something to do, a change. It would give him another chance to study the cooper in his own jealously guarded bailiwick. And finally, Sal could see that Gunner Webster was disgruntled by the decision to ask for further advice, and decided to butter him.

Webster had said that it would take a dozen men the better part of a week—and such men could not be spared—to jettison those cannons. Sal blandly agreed.

There were a minion that might have weighed 1,200 pounds, a 10-foot saker of 4-inch bore, perhaps 1,800 pounds, a falcon, and two bases.

It was Sal's private opinion, anyway, that it would be better to leave the guns where they were. They had been well lashed, and being stored far below they must serve in part as ballast. However, he said nothing of this. He simply endorsed Webster's opinion and won a friend.

While the Captain's party was below on this inspection tour Sal studied young John Alden.

Here was a lad of immense strength, blond, easy of movement, and not bad looking in a sullen way. If he was overaggressive it might have been because his youth and lack of experience made him unsure of himself. There was everything to indicate that he was a first-rate cooper. While the party was below he kept tapping barrels, kegs, hogsheads, and pipes and testing their hoops. He would feel all around them and on the deck beneath each one for possible defects, and he sniffed continuously— though how he could have hoped to smell anything above the blast of the bilge it was hard for Sal to see; perhaps coopers had keener noses than gunners.

Alden didn't do this just to look busy in the presence of the skipper. He owed the skipper nothing. He had been hired not by the Mayflower but by the saints themselves, and it was their stores, not the mariners', that he strove to save. It was clear from his manner that he worked like this all the time.

Not only the water, wine, beer, and spirits the colonists carried with them, but much of the food as well—the biscuit, oatmeal, salt beef, beans, and even cabbages—was largely stored in barrels of one sort or another. If air got in, or if salt water did, or bilge, it would be ruined. Since the company would land in the New World in winter, these supplies must maintain them at least for six months. Young Alden was quite right to take his duties seriously; and Sal, though he still didn't like the lad, watched him with a new respect, a respect that was heightened a bit when Sal learned that the cooper, like himself, was an orphan.

Nevertheless they scowled at one another when they passed.

After the inspection the officers conferred, and a decision was reached.

They wouldn't turn back. Mayflower would fight on.

Chapter Ten

Nothing like the dramatic suddenness of its entrance marked the storm's departure. There was no clicked finish, no point-at-able ending. The blow, it might be said, dribbled out.

Bad weather went on. The sky was dark and low. There was a great deal of rain, in angry bursts, very cold. The sea did not at any time resemble a fish pond; but water no longer slashed across the waist, and though Mayflower rocked and pitched she did not again stand on her beam-ends, while the squeal of her timbers, if unremitting, was less hysterical.

People began to reappear, blinking, from below. They were ashen, their hands trembling, their eyes red, as they lifted their faces to Heaven—a low, mean, discolored Heaven—and gratefully drank the air.

What with wreckage, the lines, the gaps in the gunwales, the bustling mariners, the waist still was no Paradise; but anything would be better than the cabin below. Even those who were too weak to climb the ladder begged their friends to carry them up, so that they too might feel air that wasn't foul, that didn't stink. Weak, panting a little, heedless of the seamen's steps around them, as of the shrill cries of children, they would lie looking up; and their lips would move in prayer.

Others, the stronger, when they were not huddled in circles

for meetings, would lean against what was left of the gunwales and gaze fixedly at the sea. They had done this too before the blow, Sal observed. Landsmen who found themselves afloat often did. He couldn't understand it. The sea was the sea. It was always there. True, you tossed it a look now and then, to learn whether anything ugly was making up, just as you might toss a look at the half-hour glass if you chanced to be passing the bittacle, to see how near food time was; but you wouldn't stand and stare at the sea by the hour—not if you were in your right mind—any more than you would watch all the sands run through the glass. But these people did.

For one of them it was too much. Like the others, young William Button, Deacon Fuller's servant, survived the blow, but soon afterward he died; and they prayed for him and slid his corpse over the side sewed in canvas, lead weights at his head and feet.

The company of colonists remained the same in number, however, one hundred and two, a baby having been born to Mrs. Hopkins in the poop house at the very height of the storm. Christened: Oceanus. They gave queer names, these people, Salathiel Boyd thought.

Among the first to stagger forth from the poop house, where their suffering had been only slightly less than that of those in the cabin, was Priscilla Mullins. She was pale, she had been shaken, but she gave Sal a smile while he was helping to carry a sick man up from below, after which she went from one to the other of the emerging cabin passengers to ask if there was any way in which she could help.

Sal settled not to go to her right away, though he longed to. He missed her.

When she had made the circuit, another of those impromptu praisings was about to form. She joined in, and afterward went to the starboard gunwale, and like so many others settled herself to stare out over the sea.

Sal shrugged and sat down. A few minutes later she sat beside him, as quiet as a sprite, and grinned at him.

"It's good to be out," she said.

"It's good to see you again."

They might have looked a mite foolish, beaming at one another.

"You could have come to our place more often if it wasn't for that Mr. Clarke. He don't seem to like you."

"That's the way I feel about him, too."

"You should never hate your fellows."

"There's exceptions to every rule. D'ye feel better now?"

"Oh, yes. Look, Mr. Boyd—"

It caused him to thrill, being called Mr. Boyd, if only because he did not rate the title.

"—speaking of Mr. Clarke, you had words with him that time you did come to our cabin, last week."

Sal nodded. He had restrained himself admirably on that occasion, he thought. Had he told Mate Clarke what he really thought of him the words might have horrified nearby saints. Sal could not see any profit in that. The mariners, and especially Sawn Matthews, went out of their way to swear and blaspheme, raising their voices, when there were any saints in sight; but to Sal this was childish.

"You said something about having fallen overboard," she pursued, "and Mr. Clarke opined that he wished you'd stayed there."

"Well, I guess that's the way he feels. No harm done. I didn't stay there."

"He shouldn't utter things like that! 'Vengeance is mine, saith the Lord.' "

"Well, I guess he feels that way all right."

"But—tell me. Were you hurt?"

Without thought, she had placed a hand on his left forearm.

He let it stay there, not even daring to look down at it lest she take it away.

"Not much. I wasn't hurt much."

"Tell me about it."

He did so, since she insisted. And the hand tightened on his arm, so he strung the story out.

"You got back! It was God's doing!"

"Yes, I suppose it was."

"Have you thanked Him?"

"Not directly. Just in a general way."

Sal frowned a little. On the other side of the deck Cooper Alden had come up from below, to blat like the rest, lifting his face; but Alden was aware of this pair.

Why did they need to be talking about prayer? There was too much talk about prayer on this vessel already. It always came around to that. Sal Boyd, today, would have preferred to talk about themselves, and her in particular.

"You should have done so right away! It was an example of God's mercy, and He should be thanked. Let me call the others and tell them about it, and we'll have a meeting."

"Oh, no, please don't do that."

"Why ever not?"

"Well, I never admired to ask the Creator for favors. It seems to me it's all right if He just lets me go on living a little longer. I—I wouldn't bother Him about such a small thing."

"Nothing that happens to one of His children is small in the eyes of the Lord."

"Yes, maybe. But even so . . . I heard one time that there's two kinds of prayer, but I can't remember their names."

"Adulatory and supplicatory?"

"That's it. And the first one is the only one that I guess I have much use for. Oh, I believe in praising the Lord all right. Sure! But I never thought it's quite right to bother Him about so many small details, like I said before."

She looked at Sal for some time, very earnestly. She had taken the hand away, but there was something protective about her, this girl who faced a pirate. She shook a slow, all but incredulous head.

"Strange," she murmured. "Strange . . ."

"What's strange about it? It's just the way I feel."

"Look—"

From under her cloak she fished a Bible. It was not large, as Bibles went. And Bibles went almost everywhere, here in the Mayflower, where at any moment your neighbor might whip one out and start to read—perhaps to himself, perhaps aloud. Yet you seldom saw one in the hands of a woman. Sal was not sure that he liked it.

"What I want . . . It's in Malachi . . . yes . . . Here!"

She thrust the open book into his lap.

"Read it, and you'll see what I mean."

"You read it," he suggested.

"No, you do it. That makes a deeper impression, when you hear the sound of your own voice."

"Preachers think so, anyway."

She shook the Book.

"Go ahead."

He looked away, feeling the tips of his ears go hot. And then that hand was on his forearm again.

"Oh, I'm sorry! You can't read?"

"Never could," he mumbled.

"Oh, but millions of people can't!"

"That doesn't make it any nicer for me."

"You shouldn't feel—"

"Never went to school."

"I never went to school either. Girls don't."

"No."

"But my mother and father— Didn't your mother and father want you to learn to read?"

"Maybe. I never met them. I guess I must have *had* a father and mother, but that was long before I knew anything."

He rose.

"Well, it's too late to do anything about it now."

"Not at all!"

"Eh?"

She had sprung to her feet, facing him, and he gawped at her.

"You aren't too old to learn," she ran on. "You aren't more than— Well, how old are you?"

"I don't even know *that*."

"It don't matter. If we have a lesson every morning and another one every afternoon—"

"Ma'am, that would take up so much of your time."

"What else have I got to do? For that matter, what else *could* I do that would be as good a thing as opening the Lord's Book up to one who had not been able to see?"

"Oh, I can see all right. Only—"

"Sit down. We'll have the first lesson right now."

"No."

"No?"

"Not right now."

"Why not?"

Sal waggled his hands. He was touched, truly. He shook. Swallowing, he turned away.

"I—I've got something else I have to do right now."

He went from her. That his step wasn't steady might attract no notice, since none of them was yet walking straight.

As he made for the cabin ladder—he didn't need to use a bucket at all; that had been simply the first excuse he thought of—he noticed Alden making a way toward the place where Priscilla was.

Well, let him! There were different ways of fighting.

Sal brought up a deep breath and went below.

Chapter Eleven

Men of the sea are addicted to drawing dire conclusions from trivial signs, fond of yarns about monsters and mermen, and firm in the belief that they can foretell certain aspects of the future. For instance, many swear that they know more surely than instruments when land is just over the horizon. Some of these say that they can *feel* land coming—feel it in their bones. Others declare that the air grows denser: they know it in their lungs. There are those too who claim to be able to see the reflection of earth, a vast distance away, upside down on the lower part of the clouds, a faint greenish shimmer, a system they insist is infallible. A majority, however, connect this uncanny sense with their noses. They aver that they can smell specific things, though hundreds of miles away—the mud of the Low Countries, the olives of Spain, frangipani and other flowers of Polynesia, and off the East Indies pepper, cinnamon, cloves.

Salathiel Boyd was one of the bones group. His joints reported to him that America was near. But he said nothing of this.

America must be a mighty cold place, he reckoned. As he understood it, the land of Virginia, to which they were going, stretched between Florida on the south, Spanish territory, and the Grand Banks. How far that was Sal didn't know, and he did not suppose that anybody else knew either—some said hundreds of miles, some said thousands. But clearly they were headed for the northern part. The winds, from the west and northwest, were sharp, wet, and most marvelously penetrating: They worked their way into every crevice of raiment, slipping through cracks and slits, wriggling like a snake, remorseless, unflagging, inescapable, harsh.

It sometimes seemed that Mayflower must be pushed backward, making for the east, for England, rather than for the New World; and it was certain that at times they reached only one mile in the right direction for every four or five miles they covered. This must have made it hard on the man with the astrolabe and charts. But Sal was no navigator. He depended upon those susceptible bones.

There were others who seemed to depend upon the sea itself, which they contemplated for hour after long hour, motionless, entoiled in its might and majesty. But Sal Boyd turned his back to the sea, and spent most of his time seated on deck, out of the wind, propped against the weather gunwale, while Priscilla Mullins sat beside him, so close that their shoulders touched for warmth, and the Book they held rested partly on her left knee, partly on his right.

It was good that way. You forgot your shivers.

An impartial observer might have remarked that the arrangement was unfair to John Alden, who because of the battering they'd taken had to spend most of every day among his barrels in a fetid hold. Sal didn't see that. You grabbed what you could get whenever you could get it, if you had sense. A pity about John Alden. But any time he wanted to fight—

Besides, the business of learning to read was proving even harder than Sal had expected.

They started at the beginning, with Genesis.

" 'Afterward the man knew Hevah his wife which (a) conceived and bare Kain, and said, I have obtained a man (b) by the Lord.'

"They don't tell you when they're talking," Sal complained.
"You're supposed to know that."

"How?"

Priscilla was silent.

Sal went on: " 'And againe she brought foorth his brother Habel, and Habel was a keeper of sheepe, and Kain was a tiller of soil.

" 'And in the processe of time it came to passe, that Kain brought an (c) oblation unto the Lord—'

"Why do they have those numbers and marks and little squigetty things?"

"I don't know. But they always do."

"And all that tiny print off to one side and down below there. Do they have that in other books too?"

"No. Only in the Bible."

"To make it harder to read?"

"I don't know. But—go on. You're doing fine."

Alden might have resented the lessons, but nobody else appeared to. Saints and strangers alike, and even the mariners, smiled as they stepped over Priscilla's and Sal's feet, and he was often asked afterward how the good work was going, and praised for his progress. Though by no means all of the colonists were literate, the leaders were; and his attainment, slow as it was, seemed to bring Sal closer to them.

Also, he was mixing. The mariners never condescended to answer questions, and Sal as a seafaring man often was approached for information about Mayflower's ability to weather the storm.

"You understand that we don't *fear* to go down. We are all in the hands of the Lord."

"Oh, of course."

"It—it's just that we would like to clear our souls of every last smitch of sin, if the end is to come soon."

"Yes, I see. Well, I don't think you need to worry. She's a sound vessel, this one. She's taking it like a lady."

"You—you really mean that, Master Boyd?"

"Why, of course I do."

He didn't, so he was lying; but it did no harm to make the others feel better. All of these colonists who were crossing it had a far-ranging ignorance of the sea, and their blatant lubberliness in matters nautical shocked Sal, who winced to hear them speak of "the right-hand side" and "the left-hand side," "the front of the boat" and "the back of the boat." Out of pity, he strove to set them right; and he was flooded with dismay when they failed to be impressed, in a few cases even saying that they thought all those technical terms a lot of bubble. It was hard to know how to talk to people as bigoted as that. Priscilla, however, took him seriously, and she begged him to correct her whenever she miscalled anything. *She* had some sense.

None of these passengers had had fine clothes to begin with, and what with the movement of the ship and the shortage of water they had become a seedy lot. Sal, on the other hand, blossomed. Since his first meeting with Priscilla he had taken pains with his appearance. He shaved three times a week, using for each shave half a mug of water provided by his friend Harris, the cook. As Mayflower passengers went, he was positively spruce.

They liked too his advice against jettisoning their artillery. To have been dumped into the New World without cannon would have made the venture more perilous. Moreover, it could be that they hoped Sal would help them to set up these guns. Certainly *they* didn't know how.

They were not plunging all defenseless into the wilds of North Virginia, these meek men. Sal Boyd was scarcely awed by their weapons—pikes, swords, muskets—nor yet by the breast- and backplates and the morions they sometimes tried on, though seldom cleaned. They didn't *love* their killing tools, as fighting men should. They didn't swab and polish them, sharpen them, oil them. Some even handled the things gingerly, as though picking up a snake. This disgusted Sal.

Like any rover, he was accustomed to large numbers of well-maintained weapons. A display of ferocity and of might was part of a corsair's method. The more blades the better, the more steel, and keep it bright. Sal didn't think that the saints were well equipped; but he was astonished to find them equipped at all, and in this he was not alone.

"Do we not have a surplusage of instruments?" he overheard a quavering, worried William Mullins ask of Elder Brewster on the occasion of the first drill.

The elder's answer was prompt. Though there was a pike tucked beneath his left arm, he still held the Book, and now he allowed this to fall open.

" 'But wee our selves will be ready armed to goe before the children of Israel, untill we have brought them into their place . . .' "

"Um-m."

"Then here again: 'And Moses said unto them, If ye will doe this thing, and goe armed before the Lord to warre:

" 'And will goe every one of you in harnesse over Jorden before the Lord, until he have cast out his enemies from his sight:

" 'And until the land be subdued before the Lord . . .' "

Priscilla's father screwed his little finger into his ear for some time, and then brought his finger out and regarded it resentfully.

"Yes. But mightn't it be better, brother, if we offer them the thing that you hold in your hand rather than the thing that's tucked under your arm? I—only ask."

"If this can be done, be assured that we'll do it, brother. Oh, be sure of that! But the savages might not understand, at first."

"I see," said William Mullins.

Sal, however, was not asked for his opinion of the armor and small arms. These were the province of a small, peppery soldier hired for that purpose, one Captain Standish. "Captain Shrimp" the disgruntled strangers called him, both because of his small size and because of the fact that when his anger rose, as so often it did, his face and neck became as red as the wattles of a fighting cock. Sal distrusted Standish, as he instinctively distrusted all soldiers. The best thing about Miles Standish, as Sal saw it, was his musket. The other muskets—there was no pistola that Sal ever saw aboard Mayflower—were, of course, matchlocks. Wheel locks would have been too expensive for these men. But Captain Standish had a new Dutch snaphance. Sal, who had heard of these guns but had not yet seen one, eyed the thing with respect.

It was very long—much longer than Standish himself, who looked ridiculous when he held it—yet it was so light, Sal was told, that it could be fired without the use of a barrel rest. If a knife was screwed into its muzzle it could be made to serve as a pike, and its stock was heavy enough, and its barrel light enough, to suggest clubbing possibilities. Best of all, it wasn't burning all the time, a constant care that might be put out by rain or might give away your position in the dark; instead, it brought about a shower of sparks the way a wheel lock did, though in a simpler and cheaper and much less sensational fashion, using the flint and steel familiar to every kitchen.

Sal would have liked to handle that snaphance, maybe even fire it a few times, but he wouldn't lower himself to ask a favor of a soldier.

So it was that he no longer loitered about the fringe of this company, but entered in. He belonged. He even fancied that a few of the saints were beginning to like him, which made him warm inside.

Chapter Twelve

" 'So when men began to be multiplied upon the earth, and there were daughters borne unto them,

" 'Then the (a) sonnes of God saw the daughters (b) of men that they were (c) faire, and they took them wives of all that they liked.' "

She slapped her knee in delight, and then slapped his.

"Wonderful! I hardly helped you at all that time!"

"I still can't see," he muttered, "why they break it up like that, and put part of it on one side of the page and part on the other, and then all those little letters and numbers and things ... How many times have you read the Bible, Mistress Mullins?"

"Four times. This is the fifth."

"Clear through?"

"Oh, yes. Even the begats. They're mostly in Chronicles."

Sawn Matthews went past, openly sneering. He spat. He would not dare to spit on Priscilla's feet or Sal's—he had too much respect for Sal's fists—but he came close. Priscilla gave no sign of having seen, and perhaps she really hadn't. Making a mental note that he must speak to Sawn later, Sal moved one foot in such a way as to cover the spittle, the existence of which he did not otherwise acknowledge.

"I should think," he went on slowly, "that if, like you say, if other books don't have columns like that, and all those marks, and that smitchety-smitch in the margins and at the bottom—I should think they'd be more pleasure to read, now ain't they?"

"You don't peruse God's word for pleasure, Master Boyd."

"Maybe not. But—ain't they?"

"I don't know. I've never read any other book."

"You mean, you just go on reading this one over and over again?"

"Why, of course."

"I see."

The shadows were long when these two scrambled to their feet for evening prayer, and Sal noted that two lookouts were being sent forward, instead of one. This had happened each night for half a week, as Sal, who spent most of his time on deck, and who from the shelter of the longboat could hear a deal of what happened, could attest. Moreover the lookouts, one in the bow, one aloft, did not stay there all night. They were relieved twice.

Perhaps it was these precautions rather than any feeling in his bones that convinced Sal that Mayflower was nearing her landfall. Captain Jones, he'd overheard, was one-quarter owner of this vessel, a man planning to retire soon, maybe at the end of this very voyage. Christopher Jones would not risk those twin bugaboos of sailing masters who approach shore—breakers and a sleeping lookout. As Sal knew, Captain Jones these last few nights had taken many more than his usual few turns around the poop deck. He often went forward as well. He was checking his sentries.

Also, the anchor cable had been reflaked, and the dipsy and line brought up from below.

It meant something.

Sal was out from under the longboat a bit before dawn. He walked back and forth, trying to get warm.

The wind was northwest, as usual. Mayflower was on the starboard tack, bowling along, every inch spread, the sails standing out dark gray and fat in the moonlight. For there was yet a moon, a waning crescent in midsky, some seven hours high, its horns pointing due west.

Sal had never felt more wide awake. Walking with measured stride, as though he was a marcher in some solemn ceremonious procession, he went up to the prow deck, a tiny triangular place. He was often up and about like this before first light, but ordinarily he used the occasion to take a walk in the waist, that being the only time a man could stretch his legs. This morning it was different. He didn't feel like walking. He felt like thinking about Priscilla.

The sky was dark, and the lemon-colored stars twitched out one by one, leaving only that sliver of moon. The horizon was a smudge, very close. Below Sal Boyd the Mayflower's apple-cheeked bow rose and fell sighingly, suckingly, and with a sad hiss.

There was a step behind him. He wheeled around, edgy as any race horse.

"Is that you, Mistress Mullins?"

"Yes. Couldn't you sleep?"

"I can always sleep."

"You must have no sins on your conscience, then?"

"I've got a few. But—what about you? Or did you want to be one of the first to see it?"

"See what?"

"Well, there's a chance—"

"You mean we've sighted *land?*"

"Not yet. But we're going to. Mighty soon."

"How do you know?"

Sal sighed, for he was weary of being deferred to as a seaman.

"I can feel it in my bones," he said at last. "And—look at that moon up there. You see which way the horns are pointing, don't you?"

It was spooky, standing in the shadows talking to her when he could scarcely see her face. It was also extremely cold. Sal flapped his arms, and blew upon his hands.

"To take the moon as a sign," she said carefully, "would be plain pagan superstition."

"All the same, I'll bet you—"

"I don't bet."

"Sure, sure. What I meant was—"

He paused, suddenly embarrassed, all but choking.

"Yes?" she offered.

It had occurred to Sal that this was the first time he had ever been alone with Mistress Mullins. He was frightened.

"What I meant," he resumed, in an even lower voice, "was that you have been very kind to me—Priscilla."

He heard her gasp and saw her sway, but she didn't go. He hiked up a long breath. He put his hands on her shoulders. He thought that he could feel the beat of her heart as he stepped closer to her.

The deck was sodden, drunk with dew that gleamed like pewter. Below them the bows rose, splattering seadrops. Above, the man in the crow's nest shifted his feet, cleared his throat.

"I'm not much of a hand for saying thanks," Sal managed to say. "But—thank God for you, Priscilla. And I mean that."

She lifted her face, the lips falling open. She too was frightened. She had to swallow before she could speak.

"What—are you going—to do?"

The man in the crow's nest whirled around, stamping his feet as he faced aft, and put his hands to his mouth, awakening the whole vessel.

"Land ho! Land HO!"

They had reached America.

Chapter Thirteen

It was at first no more than a fuzziness, a thickening of the horizon, unreal, a thing that might disappear in a blink; and indeed there were many, Priscilla Mullins among them, who vowed that they could not see it at all and doubted that it was there—there, that is, for eyes strained from horizon-staring.

Salathiel Boyd never questioned it, nor did the mariners, the moon having pointed the way. Soon, when canvas had been raised for furling on the spars, and Mayflower had been put about so that the sea no longer spanked her bows, the ear confirmed the report of the eye. Through air that was reluctantly lightening, a land breeze brought the bumble of surf in a rich sound, musical and beautiful to the man on shore, horrible to a man who is at sea.

They had been driving right toward those breakers, now disclosed.

"It was the will of God that stopped us," Master Carver murmured.

"The lookout might've had something to do with it too," said Sal.

That first shout had been a tocsin to turn them out of their blankets and tumble them upon the deck like dice tossed from a dice box. Almost before they fully realized what had happened, Priscilla and Sal were inundated by would-be settlers, who climbed even to the prow deck, a place by day denied them. They always had been a talkative lot, not glum; but now they fairly chattered like magpies, and their eyes shone with eagerness, their mouths worked. Poor dried-up little pale men! poor scrawny, homely, overworked women! After sixty-six days of torture they would have cheered the appearance of anything solid, had it been but a pestilential swamp. Their hands trembled, and their nostrils. Of course they prayed, pouring forth their thanks; but just at first, for a little while, they only gazed, their hearts throbbing.

This was not permitted for very long. Christopher Jones, like a good master, was topside among the first; and from the poop, high above them, he shouted orders for all passengers to go below. This was to give his men a chance to take in canvas, a complicated process that might have been all but impossible while strangers and saints swarmed antlike across the deck. Soon Clarke and Coffin, the mates, were moving among them, none too gently shoving them toward the hatch, the opening to the black hole below. As a rule, on such occasions—and Sal thought them much too numerous—the passengers responded with meekness, even alacrity. This morning it was not so. Their heads turned, their necks craned, they stumbled. Fluttering and squawking in much the same manner, they were stuffed below like live fowl at a fair being shoved into a poke for sale.

However, nobody laid a hand on Sal Boyd. This was in accordance with the custom, for it was generally realized that Sal was a special passenger and not subject to the usual rules. He could keep out of the way, and even from time to time lend a hand with a line, a sheet, a capstan bar.

So Sal was left, hugging the gunwale, gulping the shore.

Dead ahead loomed a clump of low, dark hills that appeared to be covered with brush or perhaps trees, but on right and left the land was flat, only scantily scattered with low trees or thickets, and splotched with dark spots that might have been pools, even bogs. Nowhere was that line of white foam—it kept appearing and disappearing as though some giant drew it erratically with a great piece of chalk—broken in such a way as to hint of a harbor. Nowhere did this land say hello.

The ship lolled, moving, if it moved at all, a little away from shore, since the breeze was from the northwest. Christopher Jones wanted a better look before he got in close.

After a while Sal too went below.

"You're not missing much," he assured them. "This is no Eden."

"It may prove so for us!"

"Amen, amen!"

Pressed for details, he went on.

"Well, the sky's about the color of a rusty cutlass, and the shore's the same, what there is of it, only a little more gray. No, I couldn't see any smoke, or anything moving around. Matter of fact, it looks like a desert—only cold and wet."

"Surely there must be a sign, somewhere? Some evidence that it was destined for our uses?"

"Well, I didn't see anything like that, no. But I'll go topside and take another look."

No sunlight came, but when it was light enough for a study of the shore they cracked on some canvas—not much, no main course, only a couple of topsails and a spritsail—and lumbrously, as they gathered way, they turned to larboard, south.

Still the passengers were not permitted the upper deck. A man never knew what he might meet off a shore like this. Mayflower moved half a dozen miles from the beach, and parallel to it. She moved gingerly, warily, like some cat walking down the middle of an unfamiliar alley.

Nowhere the length of that desolate sandy shore to the right was there any house or even hint of humanity. Nowhere did smoke stand against the sky.

At six bells Captain Jones sent for sundry of the leaders among those who would settle this drear land. At the same time, Sal Boyd went to the poop cabin. He had been below several times, and those in the poop, after all, did have windows; but he wanted to see Priscilla—he believed that he would know when he looked at her whether or not she wished that they had kissed —and he had as an excuse that he could offer, again, to return Mistress Bradford's cloak. He did not fear that Mate Clarke would intervene. Clarke and the other pilot mates, Coffin, Williamson, Parker, were much too busy on deck, keeping their eyes and ears peeled.

Dorothy Bradford had been weeping. Sal saw this instantly— though the light was dim—and he wished he hadn't come. Priscilla Mullins sat by her side, an arm across her shoulders.

The cabin not only was dim, it was hushed, which seemed odd on a day of excitement. They were mostly women there, the men, including William Bradford and William Mullins, having been called to the Captain's cabin.

Mistress Bradford shook her head, smiling determinedly, and looking, Sal thought, worse than ever, with her hair half down, her eyes red.

"No," she whispered. "You must keep it."

"But when we go ashore—"

"Even then, I have clothes enough."

She did not explain her tears, though she did try to control them; but Priscilla, as though in defense, passed on to Sal the rumor from the Captain's cabin. They had not raised the mouth of Hudson's River, as planned, nor were they anywhere near that: they were much farther north. Captain John Smith's map of six years ago showed bad shoal conditions just south of the land that they were passing, which Captain Jones believed was what had been called, after the fish, Cape Cod. Christopher Jones was warning the leaders of this, it was believed. He feared to continue south, but what with Mayflower's strained condition he feared as well to put out to the open sea again. They might have to land, they might even have to settle, in this savage place north of the territory covered by the Virginia Company's charter, the district marked on John Smith's map as New England. What their rights would be then, since they would not be operating under any charter, he didn't know.

Now these were grim news, but to Sal, who never had had much truck with navigation anyway, they were not grim enough to induce tears. Still, it was none of his business. Priscilla was giving him a significant look, and he rose, muttering apologies.

He was about to step out on the half deck when there came a shout of "Breakers!" from half a score of throats.

They were dead ahead this time, not to starboard, where they had been throughout the morning. It looked as though the sea had gone mad. Water raced and spat, whirling in eddies, throwing out spume, steaming, hissing. There must have been a strong current there—they were drifting right toward it—and thousands of rocks just beneath the surface.

Christopher Jones burst out of his cabin, shouting orders. Mate Clarke ran across the half-deck, bumped into Sal, and grabbed him by the shoulder.

"What were you doing in there? Well, never mind now!" He pointed to the mainyard, not fully manned. *"Hop it!"*

Sal hopped it.

They yawed, as skittish as a camel going downhill. In a real blow it would have been chancy; but there was little enough wind, and they made it, though they were drenched with spray and passed so close to some of the pounding that it was like mallets against their very ears. When Sal dropped to deck again they had their nose north, and the air still was filled with a million minute rainbows.

That night they stayed outside, and with the dawn there was nothing of land to look at. But they put in again, as carefully as before, and raised a low sandy point a little distance north of their hilly landfall of the previous morning, as near as Sal Boyd could make out. He was on deck all the while. He hadn't even slept.

There still was no sun, and the breeze was bitterly cold, but the seas were not running high—they could use their spritsail— and no white water could be seen.

Again Mayflower might have been a cat, a crouching one this time, as she approached that small low sandy spit. It looked like an island, though Sal was told by Robert Coffin that it was in fact the tip of a long sandy peninsula. They moved upon it from the east, then swung around to the north, then to the west, where obviously they were under the lee of a headland and the water might have been that of a lake.

And there at last, at seven bells of the morning watch, there came a shriek of cable and a great thumping splash, which told that they had let go the anchor.

It was Saturday, November 11, 1620.

Chapter Fourteen

Closer, the coast was no less desolate. You might have said that here was a land forgotten by God. Once canvas had been struck and the cable made fast, the skipper relaxed his restrictions, permitting hatches and ports to be thrown open, so that sunshine and fresh air got to places unvisited by fresh air and sunshine these many weeks, while the passengers once again lined the gunwale, eagerly pointing out plants that they could identify at this distance—scrub oaks, boxberry, aspen, beech, wild plum, juniper.

Despite these familiar growths, however, the tip end of Cape Cod in no way resembled Kent. Under a glum sky the trees and bushes showed stunted, grotesque. They looked as though they were in pain, desperately hanging on, clinging to the earth, their lives a pauseless battle against wind and the lack of sustenance. The shore itself, humped in dunes, was decorated by nothing more than a dry, dull, brittle, juiceless grass or sedge that none of them had seen before. The oaks were few, and farther back. They were not grand, as oaks should be, but dwarfed, for they leaned in agonized attitudes as though bent by an unceasing struggle against the weather, and their limbs, lumpy with knots, were twisted, misshapen; and of course they held no leaves, for winter came early here.

Worst, except for the gulls that wheeled and scree-ed querulously overhead, nothing stirred. No woodpecker rapped an impatient staccato, no hare flitted through the thicket, no crab scurried. As had been the case with the same scene as viewed from the other side of the peninsula, the sea side, the previous day, there was no column of smoke and indeed not the slightest suggestion that any living being ever had set foot on this cold, inhospitable cape.

"And you're going to *plant* here? You're going to *farm?*"

"The Lord will provide a way," Priscilla replied.

He glanced at her sideways, withholding comment. He could not tell, as he had hoped to tell, whether she was in any way affected by his near embrace just before land was sighted. This puzzled and troubled him. Long ago he had cast aside the notion that Priscilla Mullins was a simple girl, straightforward in her thinking, and utterly innocent. Yet he had thought he knew her well enough to detect any inner agitation. Had she been somewhat less than half awake that morning? Had it meant nothing to her that he'd called her "Priscilla" for the first time? He couldn't know.

He supposed, sighing, that the reading lessons would cease. He had done wonders, showing a quickness of grasp that amazed both of them, but there would not be time now for all that. In the poop cabin, in the waist, housekeeping arrangements had been of the simplest, for the food was scanty, monotonous, and easily prepared, when it was prepared at all. The shortage of water had caused all washing to be prohibited, and Priscilla's young brother, Johnny, habitually was under the eye of some older person. When these separatists landed, no matter where, it would be a different story. Then there would be everything to be done, with never a moment to spare for education.

Startling him, as though she had read his thought, she turned with a smile:

"Isn't it time for our lesson?"

"But—" He waggled his hands. "Don't you want to look at the New World?"

"There isn't much to be seen," she pointed out. "And besides, we have plenty of time. Come along."

"Why, sure."

John Billington intercepted them as they started for the larboard gunwale, deserted now. He would like a word with Sal.

This Billington had a wife aboard, and two holy terrors of children. Like Sal himself he was a London man, a Cockney, born within sound of Bow Bells, but unlike Sal he was narrow, suspicious, cantankerous, a complainer.

"All right," Sal said ungraciously.

"I'll get the Book," said Priscilla.

Billington did no beating about the bush.

"This patent we're supposed to be working under—you've heard what the men're saying about it?"

"Couldn't help hearing. But—how many men?"

"Enough."

To Sal it was sickening that a company of men and women should travel so far, only to start squabbling when the anchor was dropped. True, they weren't used to stench, salt food, watery beer, and the rasping relations bound to result from such close, uncomfortable quarters; but they ought to have taken this into consideration and kept their mouths shut.

They hadn't. As soon as the word leaked out that they were about to disembark, not at the mouth of Hudson's River, but at a point some miles north of that—and well above the forty-first parallel that marked the northern boundary of the Virginia Company—there were those who muttered that this would relieve them of their obligations. New England, as this territory was marked on John Smith's map, had not been assigned by the crown to any joint-stock company or any nobleman. Why then did they have to go on obeying their masters?

John Billington was not a servant, and neither was he a master: he didn't rate that title. He belonged among the "good-men," who customarily were cautious, conservative, since they aspired to masterhood and servants of their own. He wasn't an adventurer—that is, he had no money invested in this enterprise but must pay for his share with his labor.

There were eighteen servants aboard who might as well have been slaves, for they were indentured, most of them, for seven years, during which time they were buyable, sellable, and not paid. Eleven of these, one sixth of the adult company, were strapping young men who would certainly and quite properly be expected to do the heaviest work. If these lads got it into their heads that a descent upon the shores of New England would free them of their contracted obligations—or if somebody *put* that idea there—Sal shuddered to think of what might happen to this venture.

"I don't know why you broach this to me," he said coldly. "I'm no separatist."

"Neither am I."

"I'm just a simple Sallee rover."

"But you've been about! You know something of laws!"

Billington spoke it "ab-ow-it," as he would have said "gun-powther" and "escipe" and "Gawd," locutions Sal had worn out, unwittingly, while he went around the maritime world. Now it occurred to Sal that his own parents, whoever they had been, no doubt had talked that same way. He winced.

"Laws?" he said. "You mean, I know how to break them?"

"I didn't say that! Go to, man! Ain't you interested in this movement? Ain't you going ashore with us?"

"I haven't decided," Sal lied.

"But if you—"

"I'll wade no farther into this," Sal said firmly. "Besides, I have an appointment with my teacher. So—take thyself away from here, hackster, before I tickle thy prat with the toe of my boot."

Sal had a sufficiently ferocious scowl, one he had often prac-
ticed. Billington went away.

When Sal turned to greet Priscilla the scowl was gone. It
would have evaporated anyway, without effort, at sight of her.
She wore gray-blue muslin caught up with scarlet, and a pert
white bonnet. With Mayflower motionless they were able to
move about more easily, not spreading their legs. It made a great
difference in Priscilla's stride. She could swing her hips a bit
now, and she did, perhaps unconsciously, perhaps saucily. It was
provocative, and he enjoyed being provoked. He grinned.

The grin was as far away as the scowl when they sat on the
deck, their backs to the gunwale, and started the lesson.

" 'Moreover, the Lord spake unto Moses, and unto Aaron,
saying:

" 'Speak unto the children of Israel, and say unto them, Who-
soever hath an issue from his flesh, is uncleane, because of his
issue.

" 'And this shall be his uncleannesse in his issue, when his
flesh avoideth his issue, this is his uncleannesse.' "

Priscilla threw her arms out.

"Wonderful! Wonderful! That's a hard word, too—unclean-
ness."

"I guess it comes natural to me."

Robert Coffin, a mate, stood above them, and he crooked a
finger at Sal.

"You, pirate. They're putting the longboat over, and you're to
go ashore with the party."

Priscilla scrambled to her feet as fast as Sal did to his. She
clapped her hands.

"You'll be one of the first to set foot on America. You are
greatly blessed, Master Boyd."

"I am," he admitted.

"Why d'ye suppose they picked you?"

"I think I know," Sal said sourly.

"Come on," said Robert Coffin.

Just before he slid down into the longboat—he had a leg over the gunwale—Sal grinned at her again.

"Be careful," she whispered. "Don't get caught by some savage."

She tried to make it sound mocking, but did not altogether succeed.

"Would you miss me?" he asked.

"Yes," she said simply, "I would."

There were tears in his eyes, as there was a lump in his throat, when he hand-over-handed down the line and took his place at an oar. He covered this weakness with song, for he was very happy.

> "Love is a bable.
>   No man is able
> To say 'tis this or 'tis that."

He turned in his seat, and raised a dripping oar toward the beach.

"Look out, America! Here we come!"

Then he resumed his lay.

> " 'Tis full of passions
>   Of sundry fashions,
> 'Tis like I cannot tell what."

"Let's have less music and more rowing," said the mate.

Chapter Fifteen

The tide was out and they could not bring the boat clear to shore, so they sloshed the last few hundred feet through ankle-deep, stunningly cold water. The footing was sandy, and indeed there did not appear to be any rocks at all in this scrawny country. Now and then one of the men would step into a clam hole, and there would rise gurgling bubbles; but they paid no heed to these, for their eyes, bugged out, straining, were directed to the beach, where everything was still.

It was thus that they approached America—wading, paddling, gasping, huddled, gripping their muskets, while their hearts thumped.

Though he had pulled an oar, Sal learned that he was here not as a seaman but as a member of the foraging party. Moreover, the moment the keel grated, the mate, Robert Coffin, no longer was in charge, and Captain Standish took command.

Sal had no fondness for this Captain Shrimp, and had tended to avoid his company, something that was easily done, the Captain being no mixer. He was an arrogant small man, in Sal's eyes. He was gruff, touchy, and when he flew into a rage he reddened like one who was about to burst, and shuddered all over, shining with sweat.

The process of settling into a strange life, and later the equi-

noctial storms, had given Standish little chance to drill the passengers, nor had he experienced any notable success with the
drills he did have. Nevertheless, he took over when they tumbled
timorously out of the longboat. He allotted weapons. He told
the men how to march, and how fast. He gave the word to go.

There was nothing hortatory about his address.

"If we're attacked, remember it's better not to run. Try to
look toward me. I may not know what to do, but I'm more likely
to know than you are."

Sal made a note in his mind that the party of twelve included
most of the male indentured servants, and especially Edward
Leister and Edward Dotey, the hot-heads most noisily argu-
mentative about landing in New England. This confirmed Sal's
suspicion that he had been brought along because he was
thought to share their views. He'd been seen a little while ago
head-to-head with John Billington, and it was assumed that he
was one of them. The leaders among the saints—Carver, Brewster, Winthrop—were not fools. They knew what was going on.
At this very moment, as everybody was aware, they were con-
ferring on the subject in the main cabin, and what could be
better suited to their purposes than that the landing party
should consist of those who muttered mutiny? If anybody was
to be killed by red Indians it might as well be these. Also, this
would give the elders more time to perfect their plans.

Sal knew a shock when they were arrayed and the weapons
passed out. To him went a spade. He should dig, he was told,
to see how the soil was, or perhaps to try for water. He bridled
at this.

"D'ye think I'm not to be trusted with a musket, then?"

Captain Standish, the uppish, snappish man, did an amazing
thing then. He leaned forward and put a hand on Sal's arm.
He spoke in a low, placating, caressive voice.

"Boyd, you're here because I asked for you. Fighting men

should stick together. Not in so many words, no, but in all truth I'm counting on you as my adjutant."

"Oh."

"Muskets will give confidence to the others, but you don't need that. You've got no fear."

"You think so?"

"Besides, if there's a fight, Boyd, don't ye suppose that at least half of these clods will drop their guns and run? You'd have a choice of weapons then, eh?"

"I—I suppose so."

"What's more, if it did come to a fight I'd rather have you by my side with a spade than most of the others with muskets."

Sal swallowed hard, being embarrassed, bewildered.

"Well, that's all right then," he mumbled.

Standish gave a knowing nod, then proceeded to arrange his men in a single strung-out line, instructing them not to walk too close together. After a final pitying look, he took his place ahead of them and led them toward the shore.

This took courage, and Sal Boyd, angry, resentful, despite himself admired that little soldier. It was not the peril of being first that might deter Standish from taking his proper place— an arrow would reach any of them—but rather the chance of being shot in the back. The muskets were all loaded, and the men who held them were nervous, twitchy. If one of them stumbled . . . Yet Miles Standish did not pause.

Glaring at a backplate, Sal smoldered. He didn't think he liked to have a man he didn't like like him.

On the beach was a quivered line of shell chips and stale drying seaweed, which stank. They reformed their ranks, for they'd drawn close together, as men will when they are frightened. They kept gazing upon what thicket there was, the runtlike trees, the hollow spots. Even Captain Standish, as he rearranged them, more than once glanced over his shoulder.

They had all heard that the characteristics of the wild men of

America were ferocity, cruelty, the cunning of jungle beasts, and above all an extraordinary stealth.

"All right. Now, don't go too fast. Don't get too close behind me. And stay spread out! Try to keep in step. That may not mean much to you, but if we're being watched it could mean a lot to the watchers. We must look as if we're without fear."

How well they succeeded Sal didn't know. Sal was near the middle of the line, and from time to time he would glance right or left, studying his companions. They were so tense, so taut, as they scanned the wilderness all about them, that not many even commented upon a sensation that must have been new to them, though Sal Boyd from long experience had expected it— the sensation of walking on stationary ground for the first time in weeks and feeling it buck and sway beneath your feet like the deck of a ship. A few did reel, astonished, and then stop, frowning at the earth as though it had played them a dirty trick.

"Got to get your land legs," Sal called. "It won't take long."

It was astounding, he reflected, that these men with their pinched, pale faces, their thin lips, these weavers and drapers and clerks, spindly indoor workers, with weak eyes, most of whom probably never had touched a musket before, should yet keep going. Tremble they certainly did; but they did not come to a halt until Standish so commanded.

"You may rest."

This they did not do. They stood in silent small groups, faced out from the middle, always with their eyes darting back and forth, back and forth, their fingers never far from the triggers of their guns.

Sal nodded, thoughtful. He himself felt, as he always did in a dangerous place, when fighting might at any minute break out, tight at the throat, a mite tight too across the chest; but he wasn't so frightened that he could not spit.

Not only were there no fires, there were not even the remains of a fire. They saw no abandoned camp, no footprint, no discarded tool or weapon, in short no scrap of evidence that mankind ever had dug here, or hunted, or fished, or fought. Still, they had the feeling that they were being regarded.

Time after time Sal spaded the earth, without results. No marvel that the plants were stunted! Such as it was, the earth was dark and looked rich, but there was never more than an inch of it, seldom that, and then—sand, sand.

Several of the men had axes, for firewood was one of the chief purposes of their party, and these kept cutting juniper, not only because it was plentiful, but because it was fragrant and would sweeten the cabin of the Mayflower.

Their feet might have been encased in ice.

Standish strode ahead, that long snaphance over his shoulder, his morion and breast- and backplates glowing determinedly. He never turned his head except to shout an order. He did not have many inches, but he made the most of what he had: he held himself uncompromisingly erect.

If there was no sunlight, at least there was no rain, nor was the air wet, so that they did not need to fret about their matches, blowing on them intermittently to keep them lit.

They skirted salt marshes and saw no flowing stream, but unexpectedly they did come upon a fresh-water pond not far from the beach upon which they had landed. This was good.

Returning to that beach was harder than walking away from it. Even Sal had the creepy conviction that he was being stalked. He would have been happier to walk backward, as some of the men did do, but his position as second-in-command of course precluded anything like that.

It was good to be aboard Mayflower again.

For all their jangling, they sensed instantly that something momentous was about to happen. Miles Standish was summoned to the main cabin, from which the others were excluded. But the others were summoned there too, or most of them, later. Sal was the last to go, along with Edward Dotey and Edward Leister. He thought the connection significant, and was prepared for insult.

Brewster, Carver, Winthrop, they were all there, looking portentous; and not only the principal saints but some of the strangers as well, William Mullins for one, and Miles Standish, and even John Billington, who looked sulky, dissatisfied.

Elder Brewster smiled upon the newcomers, and delicately cleared his throat.

"It has been thought by some of us, nay most of us, virtually all," he started, "that before we go ashore, wherever that may be, and whenever, we would do well to have a distinct understanding as to our government. I mean, how we should rule ourselves."

"Rule *ourselves?*" cried Sal, flabbergasted.

"How else? We are three thousand miles from Court and King, and three thousand miles from the remainder of the adventurers. We must needs make our own court. Surely you see that?"

Sal was frowning.

"Go on," he said.

Elder Brewster picked up a paper. It was a simple thing, with no seals or stamps, no ribands attached.

"We have framed this, uh, well, charter."

"Only the King can grant a charter," Sal pointed out.

"Why, I suppose you'd call it a compact, then. Anyway, all of us here have signed it, and some others. That does not mean, you understand, that you three young men will be expected to do the same. It's entirely up to you."

Dotey and Leister, their master's eye upon them, and realizing that it was too late to object, nodded submissively.

"Why don't you read it?" Sal asked.

"I was about to do that. Now:

"In ye name of God, Amen. We whose names are under-written, the loyall subjects of our dread sovereigne Lord, King James . . ."

"Um," said Sal.

". . . having undertaken for ye glorie of God, and ad-vancemente of ye Christian faith, and honour of our king & countrie, a voyage to plant ye first colonie in ye Notherne parts of Virginia, doe by these presents solemnly & mu-tually in ye presence of God, and one of another, convenant & combine ourselves togeather into a civill body politick for our better ordering & preservation & furtherance of ye ends aforesaid, and by vertue hereof to enacte, constitute, and frame such just & equall lawes, ordinances, acts, con-stitutions and offices, from time to time, as shall be thought most meete & convenient for ye generall good of ye Colonie, unto which we promise all due submission and obedience.

"In witnes whereof, we have hereunder subscribed our names of Cap-Codd, ye 11 of November, Ano: Dom. 1620."

There was some silence, while Elder Brewster put the paper down. Everybody looked at Sal, excepting John Carver, who looked at his servants. After a moment Dotey and Leister, all fire gone, stepped up and signed. Then they left.

Elder Brewster sanded the signatures, and proffered the pen to Sal, who shook his head.

"It is not necessary that you write your name," the elder said in a kindly voice. "Somebody could write it for you, and you could make—"

"Oh, I can write my name all right. I could do that even afore I came aboard this vessel. But—I'm not going to write it on a paper like that. It sounds against the King."

"Boyd, it is not meant to be."

"Well, it sounds that way. It sounds *illegal.*"

"But if—"

"It ain't natural. How could we set up our own government? How?"

"It may not be natural, but it's needed. You'll notice that we specifically avow our allegiance to King James."

"I noticed that, aye. But it still looks illegal to me."

"And you won't sign it?"

"No, sir. I'll do almost anything else that most of you others think is right, but I won't put my name on something that speaks against the King."

"But—it doesn't."

"I think it does," said Sal, and he went out.

Chapter Sixteen

The next day no work was done, for it was the Lord's Day. Even Captain Jones, though there would be repairing, reflaking, refitting, allowed his men to loaf. The weather held, grim, unpleasant, but not severe; wet, smelling of a snow that never did fall.

The saints, when they were not holding services, clustered around their braziers in a cabin that now was redolent of the sweet inspiriting smell of juniper.

Nobody went ashore. Few even looked in that direction, so chill was the prospect, making them feel, now that they were motionless, excruciatingly lonely.

Because there were no longer the pauseless squeal of timbers, the cursing and clatter of mariners at work, the sough of wind in the shrouds, the thud of water at the bows, the swish of water at the stern, Mayflower seemed eerily quiet, a circumstance that heightened what sounds there were—the psalms nasally chanted, the high, shrill, discordant, inane screech of gulls, and the coughs, sneezes, snivels, nose-blowings. For a large number of them had colds, and in addition seven were laid up with advanced scurvy.

Three of the seven in sick bay were mature men—no children were ill, even with colds—and these, all but helpless, were the only ones among the adult male passengers, excepting always Sal Boyd, who had not subscribed to Elder Brewster's compact.

Not a word of reproach was spoken to Sal, nor was he sneered at, or scowled at. Priscilla, though she must have known of it, and puzzled about it, made no mention, at their lesson, of the refusal. Such matters were not for females.

Uneasy, in the middle of the morning Sal sought out Elder Brewster and asked for another look at that paper. This was a request granted readily, and Sal, his lips moving, his forefinger shifting from word to word, read it. It was the second thing he ever had read, the first being the Book of Genesis, and the only thing that he had read unassisted. Elder Brewster congratulated him.

But Sal shook his head.

"No," he said again. "I can't go with that. It's against the King."

Brewster did not attempt to argue, but sighing put the paper away, and Sal went back on deck.

An exception to the general reluctance to gaze upon the New World was Dorothy Bradford. Sal saw her on the high poop deck, seated on the taffrail, looking toward shore. That was also toward England. Was she thinking of her son at home?

This was a place withdrawn, now that there was no watch, and a place moreover where she had no right to be. Either she had not been seen, or, having been seen, she'd been so pitied, what with her pale pinched face, her red eyes, the hands folded in her lap, that even Christopher Jones did not have the heart to shoo her away.

Sal went to her, as though in an offhand way. He felt sorry for Dorothy Bradford, married to a dry stick. Oh, no doubt William Bradford was a true believer, a faithful spouse, and a highly admirable man. He was no more holier-than-thou than any of his companions; he was at least as well educated as any of them, far better educated than most; and he was a tireless worker, honest, conscientious. But he was dull. He looked as if he had never laughed, and never would. What Dorothy wanted, poor dear, was a nudge in the ribs, a chuckle, a playful slap on the butt. She'd never get those things from her husband.

"Thinking of taking a walk? Do some shopping, maybe?"

She responded with no more than a wan smile, a smile intended to thank him and which disappeared almost as soon as it had come. She didn't feel like talk, and Sal—who himself had no business on the poop deck—sauntered away, whistling as he went, to let her know that he wasn't hurt.

Priscilla, for a change, was busy. Standish was aloof. A group of the younger men still nattered on about their exploring experience of the previous day, but Sal, already bored by this, strolled off.

He thought of taking a swim. He could not remember ever *learning* to swim. As a boy he had been from time to time tossed into the garbage- and sewage-strewn Thames, and staying afloat and getting ashore seemed as natural to him as walking. More, he always enjoyed himself in the water. This made him a freak among mariners, a sport, for few of them could swim at all, and none would dream of going into the water just for fun. In quiet semitropical hideaways, especially if there had been any fighting and he was dark with powder smudge, Sal not infrequently used to amuse his fellow rovers by stripping and diving overboard, to romp and play like any porpoise. He'd laugh. He'd clown. He would fish things up from the bottom, while the boys cheered him.

Such behavior by the side of the sedate Mayflower would not meet with the approval of the saints, even on a weekday and much the less so on the Lord's Day; but Sal was a bit weary of deferring to the saints.

However, when he looked at the water, as still as ice and doubtless almost as cold, and remembered how it had felt on his feet and against his ankles the previous day, he changed his mind.

He refused yet another invitation to join a lugubrious group engaged in praising the Lord, though he did pause to listen a little while.

"Jehobah feedeth me; I shall not lack. In folds of budding grass He maketh me lie down; He easily leadeth me by the waters of rest . . ."

Sal sighed. There was not even, for him, his old refuge, his haven, or *sanctum sanctorum*, the inverted longboat, for that was in the water.

At least, it being the Lord's Day, the children weren't permitted to play.

Sal drew Dorothy Bradford's cloak close around him, and slid to a sitting position at the foot of the mainmast, against which his head rested. He propped his feet upon the knight. He grunted, belched, closed his eyes, and went to sleep.

Chapter Seventeen

The Monday bustle began before dawn. The women had been asking many questions about that fresh-water pond. Having gone more than two months without a wash day, they were eager to be at it. However, they could not be allowed to go ashore until full light, and even then only when surrounded by a guard, of which Sal Boyd was one. Yet they got there before the men with the shallop.

The shallop, a one-masted, half-decked boat, had looked huge in the hold, where it served as sleeping quarters for a large number of strangers and saints alike; but once it had been hauled, piece by piece, out on deck, and there half assembled, it showed as a scant thing indeed.

At first there had been another ship, Speedwell, smaller than Mayflower but many times larger than this unnamed shallop; but when it had proved unseaworthy and perforce had to be left behind at Plymouth, they became dependent upon the shallop. It came topside in sections, and the original plan had been to assemble it right aboard Mayflower, launching it from the waist, but one look at it when it had been dragged into the open was proof sufficient that a great deal of work must be done before it could be trusted to the water. The wet air of the hold, and even more the fact that so many persons slept in it every

97

night and climbed in and out of it, had done the shallop no good. The seams were sprung: the thing would be a sieve. Besides the work of assembling, it would be necessary to build in many braces and to recalk completely. Therefore it would have to be taken ashore, at whatever cost of labor. Captain Jones refused to permit his deck to be cluttered with the ungainly craft for days on end, perhaps a week. He had his own work to do, he said.

For the men assigned to the setting up of a framework on shore in which to lodge the shallop, the day was one of unremitting labor. For the others, the women, the guards, that day had about it, unexpectedly, an air of merriment. They felt good. They stretched. They hummed, and some even sang. In the middle of the morning and again for a little while early in the afternoon the sun came out, and they lifted their faces to it, basking.

As the day advanced and the cleansed clothes and bedding were sent back by repeated trips of the longboat, Mayflower, all hung with it, took on a positively festive air.

Many of the men working on the beach succumbed to the temptation to eat some mussels they found there, and they were violently sick, but back by the pool the scene was all but idyllic.

The guards walked about, their muskets over their shoulders, sometimes stopping to talk to the women, sometimes scouting a short distance for a possible rabbit or squirrel, which they did not find. Unless the sick got fresh food, which they all craved, it was agreed that they would be worse and there would be more of them. But the guards, on orders, didn't stroll far; and they found nothing.

Priscilla was one of the women sent ashore, and she worked around the pond with the others, chattering, beating, scrubbing, wringing. Her sleeves were rolled high because of the nature of this work. It was the first time that Sal Boyd had seen her arms. They were lovely.

She would make a wonderful wife. And she must be thinking

of that. She was at least seventeen, maybe even eighteen. She'd have to get married soon.

"Is this what we call alertness?"

He jumped. He had not heard Captain Standish come up behind him. The Captain, however, though on a sentry-inspecting tour, was not inclined to be censorious. Like the others, he seemed to be affected by the day, and if he did not go so far as to smile he did nod warmly to Sal Boyd as to an old comrade. He shook his snaphance as though it had been a spear.

"I've noticed you looking at this with eyes of love, Boyd. Would you like to shoot it sometime?"

"Say, I'd admire to do that, sir!"

"All right. But not today. It might break the spell, eh? Or cause a riot."

Sal grinned.

"The children were up here a little while ago, sir."

They were still landing children from the longboat. These had been told to keep out of the way of their mothers and sisters at the pool as well as of the men who were erecting the frame for the shallop, and they had been warned also not to stray far from the beach. This limited their activities, but anything was better than the waist of the Mayflower.

"What did they want?"

"They wanted to know if they could go over by that oak and dance around it. They always like to have something to dance around or walk around."

"So I've noticed. And what did you tell 'em."

"I said no. My orders were they wasn't to go any farther than right here."

"Good."

There was some silence. This was in the middle of the morning's brief sunny spell, and Miles Standish actually squinted as he gazed down toward the beach, where the men under the ship's carpenter, Francis Eaton of Bristol, were stacking planks.

The cooper, John Alden, was one of them, Sal noted. It kept him away from Priscilla.

"Boyd, why did you refuse to sign that compact?"

This jolted Sal. The average Mayflower passenger ordinarily was willing to debate with you at the drop of a hat. The saints especially loved argument for its own sake. They could wrangle by the hour, with very little hard feeling and never an oath or even a raised voice. Their councils seemed interminable. But Miles Standish, like Sal himself, by habit stayed away from those discussions, reserving his decision until he was asked for it.

"I don't know, sir. I just don't like it, that's all. I looked at it again yesterday morning, and I still didn't like it. It smacks of—well—"

"Not treason, surely?"

"Well, maybe not really treason. But something mighty close to that. You know yourself, sir, it ain't right for the likes of us to try to make up laws for ourselves. It ain't natural. That's for a king to do, under God."

"But we haven't got a king here."

"That's not my fault. I didn't ask to come."

Again Standish was silent for a while. Clearly he had been thinking about this compact he'd signed.

"It could be that I feel somewhat the way you do, Boyd," he said at last. "Oh, just a little bit! But—have you ever heard the old saying that when in Rome do as the Romans do?"

"We're not in Rome," Sal pointed out.

At this point further conversation was cut by a group of children who, since this was the outside rim of their playground, which contained no trees, used the next best thing. Solemnly, holding hands, they began to encircle these warriors, singing as they did so.

"Molly go round the sun,
Molly go round the moon,

Molly go round the chimney pots
On a Saturday afternoon."

It had been a good day, Sal reflected as he herded the last worker to the beach, to the longboat, just before sundown. He hoped that there would be other days like it.

Chapter Eighteen

It came on colder, and there were complaints. For several days they toiled willingly, even enthusiastically, the women at the pond, the men on the shallop, while Standish and Sal and others stood guard, and the longboat plied back and forth between ship and shore. An outsider, viewing this scene, might think that all was well.

An outsider would have been wrong. They were split not only into strangers and saints, with the strangers resenting the control that was exercised by the saints, the Leyden separatists who, though not overweening about it, were determined to keep their grip upon the company; they were split as well into masters, goodmen, employed artisans like Alden, and indentured servants. That they had signed their names did not make them acquiescent. Those who were left on the ship croaked because they were not permitted to go ashore, while those who went ashore to work on the shallop croaked because the guards only stood about, hauling nothing, hammering nothing, holding nothing heavier than their muskets, and whenever they felt like it making pleasant converse with the women. Even the women themselves might be expected to whine, once the dirty laundry ran out.

The first fine welling of elation, the initial sense of achievement, had faded. Now they were beginning to ask themselves

where they were, how they had got there, and what they ought
to do about it. "Cape Cod" meant little. They did have John
Smith's map, as well as a copy of his book, *A Description of
New–England,* but these, though recent, were of no real help.
Some of the leaders had talked with the doughty Captain himself, in England, just before the sailing, but they had declined
his offer to go with them as an expert, for they had pointed out
that his book was cheaper than his services might be. Now perhaps they wished that they had not so decided.

Surely they could not settle in this horrid land, yet neither
could they explore the shore of the bay until their shallop was
ready. And work on the shallop dragged. There was a great deal
of quiet but dogged bickering. It was supposed at first to take
three days, that operation; then five days; but now, at the end
of a week, they were still slogging at it.

The wind rose. For the most part the sun stayed away, and
when it did shine its light was watery and wan. Soon the snow
would fly. Before that time came they must select a site for their
colony, clear it, fortify it, build huts, and land all their tools and
supplies. Man needs more than bread. He needs beer, and gunpowder, and axes.

There was yet another quarter from which complaints were
made, and these increased. The mariners of the Mayflower never
had liked their passengers, whom they esteemed to be mealy-
mouthed, smug, always in the way. At Cape Cod the mariners
developed a more definite objection. They had crossed the ocean
sea, and their supplies were low. They'd get nothing here, in
this New England or North Virginia or whatever it was. Soon—
but *how* soon?—they would be obliged to cross back to England,
in the middle of winter, on short rations, the beer souring. It
was not a prospect calculated to please them; and if they had
muttered before, they growled and grumped and grumbled now,
giving the passengers many a dark look. They had completed
their work, hadn't they? Why couldn't they dump these damned

psalm-singers ashore somewhere, anywhere, together with all their gear, and then hurry home—before they froze, or starved, or both? Jones and the mates were frankly worried. Over at this end of the world there were no high sheriffs or King's commissioners, there was no Royal Navy to be called in.

Another thing: This desolate land, with its dunes, its twisted trees, its gritty ubiquitous sand, most of all the appalling absence of any sign of human life, was getting on their nerves. They leapt at trifles. Wherever they went, not only ashore but even aboard Mayflower, they moved, as Sal had heard Spaniards express it, *la barba sobre el hombro,* with the beard on the shoulder, looking backward, askance.

Of course they discussed this, as they discussed everything. Night after night in the cabin they held forth voluminously, asking God for strength, asking one another for patience. Night after night they arrived nowhere, while work on the shallop limped, and in the forecastle the grumbling grew louder.

If they were dumped—there could be no doubt of this—they would die.

"What of it?" Sawn Matthews said to Sal. "That'd be no skin off your bum, would it? Nobody *made* 'em come here, did they?"

Sal did not answer.

At last it was agreed that they should send a fairly strong party, a dozen or more men, down the peninsula. It would be a mission fraught with peril, but they were desperate, and must do something.

Volunteers were called for, and Salathiel Boyd was among the first of these.

Sal was not seeking to impress anybody. Though he would always do anything he'd been ordered to do—if ordered by the right officer—until this time he had subscribed to the old military adage: Never volunteer. It was different off Cape Cod. All rules could be broken, and perhaps should be, when you came to a land like America.

They started the next morning, fourteen of them, each with a matchlock over his shoulder, while the women waved them away. Captain Standish at their head begged them to maintain some semblance of military precision and snap.

They wore corslets and morions, which made the marching heavy. Each man, in addition to his musket, had a sword and a dagger.

They hadn't gone two miles down the beach before they met the savages.

Chapter Nineteen

There were five or six of these wild men—in the excitement nobody could be sure of the number—and they were walking north along the beach. They had a dog with them. They must have seen the sixteen soldiers at the same instant that the soldiers saw them, but the savages moved much the faster. Whistling their dog after them, they darted into a nearby wood.

"No, no!" cried Miles Standish. "Don't run! Stay in step!"

He might have saved his breath. The sight, and the immediate flight, were too much for the settlers, who broke their ranks and ran down the beach, leaving their leader with the only man who heeded him, Salathiel Boyd.

"Fools!" Standish cried, sobbing. "Oh, the *fools!*"

Not only did they run to the point on the beach where the Indians had been: they wheeled left there and plunged into the same wood at the same point, disappearing.

It could be that they disappeared—forever.

"The saints preserve us!" yelled Miles Standish.

"We'd better go after 'em," said Sal.

"Yes, yes!"

There was no shot, there were no screams or shouts. Sal and the Captain could only pray, as they leapt ahead, that this was not a trick, an ambush, but that the red men had been just as surprised as the settlers, so that their flight was precipitous and not a lure.

The trail was easily followed. Panic-stricken cattle could not have made one clearer. Yet when they did come upon their panting, scratched, baffled companions, it was evident that the pursuit had been abandoned. How could they ever have hoped to maintain it, with their steel helmets, their cuirasses, and swords and muskets and provisions, and heavy boots, Miles Standish explosively demanded to know.

The little Captain was in a rage, and despite the fact that he too had not yet caught his breath he strode back and forth, swashing his flintlock, while he scolded a sheepish, shamefaced company.

"Did ye not hear my order? If you'd come to a halt, or at the least kept a march without breaking step, then we might have made touch with these savages. Who knows, we might have bought some American corn of them, or learned where berries are to be picked? Don't ye want to *live?*"

He stopped, statue-still, though he trembled.

"But no, you gallant men, you had to rush! *Who's* the savage there? No wonder they scurried for shelter! Oh, oh, ye fools! Ye beefwits!"

He did not use profanity. There might have been two reasons for this. In the first place, Miles Standish was a most amazingly clean-mouthed man, for a soldier, and perhaps in his wrath expletives of a blasphemous nature simply didn't come to him. More likely, though, the restraint was calculated. There were as many saints as strangers in this group; and while men like Billington, who was there, would scarcely be shocked and might even be amused by an eruption of verbal filth, men like William Bradford and Edward Tilley, who were also there, would simply have been saddened, and might have declined thereafter to obey when any man of such ungodly mouthings gave a command.

Nevertheless, Miles Standish's rebuke was loud, and it blistered.

"We could have talked to them by signs, from a distance! But you—each of you must lunge forward like a bull that's been goaded in the rump! And now we'll never see 'em again. Or if we do, they'll start to shoot before they talk."

He stamped back and forth, waggling his hands.

"And I mean this not only as a soldier! *I*'ve got a belly to fill too, in case you didn't know! And look at you now: your breeches torn, your sword-belts loose—not a one of you could lug out, if we was attacked this instant—you're so winded—and the powder spilled from your priming-pans—and half of you have let your matches die! *Ugh!*"

He appealed to Heaven, reverently enough, and not undramatically, both arms raised.

"God spare me such troops! They should have stayed at home!"

William Bradford, Dorothy's husband, the dry stick, though the best-educated of them all here in this company, was a man of all but terrifying humbleness. To him the Holy Discipline was very real. It was not a matter of induced ecstacy, but a constant condition; he breathed it, ate it, slept it, drank it, *was* it. Theoretically Bradford was in command here, though it had been understood that in all matters military Miles Standish should be deferred to. Sal was watching William Bradford, and saw him stiffen. But the Bradford head remained low.

"I reckon we have a lot to learn."

"You have," said Captain Standish.

Unexpectedly, the trail was almost as easy to follow from this point on. But that's all they could do, follow it. They kept after it all day, though they had no reason to believe that they were ever close to the persons they sought. This part of the pursuit, at least, was made in step; and orders were obeyed.

They had heard about the wiliness of the American savage,

his superb woodsmanship. Had such stories been exaggerated?
Or were the savages of Virginia skilled in covering their steps
while those farther north, here in New England, were not? Or
were these creatures whom they followed so badly scared that
they forgot to take precautions? Or again—and it was this possi-
bility that troubled them the most as that day wore on—were
the footprints, the broken twigs, *deliberate?* Did the savages
wish to leave a trail that even these blundering white men could
see? Was this a trap?

Not only were they apprehensive as they renewed their march,
they were also tired, even this early; and soon too they were
thirsty. Since they had no sort of vehicle, and it had seemed best
to travel as light as possible, they had not brought any beer. The
best they had, in a few small flasks, was some aqua vitae or Hollands gin, which, though strong, was not as refreshing to the
mouth as wine or beer would have been. When late in the afternoon they stumbled upon a spring, they did not hesitate to
throw themselves down and gulp its plain water. They even
took some of this along with them, in a flask.

That night they camped between two mountainous dunes on
the ocean side of the spit, the slam of breakers in their ears. No
wood or thicket was close at hand, but they kept a fire burning
and a guard posted all the same. Nothing happened.

In the morning they could not pick up the trail of the fleeing
Indians, which the wind had carried away. But they did come
upon what looked like a grave, and with reverent knives and
swords they dug into this, finding some bones, a decayed bow, a
few rotting arrows. All of these they replaced, as they replaced
the earth.

"Only—I hope nobody's watching," murmured Sal.

Back on the bay side again, they explored a small river or
tidal inlet: they couldn't make out which it was.

Here was the best place for a colony that they had yet seen,
but it wasn't very good. There was a harbor of sorts, but the

water was shallow. The banks of the river—or inlet—were high, as land went in these parts. It was a spot that would not be difficult to fortify. The ground was about the same, a thin layer of black soil over sand. But the only fresh water was a small pool some distance inland and lower: it was so small it might well dry out in summertime.

They camped again, somewhat less timorously now, though without vainglory; and the next morning, the third, they started north along the bay shore for Mayflower.

It was then that they made a discovery that would change the lives of every one of them.

Chapter Twenty

There was a hill to their right, back from the beach. It was not a large or imposing hill, yet it was enough in this country to constitute a landmark. At its foot was a clear, somewhat grassy space that might have been called a meadow; and there some of the sharp-eyed members of the company, who could have been seeking an excuse for a halt, all of them being weary, spied what looked like graves. One in particular, they saw when they approached, appeared to have been recently dug.

Without further ado they violated this.

It was brutally and immediately done. As far as Sal could hear, no order was given. The deed was spontaneous. And once they had started, feverishly, they were afraid to stop. Standish as the military leader had no say in such a matter, and he was not even given a chance to command the halt: they did that for him.

What Standish thought of the business Sal could not guess, for the Captain stayed to one side, his face professionally expressionless.

Sal himself was shocked, and said so.

"That's a fine way to make friends!"

They paid him little mind, though Bradford himself, Sal could sense, was inwardly troubled. They sworded the earth furiously, all at once, in a wild sort of scramble that caused Sal's lip to curl. Sal indeed even thought of breaking in upon this undignified, indecent digging, stopping it by force. That might mean a fight, and probably would, but he was not sure that he wouldn't welcome a fight just at that time. He took a step forward.

"If we're caught at this," Standish said suddenly, "it will go badly with us. Dotey, go up the beach a few hundred yards. If you see anything suspicious—anything at all!—fire a shot. You, Boyd, go to the top of the hill. The same instructions."

It was the best view of Cape Cod that Sal thus far had been vouchsafed; but he cared little for this. Bitterly he turned his back upon the burrowing, molelike men, and with shoulders hunched high against the cold, his hands deep in his breeches, he surveyed the scene. How anyone would come voluntarily to a land like this was more than he could comprehend. He doubted that a fox could live here, or a rat. It was enough to give a man the mulligrubs.

He did not see any Indians. He hadn't expected to.

The men below did not linger at their task, and when in amazingly short time Sal was called back they already were refilling the hole. Not bones but corn had been uncovered, a huge basketful.

This corn was different from any that Sal ever had seen. It came in large shiny triangular chunks, some yellow, some red, a few streaked with blue. They were as hard as pellets of lead— and this though the ground was not yet frozen.

"This is American corn, the kind they have in Virginia, the kind they got from the barbarians there," reported Stephen Hopkins, one of the few in the party who had been to the New World before. "We know that it will grow here. We can't be sure that the wheat and rye seed we brought from home will. Or the vegetables. This stuff may save our lives."

He started to cram his pockets with it, as the others already were doing.

Salathiel Boyd wouldn't touch it.

"It was put here by the Lord for us to gather," William Bradford said, searching Sal's face.

"How do you figure that out?"

Bradford was troubled, and any saint when troubled instinctively sought backing from the Book.

"Is it not written that the Lord Himself commanded Moses to send men from the wilderness of Paran to spy out the land of Canaan?"

"Is it? Mistress Mullins and I haven't got that far yet."

"And does it not say 'Then they came to the river of Ethcol, and cut down thence a branch with one cluster of grapes, and they bare it upon a bar between two, and brought of the pomegranates and of the figs'?"

"I see."

"And is this not analogous?"

"Mister, I don't know what that word means. What I do know is that you'll find it says in that same Book, it says 'Thou shalt not steal.' "

They all looked up; for Sal was angry and had not striven to keep a low voice.

"Coming from a pirate," drawled John Billington, "that hath a fine moral swing."

"Speaking of swinging," Sal countered, "what d'ye suppose would happen to you if you did this in England?"

"If all the pirates—"

"I never was a pirate. I was a privateer sailing under the banner of the Emperor of Morocco. And besides, we were at least open about it. We didn't *sneak* things away."

He glared around. Most of the men looked embarrassed, but they kept stuffing corn into their pockets.

"And we always left a man something, to keep him alive till

he got to the next port. That's more'n you're doing here now."

Bradford put a gentle hand on Sal's arm. He was anything but a demonstrative man, and this showed that he was shaken.

"Boyd, we'll starve if we don't take this."

"And maybe *they*'ll starve if we *do*. Why else did they put it there for excepting to save it for next spring, for planting?"

"Boyd," quietly. "I've got my wife and my child at home to think of."

Sal shook the hand off.

"You've also got your immortal soul to think of, haven't you? I have heard of selling it for thirty pieces of silver, but I've never—poor ignorant Sallee rover that I am!—I've never heard of selling your soul for a pocketful of American corn."

It startled them all, himself included. Without ever having meant to, he was outdoing them at their own game. Yet nobody laughed. And though Bradford, when he turned away, showed hectic spots of rage or perhaps fear in his cheeks, he said nothing. Nor was Sal further urged to load up with corn. He didn't carry a kernel, while the others were so crammed with the stuff that they could barely walk, almost waddled, with their feet far apart, "as if they had the French marbles," Sal sneered.

It started to snow, large, wet, angry drops that fairly hissed as they struck.

The explorers were hailed with great gladness, a joy all but hysterical, which startled them until they learned that their chase of the savages had been witnessed and reported by the mariners who put them ashore. There even had been proposals to send a rescue party after them, a mad act that was just about to start. They were heroes, then. Their shoulders were clapped, their backs slapped, even Sal Boyd's.

Sal's response was surly, for him. William Bradford too, never a noisy man, was especially reserved. He sidled up to Sal.

"I'll raise the matter at meeting tonight. We'll pay them for it, of course! I never meant else but that. We'll seek them out."

"I just hope to hell they don't seek us out first," said Sal.

Seated on deck that night, he could hear the buzz of debate below in the cabin, another of those on-and-on-and-on sessions. They would talk about it for half the night, in the hope of justifying it to themselves. They would pass all kinds of pious resolutions. But Sal was sure that they would keep the corn.

They did.

Chapter Twenty-one

The atmosphere aboard ship had changed with the changing air. Dispute was everywhere, and no longer was it without ire. Saints and strangers alike seemed almost on the point of losing their tempers, which would have been unfortunate. The seamen cursed the passengers more raucously than ever, for they teetered on the lip of mutiny. Christopher Jones and the mates, though they were quicker to help than they had been throughout the voyage, clearly were unsure of their authority, and they had about them, when they dealt with the passengers, an ill-concealed air of urgency, impatience.

If there were fewer prayer sessions, there were more informal and by no means amicable discussions. Fists were not shaken, no, but forefingers were.

"They're beefwits," Sawn decided. "If those Indians did come and start shooting at them, they'd have to have three prayers and a sermon before they settled down to a meeting called to debate whether they were rightly instructed by God to shoot back. And by that time they'd all be dead anyway. *Merde!* Why don't you quit 'em Sal? They're not for the likes of you."

"At a time like this?"

The confiscation of the corn, more than anything else, had brought about this tightness. A moral issue had been raised, and

a moral issue to these settlers was a red rag to a bull. They broke
into many camps, each clamorous.

Oddly, none of them rallied to Sal Boyd. Rather they seemed
to resent him. Nobody scolded him, or even mentioned the
matter in his presence, but it was clear that they thought he
should mind his own business. That *he*, of all persons, should
berate one of their leaders, quoting from the Book forsooth,
caused them, whatever their internal dissensions, to close ranks
when Sal stood there.

There was no overt condemnation, but the reproach was
plain. Sal, it was implied, had overstayed his welcome.

"Should I leave the gathering and go home?" he asked himself.

He regretted this freeze. He reckoned that he liked these
travelers, by and large, more than he had ever liked any group
of persons before, and he had been proud of his own popularity
among them, feeling a glow inside when he saw their faces light
up at his appearance. He was not accustomed to this feeling,
which warmed his heart. Now it was different. They did not
turn away; they wouldn't remonstrate with him, as with one another; but it was with politeness rather than with joy that they
greeted him each day.

Then too there was his refusal to sign the compact. That
rankled.

"Should you change your mind about matters of governance,"
John Carver said to him one afternoon, "please don't hesitate
to come to me—and we can talk."

"I don't change my mind," Sal replied. "I know what's right,
and conversation wouldn't make it any different."

"In a new world—"

"It's a world that belongs to the King, isn't it?"

Even Priscilla, it seemed to Sal, had grown a trifle cold. They
still had their lessons, and still she praised his progress—they
were up to Lamentations—but as soon as a reading was finished

she would make some excuse to go back to her cabin, where Sal was not allowed.

William Mullins was one of those who upheld the taking of the corn. But Sal did not believe that this had anything to do with Priscilla's attitude. Priscilla had a mind of her own.

A doubt was gnawing at Sal's mind like a mouse at the bottom of a cheese. It had been there for some time, and it grew each day as his own spirits sank. Was Priscilla kind to him only because she pitied him? Was her goodness, her sweetness, simple charity? He would have asked her, but they were seldom together these days, and never in any private place. Perhaps he would not have found the courage to ask her anyway. But he worried about this. He fretted. Sometimes as he lay seeking sleep he would mutter little prayers; and though these were set prayers, prayers that he had been taught in the orphanage—for as he told Priscilla, he would have thought it brassy to ask God for something personal, and the saints' habit of doing so frankly shocked him—nonetheless, he did manage to give them an intonation of pleading, and his mind at such times was not altogether on his Creator.

Alden's attitude cheered him somewhat. The cooper was confused, unsure of himself, and more angry than ever. He did not say this in so many words, but he didn't have to, for his face spoke, his scowl. Until these last few weeks, since the end of the storm, John Alden had looked upon Sal only as an obnoxious intruder, an excrescence, a foul being from another world from whose company a girl like Mistress Mullins should be protected. Until lately he had not even dreamt of regarding Sal as a rival. Since he had come aboard the ship at Southampton and met her for the first time—a head start of more than a month over Sal— John Alden had taken it for granted that she would be his eventually. Indeed, it stood to reason that she'd have to marry sooner or later, if only as a matter of duty, leaving out her personal inclinations, and young Alden took himself to be the

only possible husband, the other unmarried men aboard Mayflower being indentured servants with six or seven years yet to
go and thus in no position to make a marriage proposal.

Recently, however, Alden had become perturbed in his mind.
Whether or not he had spoken to Priscilla Sal had no way of
knowing. Probably not. He wouldn't have had the chance. As
for William Mullins, *he* tossed in fever and was hardly the person to be approached just now about an affair of the heart. And
William Mullins's wife meant nothing.

Sal could be sorry for John Alden, which was good. When his
own doubts plagued him, he would reflect upon the cooper—
and feel compassionate, as he chuckled. He even thought of going to Alden, who might not be a bad lad at all if only he could
cease to feel sorry for himself, and suggesting outright that they
stop snarling at one another and shake hands. Sal Boyd didn't
fancy making faces from a distance. He'd fight a man or kiss him,
and have it over with. But Alden wasn't presently available. His
barrels, so well taken care of, could not be moved from the lower
hold until a site for a settlement had been picked, and since
there was now no motion of the ship they did not need his constant care; but ashore, where the men were still assembling the
shallop, Alden's skill with wood was in demand, and he was
busy there every day almost all day.

Work on the shallop dragged, Sal didn't know why—perhaps
because the workers were too disputatious?—and ten days after
the First Discovery, as they had come to call it, still lacking a
boat in which to explore the shore of the bay, they sent out
another party on foot. Sal Boyd, though he had volunteered, was
not assigned to join this party.

"Lucky for you," Sawn told him. "They bump into any savages and they'd turn around and run like Satan, leaving you
there alone. Or maybe you'd run with 'em? Ah, whatever's become of the Salathiel Boyd I used to know!"

"Shut up," said Sal.

The Second Discovery did less than the first, and saw no Indians at all, even from a distance, but it did dig up that basket of corn at the foot of Corn Hill (as they had named it) and carried away all that the First Discovery men had not been able to carry. This was put into the common fund.

And Sal, inactive, moaned.

Chapter Twenty-two

The Captain shot a duck one day, but he ate it himself. There was not a morsel of fresh meat for the scurvy patients, who numbered fourteen, crammed into a dim bay that was located forward, just below the galley. Sal, lacking other duties, often helped to nurse these men and women. He was, of course, familiar with scurvy—the bloody blotches of the skin, the aching muscles, the sore gums, throbbing eyes, parched throat—and as a veteran mariner he could endure just about any stench. Also, he had displayed a skilled hand at stripping young William Button, Sam Fuller's servant who had died at sea, and sewing the body into canvas and weighting it. That was an aptitude assumable in one of his past. When James Chilton died here at anchorage, not of scurvy but of a lung ailment that always had plagued him, it was Sal they called upon, again, to strip and sew up the body. He obliged. He didn't like that kind of work, but he was used to it. And anybody likes to be kept busy.

This was the reason given for excluding him from the Second Discovery. The patients in the sick bay needed his ministrations; and if they died—why, even then they needed him. He wished that he could believe this. The truth, he told himself, was that people who like to preach to other people can become almighty nettled when somebody preaches to *them*. Which he shouldn't have done. But he didn't care.

They buried poor small Chilton a short distance above high-water mark, just past the place where the shallop was being completed. The ground was frozen; it was so hard that they had to use axes on it before they could dig. While this work went on Sal regarded the corpse. Poor little Chilton, he looked so small in his canvas shroud, a midget! Not only had he been short, but, as Sal knew from having laid him out, he'd been thin of bone, slight, brittle, slim. Why had he come on this journey, that tiny old man? He'd been a tailor with a shop of his own in Canterbury, in the shadow of the cathedral, a scene so different from this one! He was not a saint, not a practitioner of the Holy Discipline. He was not known to have had any very vehement religious views. Gasping, dying, he had taken up his few possessions, and with his wife and his daughter Mary, a minx of fifteen, had embarked aboard Mayflower. Why? And now they were burying him.

The shallop, at long last, was about ready to to take to the water, yet the workers, for all their eagerness to see this event, came over to help in the burial, and stood uncovered in the drizzle while the body was lowered into its grave.

"Will you help me here a moment, Brother Boyd?"

"Sure."

It saddened Sal, who when they went back in the longboat had some trouble trying to cheer up Mary, a scared girl. Aboard Mayflower he turned her over to Priscilla Mullins, who had been attending her own sick father as well as the widow.

All talk was of the Third Discovery, which would set forth the following day, as soon as the shallop was launched and rigged, and which would be under orders not to return without a site. This trip must be decisive. The plan was to explore the whole inside of the bay, if necessary, but in particular to examine the place that John Smith had designated on his map as New Plymouth. The longboat was about to start back for shore, and the younger men, the ones who were going on this Third Discovery, to the number of twenty, were storing their gear aboard of it. Sal Boyd had no gear, but he knew he'd be going, and he would be ready. He had borrowed a whetstone, and now he sat in the waist, slowly, lovingly putting a razor edge on his knife. They'd need real men on this jaunt.

"It ought to go through red skin just the same's any other kind," he remarked, holding the knife high for Miles Standish to see.

The Captain had been about to take his place in the boat. He paused, looking down at Sal.

"You know, Boyd, maybe I shouldn't be the one to tell you this—"

"Tell me what?"

"*I* wanted you. I asked especially for you. But— Well, certain others in the company decided that you'd be of more use here aboard the ship."

Sal sprang to his feet.

"What's that you're saying, man? God damn it, you're not trying to tell me that I'm to be kept back here like some God-damn' woman?"

"I—I'm afraid that's the way it's going to be, Boyd. That's what was decided."

He put a hand on Sal's shoulder, which he shook.

"You're a soldier, Boyd. Be one. I know it's hard, but—well."

"Sure," muttered Sal. "Well."

He turned away, snicking his dagger back. He didn't watch as the longboat was pushed off. He felt a little sick, and he was afraid that his eyes might be wet. Nobody should see him that way.

It was a raw morning, the sky low, the wind high, while an icy snow-rain sliced the air. Nobody but a fool would be out in weather like this, if he didn't have to. After the longboat had gone the waist was strangely quiet, all but deserted.

Sal wandered about aimlessly, kicking things.

"Master Boyd?"

It was the Mullins kid, Joe. He was still a little afraid of this pirate.

"Yes?"

"My sister says to tell you she won't be able to leave the cabin for a lesson today. It's because my mother's sick now too, bad cold, besides my father, and that Chilton girl and Mrs. Chilton. But she told me to tell you that."

"Yes. Thank you, Joe. Tell your sister that I'm sorry about her mother, and if there's anything I can do she ought to let me know."

"Yes, sir."

Undoubtedly it was true, that message, and it had been sent in kindness, but coming as it did it didn't make Sal Boyd any happier.

He drifted below. There a brazier glowed, and it was surrounded by jabbering saints, who fell silent at Sal's approach. He passed them, nodding, to visit the scurvies.

These were, as usual, either comatose or inanely blubbering, drooling. The stink was such that it caused even Sal to cough, batting his eyes. Nothing in this world smells worse than a scurvy sufferer's breath.

Most of them did not know him, and none of them cared. "They wouldn't listen," Sal had told Priscilla when she offered to read the Book to them. He made sure now that at least they were all alive, and he emptied and replaced a few pans. Then he went up on deck again.

The snow-rain had ceased, but the day still was dark, the wind sharp. The only person in sight was Dorothy Bradford, husbandless for the present, since William Bradford was ashore supervising the launch of the shallop. She sat, as she so often did these days, on the taffrail, staring in the direction of England. It was a precarious position, but Sal was tired of cautioning her; and clearly today, as so often before, she had no wish to chat, so he went below again.

This time he went all the way down, to the lower hold where the barrels were. He hadn't visited that place since his inspection of the cannons.

It was neat. He snooped, nodding approval. The light was poor, a mere filtering from above, but his hands told him that everything was in order, each barrel tight, the air spaces carefully kept.

A keg was on its side in the middle of the cleared space where Alden probably did most of his work. Beside it on the deck was a small iron tube that coopers called a straw. It was a testing device. If they wanted to know what a given barrel contained, all they needed to do was put it on its side, work out the stopper, and sniff. However, in the case of beer, if they wanted to learn whether it was going sour, an important consideration in what should be moved down here, the surest way was by sucking some of it up through this "straw."

But this couldn't be beer. It was too small a container.

Sal went to it, unplugged it, put his nose down.

There was no mistaking the odor of Hollands gin. Sal beamed. He took up the straw and thrust it into the hole and gave himself a good, long, burning drink. He smacked his lips, while his eyes started to smart.

Since that last night in Plymouth, when it had played him false, and excepting for the time of the First Discovery, Sal Boyd had known no gin. Aboard Mayflower he'd confined his drinking to the ship's beer, a thin, weak, malt-tasting fluid that might almost have been water. Now the Hollands tasted good. He took another drink.

He let it frolic inside, as he nodded knowingly.

He was not stealing anything. This was not ship's property, it was company's property, and Sal could always partake of the common fund.

He cocked his head. There was that pauseless bumble of talk from above, where the remaining saints and strangers were huddled around a fire, discussing dogma.

Sal had put the plug back—no use letting the stuff evaporate—but after a while he worked it out again, and took another drink, just a small one.

He sat on the keg, palms on knees. He was beginning to wonder whether he hadn't ought to feel ashamed of himself. What, after all, had he made of his life?

He thought about this for a while.

He wasn't even a first-class freebooter, really. And as soon as he found himself in the midst of this flock of separatist geese, what did he do? Did he tell them to go soak their heads? No, he gave them disquisitions on the Decalogue. That was it. He snickered. Those were delicious, those disquisitions on the Decalogue.

Sawn was right. They weren't his kind of people, and why should he try to pretend that they were?

Well, when he got back to England, bugger them all, he'd know what to do. Would he "preserve better walking"? Hell, no. He'd cut loose, and pitch all this praise-be-to-the-Lord yammering down the necessary.

He took another drink.

The air was close down there, and relatively warm, and it could be that Sal fell asleep. Not a real sleep, only a few nods. The voices from above had long since ceased to mean anything to him, but he was brought to attention, his head snapping up, his eyes popped, at the sound of John Alden, who had just come down the ladder.

"What the Devil are you doing here?"

Sal waved a negligent hand.

"Go jump down the jakes," he suggested.

Alden started forward, raising his fists, and Sal, with a glad little cry, lurched to his feet.

Alden slammed for the face, a long overhand right. Sal lifted his elbows to avoid it, but he didn't lift them fast enough. Blood spurting from his nose, streaming hot over his mouth, he was slammed back against a barrel.

"Merde!"

He went right in again, head down, both arms swinging. He was hit twice, once over each ear. He fell like a tree.

He knew that he was on the deck. But he couldn't do anything about it. He could not even move.

He assumed that Alden would jump on him with both heavy boots and stamp out his consciousness, along with a good deal of his skin. Sal couldn't help that. He just had to lie and wait for it to happen.

Alden was an ass. He turned away, with a curious little sob from deep in his throat, the sound of a man who is frightened. He scrambled up the ladder. While Sal blinked, dumfounded, his bloody mouth open, the hatch was slammed.

Chapter Twenty-three

Sal lay still for a little while, being in no hurry to go back into the world. He was dizzy, but not dangerously so. The two ear blows, though heavy, and though they had certainly knocked him down and started his head aching—or was that the gin?—at the same time, paradoxically, had cleared that head. He was weak, he was abashed, but he was no longer muddled. He knew what had happened, and why. Nor did he find in his heart any blame for John Alden, who after all was only protecting property entrusted to his care.

What Sal could not grasp was the reason for Alden's sudden departure. Why didn't the fool stay and finish the job, the way anybody else would have done? And what was the meaning of that small, throaty, lemon-shaped sound he had emitted as he fled?

This much Sal did know: John Alden was afraid of him. Alden had attacked in a moment of rage, and now he trembled to think of what he had done—and what might be the consequences.

Was this because Alden was *physically* afraid of him? It seemed unlikely. The cooper was taller and somewhat heavier, and the way he had punched showed that he knew how to use his fists. On the other hand, Sal Boyd, though only a few years older, had behind him all the dread prestige of piracy. Sal was known to have a violent temper when drunk, and to carry a knife; but more important was that murky background. From Alden's point of view Sal could be said to come from a different and much darker world, even from a different age. Almost anything might be expected of a man who had served with the Sallee rovers.

There was another possible explanation, and Sal quaked to think of it, wishing that he could believe it.

John Alden, sobered by the blows he himself had delivered, brought to his senses by the stinging of his own fists, might have gasped to realize he had knocked down—could he have reasoned thus?—one of the most popular persons aboard the Mayflower, a man who had a host of friends. It would be almost like knocking down the skipper, thought Sal, elaborating—indeed, in many ways worse, for nobody liked Christopher Jones. Similarly, there were few who cared for the surly cooper.

This was a pleasing hypothesis; and though Sal could not quite believe it, even as he lay there in that dim place, he gave a tight little blood-smeared grin. The very fact that he had dared to think such a thought in passing stimulated him.

Not consciously but as a matter of course he decided that he would not go after John Alden. He certainly would not apologize, he wouldn't ask for more: That other-cheek behavior might be all right for such as Elder Brewster, but in Sal Boyd it would have smacked of cowardice, an emotion Sal couldn't afford. But he would drop the matter, publicly. And if the cooper renewed hostilities—well, Sal would be steadier the next time, better prepared.

The closing of the hatch had made it very dark down there. Sal got to his knees. He shook his head. With the back of a hand he wiped his mouth. At last he rose.

Tottering a bit, he found the ladder with his hands. He

climbed slowly, doggedly, and with his head pushed open the hatch, a mere trap door.

Again silence seized the group around the fire. John Alden was not among them. Sal nodded easily, affably, as though a bloody mouth was an everyday acquisition, and went up to the waist.

It was deserted. As before, the only person in sight was Dorothy Bradford, and as before, though he desperately sought sympathy, he respected her privacy.

He sat on a snubbing post, put his elbows on his knees, his head between his hands. He was lonely, desperately lonely. For all anyone cared, he could throw himself over the gunwale—there, like the splash he had just heard—only he could swim too well.

This was silly! He was feeling sorry for himself. Gin, he knew, made some men maudlin: did it have this effect upon him?

He looked up startled, though there had been no noise. But a little earlier—his responses were slow today—a little earlier there *had* been a sound, a splash, astern of Mayflower. A fish jumping? It wasn't that kind of splash, not hollow, not a spank. It could hardly be the longboat, for that was ashore with a firewood party.

Then suddenly he knew what it had been. He sprang to his feet, whirling around.

Dorothy Bradford no longer sat on the taffrail.

She was nowhere else on the poop or half deck, and she could not have reached the door of her cabin without passing close to Sal.

He ran up to the half deck, up to the poop, across the poop. He looked over the taffrail.

He saw *something* in the water, he wasn't sure what.

It must have been twenty-five feet down, and he closed his eyes as he tore off his boots, for he was badly frightened. He kept his eyes closed even when he climbed over the rail and launched his dive.

The water was so cold that it was like an enveloping flame, but a paralyzing flame; and he could not even be sure he could swim.

Though he knew that there was a sand bottom, the water was dark. He had struck well, yet he was quickly winded, and as he rose to the surface he starfished his limbs in the hope of brushing something.

With his head out he did not pause to yell. That would have taken too long. He gulped in a great breath, and dived again ... and again. . . .

Chapter Twenty-four

He had a horrid conviction that the woman he held was not Dorothy Bradford but Priscilla Mullins. He couldn't see her, but he could feel her; he was *sure* it was Priscilla.

He held her at arm's length, though he couldn't seem to swim any more: It was as though he had been paralyzed. But—strength might return. She was passive, never stirring. Was she dead? Oh, God, don't allow that to happen! Sal tried again to swim, at least to kick a little, holding her hard.

They were sinking all this while. No matter what he did they went down and down . . .

His ears rang. The force was almost unbearable. He wanted to open his mouth and scream in pain, but if he did that it would be the end.

Yet he did do it. He opened his mouth. And abruptly the pressure was relaxed. He knew a happy, slightly silly feeling. The world went all milk, soft, a film. Now, the world was not harsh; it did not scrape; and if this was death it wasn't pain but relief.

"Thank God!"

Priscilla Mullins he clung to, yes. But she was dry. And so was he. The only thing wet about Sal was his face, which was drenched with sweat. Priscilla, when she managed to get a hand free, wiped the face with a wet cloth.

"You're all right! Praise be to God!"

"How—how long have I been—out?"

"All day."

"*What?*"

He saw from the light on the ceiling that it was indeed sundown. He tried to rise, bumped his head, and fell back. He was in a bunk in the poop cabin, forbidden territory for him ordinarily, and he was dressed in somebody's long white night rail. Like an angel, was his sardonic fleeting thought.

"They—never—found her?"

"No. She must have been washed out to sea. The tide was flood at the time. They dragged the bottom. They did everything. They even sent parties to search the shores all around, and they used the shallop for the first time. They're only beginning to give up out there now. They're coming back."

Sal closed his eyes. He felt weak but otherwise all right. He said a small prayer for Dorothy Bradford, a woman who had quit.

"We—we were afeared that you might go too. You've been in a fever, raving."

"Um. What am I doing here, instead of in the sick bay?"

A voice came from elsewhere, answering.

"I ordered you brought here."

Sal opened his eyes and rolled them sideways. Sam Fuller stood smiling down at him. As far as Sal could see, the three of them were the only persons in a usually overcrowded cabin. The search, and now the return, could account for that.

"I told them that anybody who had tried the way you did to save a woman's life should not be rewarded by exposure to a catching disease."

Sam Fuller was supposed to be a physician. Sal was shocked.

"You can't catch scurvy from somebody else!" he cried.

"I know that, Boyd, and you know it, but they don't. Then too, Mistress Mullins here was bound and determined to nurse you, no matter what happened, and I hated to think of her being in a place where things don't—well, they don't smell sweet."

"They sure don't," Sal agreed.

"Tell me, Boyd—"

Sal had been expecting this. Priscilla already was looking the question. Sal braced himself, swallowing.

"—tell me, do you think that maybe Dorothy Bradford might —well, might—"

"Of course not," sharply.

Sal himself could see nothing wrong with self-destruction, which he took to be a personal matter and nobody else's affair; but to these people it was the most heinous of crimes, at least as bad as, conceivably even worse than, adultery, cannibalism, incest, dooming the doer straight to Hell, his family to ineradicable disgrace. They were very passionate when they spoke of suicide, these saints.

They were not, in the conventional sense of the word, superstitious. Meek and mild enough most of the time, they could yet do things that chilled Sal's blood. They would as lief pare their nails on a Friday as any other day, they cared not a fig about the physical condition of the first person they saw in the morning, and if they'd possessed a black cat they probably would have petted it. They had no fear of Obidicut, Mahu, Modo, and some of them, Sal learned to his horror, had not even *heard* of Hobbididance. But when it came to a man killing himself they turned pale to the lips, and hastened away, muttering. It was a religious matter with them. They saw that the Book forbade it; and if Sal, who was beginning to think of himself as something of an authority on the Book, countered by challenging them to quote the prohibition, they would retreat into the Decalogue, citing Commandment Number Six: "Thou shalt not kill." When Sal would argue further that that only meant killing somebody else, not killing yourself, they would shake their heads and refuse to listen. Granted that killing somebody else was wrong—though naturally there had to be exceptions, even there—Sal would go on to insist that killing *yourself*— But by that time he'd be alone.

"She slipped," Sal resumed confidently. "I felt a little jar of the ship just at that time. Maybe a whale."

"Nobody else felt that."

"I felt it. What's more," Sal lied, "I heard Mistress Bradford yell for help. That's what made me look up. Now, would she yell for help if she wanted to kill herself?"

"Nobody else heard that."

"You were all below. Or here. Indoors, anyway."

Fuller nodded. Sal didn't think that he believed the story, but he was glad to hear it, and now he was eager to get out of the cabin before Sal amended it. He excused himself, pointing to the fact that the shallop was just drawing alongside.

Priscilla stood looking strangely at Sal, after the doctor had gone.

He hauled down his lower lip, eying her askance.

"Did I say anything wrong, when I was raving?"

She colored.

"You used some—nasty words."

"I'm sorry."

"I couldn't make out whether you was cursing the people of London or us, but I've just about decided it was us."

"Oh?"

"So you won't stay? And I suppose I can't blame you. Captain Jones would be glad to get your services on the voyage back."

"Yes, I know."

He did know. Three of the patients in sick bay were members of the crew, one being Webster the gunner.

"And I suppose you've made up your mind, if you ever really gave it a thought."

"I'll be asked?"

"Oh, yes. I happen to know that they'll ask you as soon as they have picked a site for the colony. My father tells my mother things, and I'm not always asleep."

Sal pondered a moment.

He put out: "Because they wouldn't want word to get back to England that even by accident they had seemed to give refuge to one of Oosterlinck's men? After all, Oosterlinck might be in real trouble this time. *I* might be a fugitive from justice."

"It's partly that," Priscilla admitted, "but it's also because they need somebody to mount the cannons. It turns that Captain Standish doesn't know much about such work. And it's got to be done."

"I see."

"Yet, if God should tell you—"

He waited.

"After all," she hurried on, "why should you bury yourself in a wilderness?"

"Why indeed?"

"Why should you endure all the hardships that are before us?"

"Why should *you?*"

"You might starve to death, or be butchered by the savages, and for a cause you don't have a smidgen of faith in."

Here were questions he had been asking himself for some time. They were wonderful coming out of her mouth. He paused. Not until she failed to speak further did he go on.

"Yes, why should I? Was that what you've been uneasy about lately? Was that why you wouldn't see me?"

"And besides," she evaded, "they all like you—as a man, I mean, as a person."

"Do *you*, Priscilla?"

William Bradford came into the cabin without knocking. He

was gaunt, long, stork-legged. He couldn't have been an old man, but in the hollows of his eyes there was all the woe that the world ever had known. He went right to the bunk in which Salathiel Boyd lay, the bunk Bradford himself had shared so many nights with his wife. He knelt. This was most unusual for any of these men.

"Thank you."

Sal gulped.

"I—I did what I could. I'm only sorry I didn't get there soon enough. I was thinking of something else when she cried out, and I was a little late."

"Oh, she—she cried out?"

"Sure. She cried for help. She felt herself slipping, I suppose, and she yelled, naturally."

"Naturally," exhaled William Bradford.

They tiptoed out then, giving Sal a chance to sleep. He should keep that bunk for the whole night, William Bradford had decreed. Bradford himself certainly wasn't going to sleep to-night: he would throw himself into the work of preparing for the Third Discovery.

Sal did sleep, though he fought it off, for he preferred to caress the memory of what Priscilla had said about the others liking him.

When he awoke it was dawn, and the first thing he saw by the light of the candle was Miles Standish's breastplate. That meant that they were ready to go. He wouldn't wear a heavy thing like that for any other reason.

Standish was to be in military command of the expedition, while Bradford was in social command.

Sal sat up.

"How do you feel?"

"Never felt better in my life. I haven't even got the sniffles."

In the dimness he could make out Priscilla, to whom he grinned, and William Mullins, still only semiconscious, and sundry others, some of them still asleep, while behind Standish stood several of the more influential saints. The group had the air of an announcing committee. Standish cleared his throat.

"There has been a change of plan," he started.

"You're not going?" quickly.

"Oh, we're going all right. We're starting right now. But we thought— Well, a man who knows how to use a gun could be mighty handy on a jaunt like this, and if you really feel well enough—"

Sal bobbed out of the bunk, laughing. He must have looked silly in that night rail, but he didn't care.

"Well enough? Say, where's my breeches? Where's my gun?"

He could guess the reason for the switch. It might have been in part because of Standish's persuasiveness, but it must have been largely due to Bradford's desire to reward Sal. Reward him for what? For diving into that icy water, or for lying about it afterward? It didn't matter. At least, it didn't matter to Sal just now.

Elder Brewster himself stepped forward.

"But we'd not have you risking your life unless you love us enough to stay with us. I mean, after a site has been selected. If you're willing to do that, Master Boyd—and of course nobody will do anything to influence your decision, which must be only your own— Well, in that case I am authorized to say that for taking the post of chief gunner in this colony you will be given one share of the common enterprise, as long as you remain."

"Oh, I'm going to get rich, eh?"

"We can't offer much. This'll be hard work. We will all be on short rations. We'll suffer, make no mistake about that!"

Sal grinned again at Priscilla Mullins, and he waved a hand to those who waited.

"My friends," he cried, "you couldn't drive me away with a pitchfork!"

Chapter Twenty-five

Prayers, such was the prevailing excitement, were kept short; and soon the discoverers were climbing down a Jacob's ladder into the shallop, a one-masted, half-decked, low, lumbrous ark. It was the same Jacob's ladder, Sal noted wryly, that he had clambered up to find himself on the wrong ship that memorable night in the Catwater.

He distrusted that shallop the instant his feet thudded upon her. She was as fat as a Norfolk dumpling, yet she wobbled like a duck. Her stumpy mast didn't look strong, only heavy. Her tiller was so long and so thick that it would make any movement abaft the beam, especially in dirty weather, difficult if not dangerous. She carried no sprit, and hence no spritsail; and indeed her only canvas was a too-large, square course, the yard for which was as thick as a man's waist. Having been scrubbed, and with so much new timber and fresh calking, at least she did smell sweet; but this would be scant consolation if she came apart.

There were eighteen of them, sixteen crammed into the cockpit, one at the bow to cast off, and Mate Coffin in charge of the tiller. A more lubberly lot Sal thought he never had seen. Courage they had plenty of, aye, or they wouldn't be here; but their experience, highly unnautical, had been confined to the loom, the press, the fuller's bench. Aside from the two mates, Coffin and Clarke, all were passengers. The mariners of Mayflower had been asked to volunteer, but not one had responded to this appeal; and Sal didn't blame them.

What Clarke was doing there Sal didn't know. He was the oldest of the mates, and the most disagreeable. Sal still didn't like him, though he respected the man's seamanship. Robert Coffin's interest was clear. He alone, of all the passengers and crew—though Clarke and Stephen Hopkins had been in Virginia—had previously visited New England and had poked about in this very bay. It was he who had told them of Thievish Harbor, on the far side, which he said should be suitable for them. It was the place John Smith had called New Plymouth on his map, but the men Coffin had explored it with, six years ago, had named it Thievish Harbor because the natives there stole a harping iron from them. He thought that he could find Thievish Harbor again. He hoped so. But they would try to see as much of the land as they could, hugging the shore instead of heading straight across the bay for Robert Coffin's anchorage.

Above, Christopher Jones and the two remaining mates, also the bosun, stared stonily from the poop, while the prow deck was crammed with mariners, among whom Sal glimpsed the saturnine Sawn. No saint was presently visible, for they had assembled around the mainmast in the waist for the purpose of sending off the expedition with a psalm.

"Thou doest prepare a table before me in the sight of
    mine adversaries;
Thou doest anoynt mine head with oyle, and my cup
    runneth over."

Sal grunted, though softly.

"I'd rather hear the little ones sing us off with something livelier," he muttered.

"Eh?"

The man next to him turned.

"Oh—you're here!"

Sal chuckled.

"Didn't expect me, did you? It was a last-minute decision, I guess."

What made Sal feel cheery, at just that moment, was the expression on John Alden's face. Alden was not subtle. It was easy to see his relief to find Sal next to him. He had been troubled in mind about leaving Sal Boyd the Sallee rover aboard Mayflower with Mistress Mullins. He was taking Sal seriously as a rival, and that was good to know.

Additionally, and to Sal rather unexpectedly, John Alden showed embarrassment. The last time these two faced one another Alden had clouted Sal, which fact made Alden uneasy now, though it didn't faze Sal.

"Doubtlesse kindnesse and mercy shall follow mee all
    the dayes of my life,
And I shall remaine a long season in the house of the
    Lord."

They had ended. They'd be back at the gunwale, to Godspeed their men. Sal looked up.

He picked her out instantly, and he smiled. She was smiling back, though whether at him or at Alden he couldn't tell—and neither could Alden. She waved a small kerchief that was brilliantly white on that dull, glum, gray morning: all Priscilla's linen, no doubt because her father had been a monger of it, at Dorking, was of a fine grade.

"'Ware the side!"

They were pushed off, rocking. The morning was bitter, December 6, the coldest yet, and the wind was high, cruel. Aboard Mayflower at least it had not been raining, nor yet had they known rain while they were alongside; but as soon as they were clear of the vessel the air was filled with a million angry pinpricks, spray that had been snatched off the top of the waves and was slammed against their unprotected faces. They winced, but carried on.

Crank as the craft was, in no more than a few minutes they were so far from Mayflower that they could see her only as a blur, and soon she passed from sight altogether, blotted by the cloud of small, salty, stinging drops.

Sal sighed, and settled back.

"Well, let's hope we ain't all drowned," he said.

The wind rose, shrieking. The spray redoubled, thick as a fog and twice as malicious. Already they were straining the not-too-skillfully stepped mast, and they had to shorten sail, a task in which Sal Boyd gladly helped.

There was no sort of protection. The tools and provisions had been stowed forward, under the half deck, and the cockpit, bare except for that possessive large tiller, was scarcely big enough to hold the men. The best they could do—but they had to do this anyway—was huddle close together.

"All hufty-tufty, my chuck, my sweetard?" Sal asked of Alden.

"I'll sweetard you!"

"Heavens, not when anybody's looking!"

They had appeared to be moving fast when they left May-flower, but thereafter, looking at what they could see of the shore, they crawled. To keep that shore even intermittently in sight they had to stay close to it, and the bang of breakers was hardly a soothing sound to hear. Now and then they caught sight of their principal, and now their only, landmark, Corn Hill, to larboard. There had been those who after the Second Discovery favored settling there. It was near at hand, they argued, which would obviate pushing farther afield in this season. The harbor wasn't good, but it did offer anchorage for small craft, and it could be a fine place to fish from. Also, it could be easily forti-fied. It was the highest spot for miles around.

Opponents cited the lack of fresh water. They'd have to be

dependent upon a pond that in summer easily could go dry. Then, no matter how strong their high fortification, they would be at the mercy of any who attacked.

The opponents had prevailed, after many hours of debate. That was the reason for this, the Third Discovery.

Still it did not rain. The spray slashed them like knives. They could scarcely move, and when, in a routine shift of position calculated to stir the blood, pressure was taken from one of them, young Edward Tilley, he actually toppled forward in a swoon; and they had to use some of their precious aqua vitae to revive him.

There was a long jutting sandy point, a point that marked the farthest the foot discoveries had gone. After that, all would be mystery. But at least it would block off some of that murderous wind, and the breakers there did not roar, only mumbled. Blinking, shivering, afraid, they rounded it.

Immediately they saw the Indians, ten or twelve of them, on the beach several miles away. They were doing something to a large black object of indeterminate shape.

"Go right for them," Miles Standish cried.

He had always been in favor of an immediate contact. If there was to be a fight, let it be right away, before the savages got accustomed to the noisy guns and bright swords. The first blow is always the best.

"Perhaps we should signal first," William Bradford demurred.

"Just as you want," said Robert Coffin. "But—make up your minds."

That was it: "minds." Coffin was the ranking mariner after Clarke, and as such the skipper of the boat, since Clarke had waived the command. Standish was the captain of the army, and couldn't this order he had given be called a military one? Bradford the saint was in general, social, political charge, the active representative of the Holy Discipline.

The whole arrangement was ridiculous. Fledgling militiamen

in a back-country hamlet would have thrown together a more efficient unit.

And there was still another voice to be heard—that of John Carver, the gentle small man who, after all, was Governor of the whole colony-to-be.

Deacon Carver shouldn't have been with them. He was too old. Yet they all knew that whatever command he gave would be given without any thought of his personal comfort or safety. He would die quietly and alone rather than utter any complaint or do any selfish thing. Now he paused, gasping a little. As always, he was unwilling to take his own feelings into account, and he looked around, staring into their faces. The men he saw, in all truth, were in pitiful condition, as bad as he was, though this was only the middle of the afternoon.

"Look! They've seen us!"

The Indians had. They had backed away from the black mass on the beach, and they ran for the woods, soon to be lost from sight.

John Carver's chin sank to his chest in assent.

"Make for the shore," he murmured. "Some—some of you need—fire, food—rest."

There was no dispute. They made for the shore.

Plenty of wood lay about, but they were so stiff and sore, and so weary, that it took all of two hours to build a flimsy barricade of branches and broken logs, in the middle of which their fire bellowed.

That fire was the only pleasant thing. Night closed in upon them like a band of sneaky thieves. They saw no more savages, but they did see fires twinkling erraticaly several miles down the beach, and three columns of smoke wavered against a darkening sky. Captain Standish promptly proposed that they build five or six fires of their own, and keep these going as long as any shred of daylight remained, an old scouting-party trick intended to dissuade an enemy from attack. Nobody paid any attention to him. The proposal wasn't even discussed; they were too tired to care. It did no good to scold them or to plead with them. They weren't men: they were mutes, without resistance. One by one, after they had eaten, and without waiting to be assigned to sentry duty, they flumped upon the ground like corpses, not even making a groan.

"I guess we'll have to do it ourselves, Boyd," Miles Standish said.

"I guess we will, sir."

Only one man, besides this pair, did not instantly fall asleep. William Bradford sat for a long time, his knees high, his chin on his folded forearms, gazing at the flames, which he didn't seem to see.

"Don't poke him up," Standish said, the first time he awakened Sal. "He wouldn't be any good anyway. And he's got a lot to think about."

"Sure."

"God knows how I'd feel if it had been Rose," Standish said. And he turned swiftly away.

Chapter Twenty-six

The black object that the Indians had been grouped around, on the beach several miles away, next morning proved to be a fish, or perhaps a whale. It was all of fifteen feet long. It had bristly hair, like a swine, and like a swine too it had a thick coat of fat, fully two inches of it all around. They cut away some of this fat, as patently the Indians had started to do, and they tasted it.

"Not bad," pronounced Edward Dotey, as well as he could from wincing.

The others agreed, and they proceeded to cut away every bit of the fat, meaning to pack it into sacks and take it with them.

Sal Boyd did not participate in this theft, for he was back in camp, catching up on his sleep; and when later they offered him some of the fat—which had a disgusting odor—he refused on the ground that he was yet so weary he feared he might be unable to keep it down.

He did, however, go prowling with a company that afternoon. They found nothing to show that this land, or this part of this land, would support them. The soil was as before, mostly sand. The trees were stunted, twisted as though in torture. The grass was brittle, juiceless, dry. And there was very little fresh water. They did find the remains of last night's Indian fires, which told them nothing. The Indians, it would appear, did not leave scraps behind them. Was this because they were so poor, or because they were careful?

If there was no sign that the savages lived in this sandy region, it was clear that they used it for burying things—bodies and food. The scouts from camp came upon what was undoubtedly a graveyard: it even had a fence around it, a fence formed by sticks driven into the ground at regular intervals. They refrained from digging up any of these graves, but when they came upon a mound outside the fence they attacked it with their swords—and got only a mass of parched acorns, which they spurned.

"Do they think that we're pigs?"

"Oh, I'm sure they wouldn't think that," said Sal.

Meanwhile the shallop had been sailed to a point several miles south, where there was a small fresh-water stream, and thither the land party, having found nothing worthy of mention, and certainly no site for a colony, later repaired; and there they made their second camp.

They were careful about this one. They set it up some sixty yards back from the edge of the water, where the ground was more substantial, and they drove into that ground stout stakes, between which they wove green branches, making the whole thing shoulder high. It was not a wall that would have withstood a well-handled battering-ram, but it could stop an arrow. Within its circle—the one opening was on the beach side—at last they snuggled down to sleep.

Nevertheless, and though they were better palisaded than last night, and had posted sentries, they were apprehensive, twitchy.

The night was silent, save for the spick-pick of a sinking fire, and perhaps it was half over when the two sentries gave an alarm.

"Indians! Indians!"

Certainly some of the men had not been asleep, for at least

three reached the palisade even before Sal Boyd, who had been; and each, like him, carried a musket.

Sal blew on his match, squinting over the wall. There wasn't a touch of moon, and in the light of the stars he could see nothing but low weeds and sedges between this camp and the black wall of the wood, a distance of perhaps a hundred and twenty yards. No human being could have hidden in those reeds.

A musket went off with a terrible blast, at his left ear. There was a flash of fire.

"Don't, you fool!" Sal cried. "Your gun won't carry that far anyway."

"*They* don't know that," the man pointed out, as he started to reload. "Ain't *you* going to shoot?"

"Not till I see something to shoot at."

There was another explosion, on the other side. Then another. By this time a frantic Captain Standish was running back and forth behind the line, pleading with the men not to fire. But they continued for some time. The night rang with bangs.

And when at last the men were quiet, hardly daring to talk, the tiny echoes bumped themselves to rest in the wood, and once again they could hear the stodgily spicking fire behind them.

"That," announced Miles Standish, "is another example of how not to meet an attack. "You've wasted a lot of powder, and you haven't scared anybody but yourselves. Who were the sentries?"

"Here, sir."

"Here."

He questioned them closely. Why had they given that alarm? They'd heard voices in the wood. Voices? They had both heard the voices, they said, but had decided to confer, checking each other's evidence, before they shouted.

"What voices? How'd ye know they were Indians? What did they sound like?"

One of the sentries obliged, conscientiously.

"*Woach!* Like that! *Woach! Woach!*"

Standish snorted.

"Of course. I've heard 'em in Sweden. A professional soldier gets to many countries, you understand."

"You never heard any American red-skinned Indians in Sweden, Captain, sir."

"No, but I've heard wolves. And that's what you just heard. Hasn't either of you ever heard a wolf before?"

It turned out that neither had. In fact, none of the others had either.

"You'd better get used to it," muttered Miles Standish.

All the same, he doubled the guard.

At first light, before the real dawn, they were up and active. Scarcely a man glanced over the barricade toward the wood, no more than a fussy shadow now, a cloudlike shape without edges, which had so frightened them a few hours ago. They were sheepish, and understandably eager to get away from this place. Even before breakfast, even before prayers, they started to haul the gear, including the guns, down to the shallop, which had been pulled close in to dry land. Sal saw them doing this, and immediately awakened Captain Standish.

"They're taking the muskets too! See?"

Standish saw; and he bounded to his feet with the agility of a squirrel. He did not shout an order, as Sal expected, but instead sought out William Bradford, who was standing on the beach some distance from the protection of the palisade, though short of the shallop. What Bradford was doing there nobody knew. He had a habit, these days, of going off by himself for a little while. Perhaps he was praying. They prayed standing up, and even with their eyes open, these separatists.

Standish grabbed his arm, startling him.

"You've got to order them to bring those guns back! Right now! They should never be out of reach!"

Why don't *you* order them? was Sal Boyd's thought. He had run after his officer.

Bradford blinked.

"We'd thought that the sooner— Well, the men aren't over-fond of this camp, and perhaps if— And also, it didn't look right to have so many warlike weapons around at prayer time."

"I said bring them back! Every one!"

Bradford nodded.

Standish turned to Sal.

"Call the men. Send 'em to the boat."

He himself made for the shallop, his long snaphance slung over his shoulder.

Sal started toward the palisade at a trot, shouting. He too had a gun across his shoulder, and his sword was at his left hip, his dagger at his right.

"Come back here! Captain's orders are that every—"

There was nobody near him, yet it felt as though some one had given a sharp rap to the upper part of his left forearm. He pulled up short, staring at it. There was a ragged groove in the leather. Something to his right went "thunk!" into the sand. Then the screaming started, and the air was filled with a waspish whine.

Sal turned, bending his knees.

The savages already had come out of the wood, thirty or forty of them—Sal had no time to count—and they were running toward the barricade, sometimes discharging their bows as they ran, sometimes stopping for this purpose.

Salathiel Boyd did not need to be told what to do. If the Indians could surround that rickety palisade, penning in the colonists with none of their guns, it would be the end. Moreover, they were running not at the stockade itself, he saw now, but as though to go around it to the north, as though they were intent upon taking the boat, which had been beached.

Crouching, his musket at his shoulder, Sal ran right toward

them. He wouldn't shoot until he got close enough to make it count.

He hadn't the slightest doubt that behind him Miles Standish was doing the same.

In the lead was a tall Indian, hideously painted, virtually naked. Sal felt his face go hot at the sight of him. This man was not discharging his arrows but waved his bow above his head. His mouth was open wide: he must have been yelling.

Sal went to one knee. He pointed his musket at the leader. The breeze was off the land, so he turned his head away, rather than risk having his eyes put out by a flareback. There were no sights on the barrel anyway.

He pulled the trigger—and got a flash in the pan.

It was loud, it was bright, but it wasn't an explosion.

The leader paused, looking perplexed.

Sal whipped out a toothpicker that he kept behind his ear, and goosed the touchhole, working some more powder into the pan. The match still was lighted at both ends, glowing bravely. Sal pushed back the serpentine, fastened the catch, turned his head away again, and again pulled the trigger.

This time there was a shot, and a very loud one. The whole beach seemed shattered by that tremendous sound, and the recoil all but threw Sal on his back.

The leading savage sprang into the air, terrified. The others behind him stopped. None could have been hit, for that ball weighed close to two ounces and at this distance would have knocked any man over backward; but the orange-red flash at the muzzle, the billow of smoke, most of all the noise, paralyzed them for a moment.

Immediately there was another shot, close behind him and a little to his left. That would be Standish.

Still on one knee, Sal started to reload.

This would take more than twice as long as the simple refilling of the pan and recocking of the serpentine, since he had to pour in powder, ball, and wadding, and ram it home. On impulse, he looked up.

The second shot too, though from farther back, had had its effect. The Indians wavered. Sal raised his empty musket to his shoulder. He pointed it at the leader. The leader screeched— and turned and ran back into the wood. And all the others ran after him.

Now there were more shots from behind Sal Boyd, but not thoughtfully to one side. Indeed, one sang past his shoulder so close that he thought he felt its heat. The boys back there at last had retrieved their guns from the shallop—the guns they never should have put there—and were using them, willy-nilly.

Sal fell flat.

"If I'm going to be shot one way or the other," he told himself, "I'd rather take it in the chest than in the arse."

Standish was yelling at them now, and the shooting ceased. Soon they were all around Sal, pressing toward the wood. Then they had passed. He finished his reloading and followed, cursing them.

Amazingly, they saw not the slightest sign of Indians or any other beings, animal or human, in the wood. Though they searched for some time, in better order now, keeping in touch with one another as they advanced in a strung-out line, their muskets at the ready, they came upon no footprint or broken twig, much less a weapon. They searched for more than an hour, and then, hungry, returned to camp.

On the beach, in the boat, stuck to the palisade, there was plenty of proof that it hadn't all been a nightmare. These places were peppered with arrows. The discoverers took out no fewer than nineteen—ungraceful things, short, not too straight, skimpily feathered, and tipped only with bone.

Not a man had been blooded. Two others, like Sal, had had their sleeves slashed, and one had suffered a hole right through the top of his black steeple hat; but that was all.

"Praise the Lord," John Carver cried. "Now let us have our prayers."

"Well now, at least, I've got something to give thanks for," thought Salathiel Boyd.

He shook his head, thinking it over, a little later as they were piling into the shallop to resume the shore-sail. He wondered: Wouldn't these gowks ever learn to do *anything* right?

But the episode was nothing compared to the trip that followed.

Chapter Twenty-seven

Just at first it was smooth sailing, the day cold but clear, the water not unbearably choppy.

The men sat silent, wrapped in somber thoughts, and more than a mite embarrassed. They had not shown well, and they knew it. Though Standish had no further reproach for them, they felt that they'd done everything wrong and in justice should not have survived unscathed. The exertion, the strain, the false alarm, the overconfidence at first light, the inexplicable attack, and the almost equally inexplicable rout, had shaken them. They'd been badly frightened; and sudden, intense, searing fear, swiftly removed, leaves any man with a dry mouth, a wambling stomach, and no inclination to chat.

Standish understandably was the hero, but he sniffed aside their praises, for his was not an ingratiating nature; and anyway, he knew that he had done no more than a good soldier should and that he appeared a paragon of martial prowess only because of the company he kept. Sal Boyd too they made much of. Sal would shrug, smiling sleepily. His thoughts were those of the Captain.

Sal and John Alden this morning had taken seats on opposite sides of the cockpit, and several times Sal saw the cooper studying him, impressed; but they did not talk.

The shallop clung to the shore much of the morning, though those aboard of her saw little change in the land, but when the wind freshened and the sky grew dark, and the waves rose, forming combers on the beach they were passing, they veered away, setting a course directly—as they hoped—for Thievish Harbor. Robert Coffin still was at the tiller.

It began to rain, and the wind rose. The rain turned to snow. Soon they were soaked, their clothes caked with ice, so that each one crickled when he stirred. Exposed as they were, they could do nothing but huddle together, shivering. Their feet suffered the most. They could stamp their feet where they sat, but it was forbidden—and it would have been dangerous anyway, what with that swinging tiller—to tramp about.

The shallop shivered and shook. It creaked complainingly.

They could see almost nothing. The world was all water. Spray was flying now, as it had done the first day, and it stung their eyes and their cheeks.

"Hold tight!"

The vessel reared like some beast of burden that feels the jab of a goad. Sal, pitched out of his seat, saw the tiller swinging toward him, and he ducked barely in time to save his skull. He reached up and grabbed the tiller with both hands, but it swung free, loose.

"Sweeps!" Robert Coffin shouted. Coffin himself had let the tiller go as a useless thing. *"Break out those sweeps!"*

These, long oars, had been lashed to stanchions on the deck of the cockpit. Half-frozen fingers tore at the lines, while the shallop heaved sideways, spun, then slid into the trough between two seas, wallowing, about to be engulfed. Then the shallop was lifted, water sloshing over her side, and she teetered for a terrible instant and sidled into another trough.

Sal was one of the first to get a sweep free. He did not fit it into the tholepins along the thwarts, but instead carried it to the stern and put it overside, so that he and Mate Coffin could hold it as a steering oar.

For Sal knew what had happened. They'd lost the rudder.

If they couldn't head this scow into the wind—from here, from the stern—they would capsize. She could not take many more of those sickening plunges.

He and Coffin strained at their steering oar, yelling back to the others to bring a second. In the noise and confusion they might not have been heard, but neither dared to desert his post.

The others, slammed against one another, thrown to the deck, drenched with shipped water, struggled to mount rowing sweeps on either side. These would have helped, but they could hardly have taken the place of a rudder on such seas. Several of the oars were swept overside. Men were badly bruised. One was knocked unconscious.

Even so, somebody must have seen the pinch that Sal and Mate Coffin were in, or divined it; for soon there was help, another sweep mounted at the stern, two men holding it.

Now the shallop was taking the seas head-on, clumsily, thuddingly, but willingly enough withal; and she no longer shipped water.

"Somebody ax that God-damn' tiller!"

The tiller was supposed to be removable in an emergency, but it was frozen into place, and no amount of hammering with the heels of their hands would budge it. Yet what with the two steering oars there was not room to swing an ax. John Alden, showing a quickness of thought that Sal wouldn't have supposed him capable of, fetched a saw from the stored supplies, and though he was not himself a carpenter—they didn't have one here—he made a good quick job of removing the sulky lever, which fell to the deck, where it was out of the way and might even serve as firewood if ever they landed on land again.

So they drove on through the night—or what seemed to be night. They bailed; they mounted side sweeps, which helped to keep the vessel nose-on; and they strained, four at a time, at the steering oars. It was strenuous work, but it did serve to keep them from freezing.

It was about the middle of the afternoon—though it might have been the middle of the night—when the mast broke.

There had been no warning. They had the wind almost directly behind them, and every inch of canvas was spread. The crack when it came was like the very crack of doom. It filled the whole world, for an instant even swamping the shriek of the wind.

The mast broke in two places at once, one high, the other about halfway down. The top section was flung away completely, along with shreds of the sail. The second section, with most of the course, was flapped against the four men in the stern, the men who held the steering oars. That canvas enveloped them. The shallop, released, went wild.

Splinters sprang, wounding some of the men. The wonder was that nobody was killed. The mast, though it had proved not strong enough, was thick, a heavy thing, a monster. Now they had only a stump, together with some badly ripped canvas.

Somehow they jury-rigged these, while the shallop reeled; and they pushed indomitably on, the rain-snow cutting their faces.

Late in the afternoon the snow lessened sufficiently to show them the shore—dead ahead and startlingly close. It was a smother of foam among rocks, and they could hear the boom of breakers. Hastily they made about, looking at Robert Coffin.

He rolled his eyes, as he shook his head.

"The Lord be merciful unto us," he cried, "for mine eyes have never seen this place before!"

The effect of this confession upon the men was curious, and varied. Two wept openly, unashamed. Several suggested, in shrill voices, that they drive directly into the shore anyway, ignoring the rocks until they hit, trusting to the Lord God Jehovah somehow to spare them. Anything, these men cried, would be better than staying in this accursed craft. Others disputed this, contending that they should coast to the right or to the left, on the assumption that there must be some sort of bay or cove in which they could take shelter. These, no doubt, would have been prepared to start another of those long arguments, disregarding any command from any leader. But most of the men simply sat as though stunned, staring blankly ahead, believing themselves as good as dead.

They were skeptical when Coffin, a little later, having recovered his pluck, called himself to have been wrong. He *did* know this stretch of shore, after all. And they were very near the entrance of Thievish Harbor: he was sure of it.

"That was six years ago," John Carver cautioned him.

"Sir, a sailor never forgets a good anchorage. Ah, here we are now!"

Largely with their side oars they worked the shallop in, bringing her under the lee of a high wooded shore. It was now quite dark, and though they did not see any fires or smell any smoke they decided, most of them, to spend the night in the open boat, being frankly afraid of another such reception as had been accorded to them at their last stop. But John Clarke, the mate, demurred.

"I've had enough. Get in close and I'll wade ashore; I don't care how cold the water is. I'd sooner lose my scalp than spend another hour in this tub."

Ashore he did go, and several followed him, feeling the same way about their hair. Soon they had a fire going, somehow. The sight of it was too much for the others, and they took the shallop in, beached her, and tumbled or waded ashore, where they made camp.

In the morning they learned that they were in fact on an island, which in honor of the man who had first set foot upon it they called Clarke's Island. It was small, and in a smallish bay that looked shallow. Their assignment was to explore the shore of this bay, especially the section of it that John Smith had designated as New Plymouth, but just now they were too nearly exhausted to move. They stirred a little, sluggishly. They did examine, if sketchily, the island upon which they found themselves, but they made no move toward the mainland, instead spending the day in rest. They needed rest. They needed and needed it.

The following day was the Lord's Day, so of course they could do no exploring then.

The day after that, however, they did go to the mainland, where they found the site of New Plymouth to be marked by a large granite boulder, a stone unusually large in that country of pebbles, and also by a fine fresh-water stream that chittered encouragement. This area was backed by forest, which hemmed it on three sides. There was a hill that could be fortified, an important consideration, one of the first things they were ordered to look for. Finally, there were many evidences that the Indians themselves once had lived in this place—the remains of cornfields, graves, bits of chipped stone and of pottery, some bones.

There was no evidence, though, of a living Indian. Sal knew nothing about cornfields, but some of those who thought that they did averred that in their opinion these hadn't been worked in four or five years. But they still would be tillable.

The day after that—it was Tuesday, December 12, 1620—in perfect weather, they sailed back to the Mayflower.

They announced their satisfaction with the site. The Lord, as Deacon Carver put it, had provided. Colonization could get under way.

Chapter Twenty-eight

They talked for three days before they upped anchor.

Sal never ceased to marvel at these discussions, which were almost as religious as they were political. They appeared to be an essential part of what the saints called the Discipline, or the Holy Discipline. Every man must be permitted to talk as often and as long as he pleased. They were forever saying that everything was in God's hands, yet they would debate all day and half the night, to rise the next morning and start debating all over again. The children of course were kept apart from these meetings, which had about them very little of order and no ceremony at all but a great deal of dignity because of the earnestness with which they were conducted; and the women prudently stayed away; but every grown man, even though a servant, was heard whenever he wished to hold forth on any subject whatever.

It seemed to Sal contrary to nature that human beings might presume to govern themselves. Quite possibly it was sacrilegious. If all things really *were* in God's hands, why not let them stay there? And it was a prodigious waste of time. For Sal had noted that no matter how many voices had been raised in passionate discourse and no matter how many hours had been spent in wrangling, the decision always concurred with the thoughts of a small group consisting of Elder Brewster, Governor Carver—they had elected this old man their governor, on what authority Sal Boyd couldn't see—and William Bradford, with, increasingly, that sly little London tailor, Isaac Allerton. These were all saints. Somehow they invariably had their way. They voted together, quietly. The only non-saint who wielded much influence in council was William Mullins, a man who without hesitation cast his voice with those of Carver, Bradford, Brewster, Allerton. There was a great show of fairness, but Sal noted that these men always won.

So it was that after three days of conversational preparation, and a great deal of prayer, Mayflower, towing the shallop, started west.

A freak wind denied them entrance into Thievish Harbor that night, which they spent in the open bay, but they did get in the next morning.

Unfortunately it was the Lord's Day, so they could do nothing.

Sal Boyd had known mariners who were indifferent about shore leave, but not many. Most, like himself, were twitchy to be on land as soon as the hook had been dropped, and would fawn upon officers, promising to do all sorts of extra tasks tomorrow, provided that they were permitted to quit ship then and there. This itchiness was understandable, and in the cases of Sal and most of his companions it was brought about by a desire for a wench and for strong drink. But there were no bagnios and no public houses in New England. These were not the thoughts that tugged at Salathiel Boyd as he leaned on the gunwale. He was not thinking of schnapps and a whore. Surely there was no joy in the prospect upon which he gazed, a glum one; yet never in his life had he known such a longing for the land.

Thievish Harbor was largely shallow. Mayflower could not venture far in, and she was anchored a good mile and a half from the place where it had been proposed that they settle, just off Clarke's Island.

The prospect was gloomy, yet not as bleak as the one they had left. The trees here were taller and straighter, and there were more of them: pine, walnut, birch, beech, oak, hazel, ash. There was even sassafras, which might fetch a good price back home. From a distance Sal could see that the soil was darker, less gritty. He could see too, from time to time, the smoke of a fire. These fires were far inland. Near the shore there was no sign of life save birds, waterfowl which, happily, were numerous.

Sawn Matthews ranged alongside of him, similarly staring.

"Christ's elbow, what a place! I wouldn't go ashore here if you was to hand me the whole land on a golden platter!"

"Now there," said Sal, "is where you and me are different."

Sawn was silent for a moment. Then he said: "Look, Sal, this is hard for me to believe. Do you really mean to stay here with these gowks?"

"I guess I've got to. I don't know what'd happen to them if I didn't. They haven't got sense enough to come in out of the rain, by themselves."

"What the Hell do *you* care what happens to them?"

Sal did not answer, and after a while Sawn went away.

For three days then there were parties of exploration. They touched at various points, often disappearing into the forest. One, in the ship's longboat, under the command of Captain Jones himself, went for some distance up a little river they named the Jones River. Mostly, however, the parties concentrated on two different spots. One of these was a fairly clear place, a beach featured by a huge light-colored boulder, a notable landmark in this wilderness, which, while by no means as flat and sandy as Cape Cod, was not stony. The longboat would ground just short of that boulder. The shallop could not reach it at all. The only other possible site was Clarke's Island, nearby. The island would provide better protection against the sudden attack that was in everybody's mind. On the other hand, the place behind the boulder already was more than half cleared, and it had that hill and that stream. An enormous amount of work would be needed even to clear Clarke's Island, and it was by no means certain that water would be found there.

The place behind the boulder finally was agreed upon, and yet another landing party was organized that night, the party that would really start the work of establishing New Plymouth.

They always called it that, or sometimes just Plymouth, which startled Sal, who would have supposed that people like these, when they came to set up a plantation, would entitle it Jericho or Bethlehem or New Jerusalem. After all, John Smith meant nothing to them. Others could and probably would make maps of this vicinity. And surely the saints had no cause to honor the Plymouth that was in England, the port from which their ship at last had sailed. They had never meant to put in at Plymouth, a rowdy, irreverent place, a crass commercial town that meant to them only further delay and greater expense. None of them came from that part of England. Yet—New Plymouth it unquestionably was, from the very beginning. The saints didn't seem to care much about the name. They did not even debate it.

Since the next day was December 25, Sal had assumed that he would be called upon to restrain his impatience for another twenty-four hours. He was flabbergasted when he saw the strangers and saints, at dawn, preparing to go ashore.

"But you can't work on *Christmas Day!*"

"Why not?" Elder Brewster asked.

"Why, because—because it *is* Christmas!"

"An arbitrary date arbitrarily assigned to the birth of Our Savior. It had nothing to do with that, actually. It's an old pagan feast day, pitched upon by a pope of Rome, and can you deny it?"

"Well, I don't know—but I always thought—"

"Can you assign any reason for December twenty-fifth being so stabbed at? Do you know any cause for it?"

"Well, doesn't it say in the Bible—I don't rightly know— Mistress Mullins and I haven't got that far yet— But doesn't it say that Jesus was born on December twenty-fifth?"

"No, it doesn't. Not one word to that effect. Celebrating Christmas by abstaining from any sort of work would be to perpetuate a barbaric and impious custom. The same applies to Easter, as our spiritual guide back in the Low Countries, the blessed John Robinson, has pointed out in his *Just and Necessarie Apologie*. Would you like to have me read that to you?"

"Well . . ."

"It isn't very long. Only about two hundred pages."

"Oh, not right now, thank you."

"Of course, if your conscience forbids it, we shan't *force* you to go ashore, Boyd."

"Oh, no, no, no! Hell, no! Where's that musket? Where's my powder? Come on."

Chapter Twenty-nine

They landed near the big rock, the keel grating bottom before the nose nudged the bank. They tumbled out, in no special order, an informal and rather boisterous landing; they turned to wave to those still aboard Mayflower, and then they went violently to work.

They sniffed no flowers and sought no stones, nor did they pace the ground, but pitched right in.

It was different with Salathiel Boyd, as with Miles Standish. No ax or auger was handed to them. They had their guns, and they were to patrol the neighborhood, watching for signs of Indians.

By vote it had been agreed that to carry those weapons loaded in the shallop—the party was a large one, virtually all of the male passengers—would be unsafe. Sal and the Captain, therefore, loaded on the shore as soon as they had landed. It made Sal at least feel a mite silly to be cutting bullets and measuring powder from a flask while the others were so busy.

He ripped off a piece of wadding and stuffed this in after the lead, and he rammed these home. There was no prime, so he used his toothpicker to work some coarse powder out of the touchhole and into the pan. He closed the lid over this, for the morning was windy and the air smelled of rain. He pushed the serpentine back, affixed the spring, and lighted the slow match at each end.

Not until then did he venture into the forest.

It fascinated him. The clearing itself, and adjacent cornfields, should have engrossed his attention at first, though he had heard of them; and indeed he did marvel, if fleetingly, about the remains of old fires, the shards, the bones, some of which Sam Fuller had pronounced to be human, possibly; but it was the forest that drew him with an irresistible urge, and as soon as he got his gun loaded he went there, a man goggle-eyed, his mouth an "O."

This was not only impulse. He was acting under instructions. While the others laid out a foundation for the Common House, the first building that they would construct, Captain Standish, it had been agreed, should climb to the top of the hill and survey as much of the surrounding countryside as he could see from there, being especially alert for signs of smoke, and Sal Boyd should scout the outer edges of the forest against the chance that savages were concealed there.

"If they slaughter me I'll try to yell first, so's you can get away," he had said.

Yet he was by no means jocular when he went into the forest. It gave him a creepy feeling, tickling and chilling the back of his neck, the back of his head. Peril he had faced many a time in the past, when with cutlass or cudgel he had leaped from ship to ship; but peril in a yammering crowd was one thing, while peril faced alone, amid an eerie silence, peril that you couldn't *see*, was something else.

This was not like the neat parkish woods of England. It was a tangle of undergrowth almost tropical in its lushness, which made walking no stroll. Sal, a city man, a mariner, was not skilled at this manner of progress. Leaves crisped and twigs crackled under his feet. From time to time he would come to a

halt, looking around. He saw no sign of aborigines. Once a hare
scuttled away from a point almost directly between his feet,
causing him to jump. Even so, he might have killed the thing,
had he not feared that the sound of a shot at this stage of the
work would cause alarm and even a panic among the men in
the clearing. There would be time enough for bagging game
later, when they'd all grown used to the feel of this place. He
stumbled on, musket at the alert.

There was a sharp staccato rattle, and he fell to his knees,
almost asprawl, in a spasm of fright.

The sound ceased as abruptly as it had started, and silence
again gripped the wood. After a moment Sal Boyd twisted his
head, looking up.

There was a gaunt, sardonic, skinny, brownish bird that
appeared to have been wired or otherwise fastened to the trunk
of a tree. It had a red head and a longish beak. It regarded Sal
with beady disapproval, and then, as though after a shrug, went
back to hacking a hole into the tree with its beak, producing
again the rat-tat-tat that had so startled Sal.

Sal had heard of woodpeckers. Sheepishly, all one blush, he
rose. He checked the slow match on his musket, and worked it a
bit farther out.

The woodpecker paid no heed to him. It's seen men before,
was Sal's thought. He looked around, less concerned with espy-
ing Indians than with assuring himself that none of the settlers
had followed him and been a witness to his shame.

There was no trace of any human being. The woodpecker
suddenly quit and flew away, and the forest was still once more.
Nevertheless Sal Boyd would not resume his scouting until he
had gone back to the edge of the clearing and seen with his own
eyes that all of those who had come ashore were working.

Two weren't. Captain Standish, his backplate gleaming, his
snaphance over his right shoulder, was climbing the hill to

examine its summit as an emplacement for cannons. And John Alden was standing a little apart from the rest, staring with sullen eyes at that part of the forest into which Sal a little while ago had disappeared. This was unusual. Alden, if disagreeable, in ordinary circumstances was an excellent worker. He was no carpenter, and did not pretend to be, but as a cooper he was accustomed to handle wood, and as an exceedingly strong young man he'd been, Sal was told, a great help in the assemblage of the shallop.

Why had he paused now? Was he, like Sal, fascinated by this wilderness in which he found himself, and did he gaze at the wall of trees as though he would ask what it meant? Or—was it Sal he was thinking of?

Perhaps he hoped that Sal would not come back?

Whatever the answer, this was not a time for dalliance, and Alden soon cut short his contemplation to return to the others and to resume work with a plane. From time to time, the hidden Sal noted, Alden would glance over his shoulder at the forest; but he was not alone in this, for most of the men were doing it. Salathiel Boyd was not the only one there who had felt his heart quop with fear.

Satisfied, he went back to his patrol.

There was nothing like the humped cornfields, the bits of pottery, the bones, the knife-marked sticks that littered the clearing—for the forest showed no trace of mankind—yet Sal was not without company. After he had moved about a bit, getting used to it, he became aware of many rustlings and stirrings on all sides and even above. He saw no more woodpeckers, but certainly there were birds of some sort up in those branches. Hares abounded, each of them with that maddening trick of waiting until it was all but stepped upon before making a scramble for different cover. There were many squirrels, and unexpectedly they looked fat. Sal had no doubt that there were wolves in America, and he had heard it said that there were lions as well, and possibly tigers. This did not disconcert him. He wore a helmet, also heavy back- and breastplates. The gun might fail to work, as guns so often did, but at his left side hung a sword, at his right a dagger. No lion could frighten him, now, as that woodpecker had done.

Twice he caught the flash of a flag and heard the wallop. He would have risked a shot, chancing consternation in the clearing, but each time the deer was too far away: he could not expect to kill with this clumsy weapon at a greater distance than fifty or sixty yards. It was a pity. Those poor scurvy patients in sick bay would have been stirred simply to *smell* venison.

A much better opportunity to get meat he missed because of his astonishment.

For the most part the forest was floored with undergrowth and offered few glades such as would be found in an European wood. However, there were some of these; and the one with the running birds was the largest.

Sal came upon it dramatically, surprising them.

There were eight or ten. They had been pecking at something, and when they heard him they raised their heads at once, a startling display of red.

They were the most fantastic creatures Sal ever had seen. They had long legs, tiny white and red heads, black backs and breasts, tails of a metallic brown. They were somewhat like guinea fowl, but much larger and clumsier. Not just the cock— easily distinguished by his wide chest, his huge spreading tail, his flappy, dewlappy wattles—but all of the hens as well greeted Sal raucously. They thrust out their heads toward him, stretching their necks, and they made a guttural sound that might have been *turk-turk-turk-turk*. This only for an instant, and then, before he could recover, they ran away.

They did not flap their wings, but with their long, gawky

legs they were most marvelously fast. Sal chased them only a short distance. He did not even catch sight of them again. No guinea hen, no bird Sal ever had heard of, could run as rapidly as that. Even if he had been free of steel Sal could not hope to get near enough for a shot.

He paused, panting. He was weaker than he had thought, and his knees wobbled. He would walk at a sedate pace back to the clearing, he decided. His first patrol was finished, his first tour.

When he heard the shot he jerked to attention, his eyes throbbing. It had come from a short distance ahead, the direction of the clearing. Armor and all, he ran that way.

There was another shot, and then another.

Had the savages somehow slipped past him, for all his watchfulness? Had he failed on this his first assignment? He was sobbing as he ran.

Then he saw the birds again. They were running toward him with the speed of wind; and he realized what had happened. The *turk-turks*, being like all birds stupid, had burst into the clearing. Some of the men—they all had muskets within reach—had known the same thought as Sal, and had acted upon it more quickly.

The turk-turks swerved when they saw Sal again, but he was given a second chance, and this one he seized. He went to one knee, and put the musket stock to his shoulder, pressing his right cheek against it. He did not turn his head away, as he'd been taught to do. If there was a flareback he would lose at least his eyebrows, quite possibly his sight. He took that risk, for the sake of the scurvy patients. His head low, he sighted along the top of the barrel, and pulled the trigger.

The birds vanished—all save one, the biggest, the cock, which pitched forward in a swirl of feathers and now lay still. It did not even squawk when Sal wrung its neck. After which he was surrounded by his fellow settlers, who had come on the run.

The rest of the day was less exhilarating. They had scarcely blocked out the foundation of the Common House near the shore, and Sal had completed his second scouting trip and was preparing to climb the hill with Captain Standish, when the rain that had been threatening all morning started to fall. It was bitterly cold. Each drop stung. The wind rose.

Stolidly they ignored this, for a while. But the rain was turning to snow, and the air grew colder and darker. They made themselves a few small conical shelters of tree branches and turf —"charcoal burners' huts," some of the men called them—and tried to sit it out.

This was no use. All of them, like Sal himself, already were weakened from the hardships of the past six weeks; and in the middle of the afternoon, convinced that they would not be able to get anything more done that day, they returned to the May-flower.

They were greeted with reproaches. The wind having been off the land, the shots had been heard by such strangers and saints as remained aboard, including all of the women. The ship's longboat was elsewhere, in search of firewood, and there was nothing those in the Mayflower could do but wait, trembling with anxiety, straining their eyes for a signal that never came.

They wept when the shallop scraped alongside, and some of the women went so far as to kiss their husbands. At the same time, they scolded them.

It fetched a lump to Sal Boyd's throat, and he was not verbally dexterous when Priscilla accosted him.

She did not actually touch him, though she waved her hands before him as though she would have liked to do so.

"I—I'm happy that you are not hurt."

"Well," said Sal, the lout, "well, so am I."

The turk-turk bird, delighting them, in part softened the

reproaches. Sal was a considerable hero; and they cheered him —albeit soberly—when he proposed that all of the cooked fowl should be given to the patients in sick bay. He added that if he was permitted to go ashore tomorrow—he was careful to get in this proviso—he would, with God's help, kill another turk-turk.

Chapter Thirty

There followed a weary time, a dreary time, and hard. Circled by an immensity of water and wilderness, their world was a small one—the Mayflower and the miserable beginnings of a settlement. Between these was about a mile and a half, for the ship could not get closer, and a good part of the men's time was spent in traversing this gap. The hardest work a little while ago had been waiting; now it was rowing. Though they left a "guard of honor" on shore every night, most of the workers at first went back to the ship at sundown. In addition, all their supplies must be landed.

There were times when because of high wind and rough water all communication was suspended for hours on end, even for a day or two at a time. In the first of these storms, when Mayflower was tossing like a cockleshell—dragging her anchor, so that many of the saints assumed that the Lord had marked them for an end—young Richard Britteridge, one of the scurvy victims, died. At the same time Mary Allerton miscarried.

Britteridge had not been a subscriber to the Holy Discipline, but even the strangers in the company—and this puzzled Sal— believed that there was something disgraceful about a burial at sea if it was not an absolute necessity. So Sal sewed him up, and still another trip was made to the landing place, where they buried Britteridge in an upsloping cornfield just behind the boulder.

The patients in sick bay increased in number, and their ailment was more severe than ever. This was not simple scurvy, though the sufferers showed most of the symptoms. It was something more complicated, and more terrible. The leeches had no name for it. The settlers and mariners called it The Sickness. Like scurvy, it was messy and malodorous, as hard on the nurse as on the patient.

Christopher Martin, that irascible man, died early, to be followed in a few days by his wife. Rose Standish was stricken. Only the children seemed immune to a scourge that smote men and women without discrimination. Three of the four mates tossed in fever, as did Sal's friend, the cook, and Webster, the gunner. Sal regarded Priscilla Mullins with anxiety. Her face was ashen, her eyes dull, the backs of her hands gleamed with perspiration. She did not take to her bunk, as perhaps she should have done, for both her father and mother were in grave condition.

It was known that scurvy would disappear once the patient was given fresh food and was taken ashore. It was hoped that The Sickness would react in the same way. But it could *only* be hoped. They knew nothing about it, really.

Most of the sufferers were too weak to be moved, even if there had been shelter for them on the site of New Plymouth, where the able-bodied, themselves weakened by malnutrition, toiled mightily—when the weather permitted.

As for fresh food, this land of New England did not appear prepared to supply it. Sal was kept aboard of Mayflower, and so did not have another look at the turk-turks. Some of the other men did, but none got a successful shot, and they were reluctant to pursue the birds, fearing that they'd become lost. Those left aboard did sometimes catch a few small fish, but their equipment was not enough for a big haul. It was more than Sal Boyd could comprehend, why they had set forth for a new world with such small hooks, so few feet of line, and nets that were falling apart. But this was no time to wonder about it. As they themselves were fond of saying, the ways of God are inscrutable.

The Common House was completed, and work had been begun on several other houses, which, though they were not so large as the Common House, also were to be square, of wattle-and-daub construction, and with high, steepled roofs made of thatch. Some of the sick had insisted upon being taken to land, among them Governor Carver and William Bradford. The shore party indeed was getting larger every day, though not all of them could work.

Three nights Sal went ashore with burial parties. For they were disposing of their dead by night now. Nobody had so much as glimpsed a savage since they entered Thievish Harbor, but savages undoubtedly were there, and almost certainly they had the settlement under surveillance. If they saw interment after interment they might gather their courage and strike. This is why The Sickness's fallen were smuggled ashore after sunset and hustled into their holes without any ceremony save the simplest. No stones were erected, or crosses. Indeed, not even a mound was left, for the burial squad scattered the dirt and raked the ground.

After the third session Sal was loth to go back to the ship, for he carried bad news.

Goodman and Browne the previous day had been sent into the forest to search for fallen nuts or even possibly left-over, half-frozen berries, and now, after thirty-six hours, they had not returned. The loss of two able-bodied young men in itself was a serious matter to this diminishing group, but even worse was the reflection of what had happened to them. They could hardly have survived the night, an exceptionally severe one, unless they had fallen into the hands of the savages. Perhaps at this very moment they were being tortured by fiends who afterward would attack the camp.

Nevertheless, Sal did go back. They needed him. Sam Fuller was ashore, caring for the sick, and the ship's physician-chirurgeon—his name, Heale, wasn't funny any more—was half dead from work. Besides, Sal was worried about Priscilla.

She met him at the ladder, and seized both his hands.

"I was afraid that you wasn't coming back."

He widened his eyes.

"*Dios madre!* Why?"

"I don't know . . . just a feeling."

She took her hands away, for people were staring, and she turned a shoulder to him.

"Those two boys, have they been found?"

"No."

"They—they couldn't possibly be alive?"

"I guess not. How're your parents?"

"I'm—frightened. I wish you'd come and look at them."

Mrs. Mullins, he saw right away, had not much time left in this world. She wasn't conscious, which was a blessing. Her breath was barely perceptible: Sal was obliged to put threads of silk across her open mouth to be sure that she was breathing at all.

William Mullins twisted and tossed, his eyes squinched shut, his mouth moving pauselessly, while his fingers plucked at the blanket. There were spots of hectic at his cheekbones, the only color he had.

Poor pudgy man! Salathiel Boyd thought again, as he had thought so many times of William Mullins. Why had this one ever come upon such a voyage? Was it in response to some still small voice, or was there some compulsion louder still but audible only to him? He shouldn't be here, writhing. He should be back in that draper's shop in Dorking. He should be waiting upon a customer and wondering what his wife would fetch him for dinner or whether his daughter should be permitted to go around in a skirt so short that it showed her feet, almost her ankles. He had no business in high adventure. He wasn't built for that.

"What do you think?" Priscilla whispered.

"I don't know." He rose. "He's—well, he's no worse anyway. Might even be a mite better. It's the old story. If we could only get some fresh meat . . . But with Browne and Goodman missing, they *certainly* ain't going to let me go out with a gun."

"I don't want you to either!"

He turned away. It was hot in the poop cabin, what with the brazier going full blast, and his eyes stung.

Blinking, he stared at a port. It was rectangular, large, high above the water, and it faced New Plymouth, but it was presently closed against the cold. Yet there was something odd about its edges . . . a reddish glow . . .

He ran to the thing, slipped aside its balk, opened it.

All the sky was scarlet, and a column of sparks flew upward, swaying, tumbling over one another.

Here was a heart-killing sight.

The Common House was on fire.

"It's God's will," muttered Elder Brewster over Sal's shoulder, "but sometimes it does get hard to believe. Forgive me! Half of our company!"

"The strong half."

"Aye. They'll all be killed. The savages struck in the night."

Then this good man, who had been so strong, experienced a moment of weakness. He fell to his knees. But he soon rose, raising his arms in a familiar gesture.

"There's only one thing we can do—"

"There's more than that," cried Sal Boyd.

"We must pray for them."

"Pray, hell! We can do that later. I'm going ashore!"

Chapter Thirty-one

It was like rowing across a lake of blood.

Only four men had responded to Sal's call, and this made a small company to handle a craft like the shallop. The course had been unshipped, as had the boom, so that they had to depend upon oars, two on each side—for the shallop was too beamy to permit one man to handle two oars—while the fifth, Elder Brewster himself, held the tiller. There might have been others, if Sal had lingered to exhort, to orate, and rally; but he took the moment to be too crucial for that.

The water, then, was lit red all around them as they neared New Plymouth. There was nothing merry about this light, nothing gay. It didn't twinkle, it glowered. It and the low, pinkish clouds were all that the oarsmen could see, for they didn't risk a turn. Only William Brewster could see ahead; and from his troubled face, compressed lips, half-closed eyes, and taut, seamed face, Sal gathered that William Brewster was not seeing much.

"There are men—I can see them running around."

"Naked men? Red men?"

"I can't tell. They might be. They're only black from here—no details."

"Are they dancing?"

"I can't be sure, but I don't think so."

There was a mumble of thunder, but no lightning and no rain or snow. On most nights of the past few weeks such a fire would have been promptly put out. The weather had seemed to be worked on a schedule. Each morning had been clear and bright, to wax murky toward noon, when the rain would start. The rain would be very cold, spiteful. Toward nightfall the wind would rise, and the rain might or might not turn into a slushy snow. Tonight, however, there was almost no breeze, and though rain threatened there was as yet none.

They could not hear the spit of flames, though they must be close. Neither could they hear any screaming. Sal Boyd always had supposed that American savages screamed as they attacked.

Though they moved fast, the light around them faded even as they approached the landing place, the boulder. The fire was dying, having burned itself out.

Elder Brewster leaned forward.

"I can't see even as much now as I could before," he reported.

Valiant little man! He was at least twice the age of any other in the shallop, yet he would go to the aid of his fellows. Sal had never ceased to kick himself for having punched Elder Brewster that memorable night on the Catwater.

They had no guns, no swords. The arms, like all of the gunpowder, had been taken ashore. The plan was that they were to unhitch their oars and tumble out with these held before them like pikes, while William Brewster, who of course would be the last, would unship the tiller itself and swing this as a club.

"Here we are."

Sal had been rowing stroke oar, the farthest astern, and the instant that he felt the keel grind he hoisted his oar out from between its tholepins and vaulted over the thwart, to land thigh-deep in icy water. But he immediately began to wade through it, so that he was in fact the first to mount the bank.

"May the Lord bless you and keep you!"

No painted heathen but the slim gray figure of Governor Carver confronted him. The Governor's arms were lifted.

"Are the rest all right?" Sal gasped.

"Praise be to God, yes. There were many barrels of gunpowder in that building, and we urged the others—we, the ailing—we urged them to roll those barrels out. We got out ourselves, just in time."

Brewster and Carver embraced, touchingly. William Bradford, one of those on the sick list, and gaunt as a death's head, had come from the area of the embers, along with several others. They had to have a prayer session then and there, of course; but it was mercifully brief.

"No Indians?" Sal cried, as soon as he could, capping the amens.

"No. But we kept a fire burning, outside. We thought it might serve as a beacon for those two poor lads, if they were still alive. We were careful to make it a goodly distance away, and on the leeward side, but there must have been a freak twist of the wind."

Yes. It was understandable enough, once you had heard it. But even a Londoner like Sal would know enough not to make a fire under a thatched roof. A charcoal brazier perhaps, but not an open fire.

It had started to rain. The drops, very large, bitterly cold, hissed as they struck the ashes of the roof.

"We'll take the sick back," offered Elder Brewster. "They can't stay in the open air all night."

"*I'm* going to," Sal announced. "And tomorrow morning I'm going to take a gun and go hunting."

He looked at the row of gunpowder barrels. All of them had been knocked about, and a few actually were charred.

He shook his head.

"You know," he said, "there are times when I really do begin to believe that God has you folks under His special care. Anybody else in the world would have been in kingdom-come by this time."

He looked around, shaking his head, as men hauled tarpaulins over the barrels, for the rain was coming down faster now.

"If only those two dimwits hadn't gone and got themselves lost," he muttered, "or else killed."

There was a shout at the edge of the camp. Tightening his grip on his oar, Sal looked out across the brook, across an old cornfield.

A man had broken out of the dark wall of forest, and he was running toward them—staggering, rather. When he reached the brook he tried to jump it, and failed. After that he lay still.

But Peter Browne, of Great Burstead, Essex, had not entirely taken leave of his senses. He was able to protest that they had seen no savages and picked no berries, and, more important, that the settlers would find John Goodman, linen weaver, a short distance back.

Goodman's feet were frostbitten. He was in horrid pain. He screamed when they tried to work his boots off. With shoe leather worth its weight in gold, they were obliged to cut these away with a knife, Goodman screaming all the while. Then they put the two men into the shallop, along with the other sick ones. But Salathiel Boyd stubbornly remained ashore.

"I told you I was going to stay here," he said. "Let the others go back in my place. They need it more."

Governor Carver put a hand on the arm of John Goodman, who had ceased to scream but was groaning uncontrollably.

"Tell me, how did you ever find the settlement, on a night as dark as this?"

"The fire—we saw a big fire."

"Of course!"

"The ways of God—" Sal started playfully, but he didn't finish it.

"Are you sure you want to stay here, Master Boyd?" the Governor asked.

"If you can stand it, I can."

"We have no roof now, and it'll be hideously cold. It will probably rain all night."

"I've been out in the rain before," said Salathiel Boyd.

Chapter Thirty-two

Sal hid his weapon under some leaves and climbed a tree. He was careful about this, because the gun was a good one, being indeed Captain Standish's own snaphance. He would not prop it against the tree, and that for two reasons. It was loaded, and there was always a chance that when he came down he might slip and set off the thing, killing himself or at the least wasting a full charge and scaring game away. Also, though the gun was clean and the powder and shot in it had been well rammed down, Sal feared that its uncovered presence might warn away casual animals. He was out for a deer, nothing less; and while he had no reason to think that a deer could smell a musket, still there was no use taking chances. His stay in the tree might be a long one.

It wasn't. He saw at once, and even before he got to the top, that his direction was right and that the wind had not shifted. The tree was oak, and despite the recent rains and the fact that it was in an exposed position and stood taller than its neighbors, it retained, in February, some of its leaves, as an oak will.

Thievish Harbor, Clarke's Island, the anchored Mayflower, and the raw, small settlement of New Plymouth were right where he had expected them to be.

He was no Peter Browne, or John Goodman, to get lost in the

New World. Already he had become expert in the art of keeping his bearings.

Houses and ship, at this distance, from this height, looked like toys on a nursery floor, and the bay a mirror that had fallen from the wall. Sal studied them, musing. Never having known a home, he had no sentiment about this village as such; yet he found himself strongly moved by it, the men and women who lived in it, or would, God granting. He wouldn't have thought this possible a few weeks ago. He, Salathiel Boyd, the tough one, the rover, in truth felt tenderness toward those pale, earnest, voluble clerks and merchants. He could not make sense out of their idea of religion, and did not see why they refused to play skittles with the Church of England, just like anybody else, as long as they weren't going to be Papists; he thought that a good many of their Holy Discipline notions were just plain silly, but they were a people of valor, and they were—*good*. He was still wearing Dorothy Bradford's cloak.

At times the saints so bemoiled him inside with their kindness and their courage that he feared he might do something that would make him look foolish—weep, say. It was not impossible. This was one reason why he so often came out here into the forest in search of Indian signs and meat.

There was another reason. He had been frightened the first time he ventured into this wilderness, and he was a person who didn't like to be frightened. When he was a small boy, adrift in the capital, he would find himself quailing sometimes at the mouth of an especially noisome, dark alley. Then he used to force himself to enter that alley, and walk the length of it, back and forth, again and again, until the sweat of fear had dried upon him. It was the same thing now, here. Not soon would he forget the way his heart had been overturned when that first hare jumped away from him, and the shameful manner in which he had fallen to his knees because a woodpecker spoke. Well, the first time is always the hardest. Such behavior must not be

allowed to happen again. Nor would it. Sal had learned not only
to control his trembling; he had learned even to love the forest
for its rustles. So far from starting at the rat-tat-tat of a woodpecker, now he would pause to listen to it. He admired to hear
the crinkle of leaves beneath his feet, and surely there could be
no sound so satisfying as the slow, sodden, hollow plop of a
branchload of snow that had slipped to the ground.

"I guess I must be a poet," he told himself, adding: "A poet
that can't write or read."

He had been more than moderately successful in his hunting,
having brought down two deer this past week as well as a bag
of hares and fowl, but he had come upon no Indian sign.

This whole business about the savages, or lack of them, had
the settlers twitchy. Sal too was worried about it.

No two descriptions of the handful of aborigines seen so fleetingly at the time of the First Discovery agreed. Nobody was
positive of how many there had been, whether they were dressed
and if so how, or whether they had brandished weapons and
raised any manner of war cry. As to the "huggery" of the Third
Discovery, also on Cape God, it had occurred a little after dawn
—of all times!—and it had been without bloodshed, as far as
they knew, and certainly without any apparent reason. As before, descriptions differed; nobody was sure of anything. Last
week Christopher Jones the skipper, at a time when most of the
settlers were ashore, had glimpsed, if briefly, two savages on
Clarke's Island. They were naked, he'd testified, and they had
been studying the Mayflower. As soon as they saw that they were
observed they had melted into the forest. When the longboat
returned, the skipper sent out a search party, but they found
nothing.

That was all they knew of the American Indians. There were
traces of them, to be sure; but where in Hell were the savages
themselves? Had they at the first sign of newcomers retreated
into the interior to rally their allies, and were they preparing to

strike like the lightning, wiping out this pitiful settlement in one terrible blow? If they were afraid, why? And would they *stay* afraid?

Sal was glad, anyway, that Priscilla Mullins remained aboard the ship. With all the other nonsick ones she had come ashore just once, when they had staged a sort of dedicatory prayer service in the reroofed Common House. All the rest of the time she had stayed aboard the ship, tending her mother and father, others as well.

He shifted his position, staring at the toy ship. That was the place to be. There were no muskets aboard Mayflower any longer, and Webster the gunner had died—Sal had helped to bury him only the previous night—but neither were there any signs that the bloody bare-arses, wherever they were, had ever had any kind of boat. They might butcher those on the beach, but they could hardly get to those in the ship.

Sal sighed. He dreaded the time—and it would be soon now —when sufficient houses had been built to justify taking everybody, all the saints and strangers, women and children, ashore. He would stay nearer the settlement then, and not go roaming.

Well, he must get down. There was stalking to be thought of. He went slowly, thoughtfully, limb to careful limb, until he had reached the bottom branch, on which he sat, hanging his legs over the side.

He looked down to pick a place to jump—and he froze in horror, the spit of his mouth going dry.

Directly beneath him stood a savage.

Chapter Thirty-three

Sal could not see the man's face, though he could see that it had been painted white and dark red, seemingly with some sort of herb. The shoulders were a milder red, and even in this shadow they glistened as though they had been rubbed with oil. The hair was short in front, long behind: Sal could have reached out and kicked it.

The savage carried five or six crude arrows in one hand, and across his back he had slung a thin painted bow. Very tall, he was without ornament, and his clothing consisted of a narrow leather girdle and leather leggings.

He stood within a few inches of Captain Standish's snaphance, facing in the direction of New Plymouth, but he had turned his head. Now he nodded, and waggled the arrows, as though in signal to somebody Sal could not see. Then he faced forward again, and with long even smooth strides he went on his way.

All of Sal's muscle tugged at him to jump to earth and run back to New Plymouth, shouting an alarm. He did nothing. He did not climb farther up the tree. Any motion might catch a corner of some eye. It was better to be still.

A second savage appeared almost immediately, and because Sal saw him coming, having watched for him, he got a better look at this man's face, which was bedaubed with violet and

187

green. Otherwise the man was the same as the first one. He walked with an easy, loping stride, his toes a little turned in, his hips rolling. Like the first, he made no sound among the leaves, and though he too passed within inches of the hidden musket he did not pause or turn. He vanished—and another appeared.

Sal counted forty-three of them, more than twice the number of men who toiled at New Plymouth—and who would be scattered at this hour. Except for the pigmentation of the faces, he couldn't have told them apart. They all walked the same way. They did not keep in step, as soldiers were taught to do, for they were not near enough to one another for that; but it was clear to Sal Boyd that they had an agreed-upon plan.

The most terrible thing about this band was not its nudity, which was shocking, nor yet its ghostlike silence, but that very air of purposefulness. These warriors knew what they were about to do. They no longer skulked.

At last they were gone, the wraiths. Not a leaf did they disturb, and it was difficult to believe that they had ever existed.

Sal waited a little longer, straining his eyes, and then he slithered off the branch, hung by his hands for a moment, and dropped.

Amazingly—for he had not been conscious of any strain—his legs at first refused to support him, so that he tottered like a baby and fell headlong.

There must have been a strain, after all, in sitting there motionless for so long a time.

He probably looked drunk as he rose. His calves and thighs felt afire. But he set his teeth, and brought out the Standish snaphance.

So they were more wily than the beasts of the jungle, these American savages? They had the instincts and the craft of tigers, did they? Well, Sal would not dispute that those were fine physical specimens he had just seen; but if they were so cunning, so acute, and sharp, why hadn't *they* seen *him?*

Or—had they? Was this a trap? Had the first savage spotted Sal before Sal saw him, and had the nod and the wave of arrows been a message to those who followed him and whom he was by this means ordering not to look up? Was it a plot to get Sal to disclose the hiding place of his musket?

He didn't take time to learn. Stooping low, he leapt to the left, and as soon as he dared he started to run.

The stiffness already had gone from his legs, and wherever he was able to do so he sprinted.

His plan was to get far enough to the left of these Indians so that his steps would not be heard, and then race them to the settlement. However, there might be other similar columns. And the one he had seen, when it did draw near to New Plymouth, would be obliged to spread out, to deploy in some fashion. Sal did not have a good chance of getting there at all. If he hoped to survive he would do best by squatting where he was, hiding himself, permitting the raid, the slaughter, to be held without him, and later, under cover of darkness, swim out to Mayflower and enlist for the return trip. He didn't even consider this. He ran.

His heart whammed his chest as though somebody was beating it with a spade. His eyes pulsated, flooding with water. Several times he slipped and fell, but he got up again.

"*God verdomme,*" he muttered.

Scratched and bruised, his feet covered with slime, his clothes torn, at last he burst into a clearing near the settlement—and saw that the Indians had not yet struck.

Four men were there. They were taking down and trimming trees, probably with a design of making planks. They had been working hard but cheerfully, all innocent of the band of braves that approached. Two even had been singing. They had many tools—axes, saws, augers, planes—but there was not a musket in the group.

Sal, when he burst upon them, frightened them almost as much as the savages might have done. They did not pause to expostulate. One look was enough. They dropped everything and ran for New Plymouth.

There had been some talk of walling the town with a palisade of logs spiked on top, but nothing had been done about this, there was so much other work. Similarly, no gun platform had been erected on the hill, nor had any of the cannons been brought ashore. The Common House was tolerably strong, but that should be kept as a next-to-the-last place of retreat, the last, of course, being the shallop—or rather, Mayflower. Meanwhile, the brook along the edge of the settlement—Town Brook they called it—would do for a line. The stream itself, though easily leapt, might serve as a sort of moral barrier to invasion, and by staying on their own side of it they were far enough from the wall of forest so that they didn't need to fear arrows, as yet; at least they would oblige the savages to break cover.

In the absence of Miles Standish, Sal took command. He had no authority to do this, but as the one who had seen the savages and given the alarm he was obeyed. He posted men every fourteen or fifteen yards along the brook, cautioning them on no account to cross. He issued muskets, and he issued pikes, one pike for each two musketeers. He stationed sentries, and arranged to have them often relieved. He broached another barrel of the precious gunpowder, horns of which would be carried to those in the line as needed. He set some of the older men to cutting bullets.

Miles Standish, he learned, was aboard Mayflower, visiting his wife.

"She's still alive, eh?"

"Yes, but sinking. She won't last the day."

When Captain Standish returned, summoned by smoke signal, a little later, his face told everybody the answer to the question they didn't ask. Rose Standish was dead. The body, of course, would not be brought ashore until after sunset.

Standish never had been chatty. If this morning he was even grimmer than usual, and if there was a glint of moisture in his gray-steel eyes, everybody pretended not to have noticed. The Captain listened to Sal's report, nodded approval of all arrangements, and immediately set out on a tour of inspection.

As he walked he barked orders for several things Sal would not have thought of. For instance, he equipped every man in the firing line with an alternate wooden ramrod. Soldiers could get excited in the heat of combat, he recalled, and snap their ramrods. Also, he commanded that every bit of available firewood be distributed to certain outdoor corner points, where with the coming of night, fires would be lit. He wanted enough wood at each place to keep the fire going all night. Wildcats were afraid of fire. Perhaps Americans would be, too.

There were some men who began to think that the night, like the savages, never would come. The forest showed blank. It was a clear day, the first they had known here, and they were eager to get back to their work. After the original flare of excitement, doubts began to creep in. How well did they know this Salathiel Boyd, after all? He had come aboard by mistake, because he was drunk. Had he been drunk again this morning, out in the wood, and had he *imagined* that file of painted barbarians he described? There were mutterings.

Standish shushed them. He was loyal to his adjutant. In the middle of the afternoon he announced his intention of going out to the clearing where the four men had been working—a place not visible from the settlement side of the brook—and seeing if those tools had been touched. He would take one man with him; in case he was killed from ambush, the other man would bring in both muskets.

"I'll go," Sal said.

"You will not," coldly. "You will assume command in my absence."

Standish looked around, and nodded at last to Francis Cooke, one of the saints, a meek man, a wool comber from Nottingham, who must have been forty years old. Cooke might be spared, if anybody could be.

"You, Frank. Take up your musket and come along."

The others watched them anxiously as they advanced with a slow but not faltering step, their guns at the ready. They disappeared over the shoulder of Strawberry Hill.

The two were gone only a few minutes, but it seemed hours. They walked backward on their return, still watching the forest, from which there came no sign.

They had not found Indians, they reported. But neither had they found the tools.

Chapter Thirty-four

His adjutant was watching the Captain keenly. Miles Standish always had been terse, quick-tempered, with a tendency to rap out his orders in a voice through which one could hear the cracking of a whip. Part of this impatience no doubt was professional, but much too must have been natural to the little man, whose size, again, might have been a part of the cause. Today and through all of that terrible night, he was more than ever the peppery despot.

Was this because his wife had just died? Surely most of the men thought so, and were prompted by humanity to hold back indignant retorts. Doubtless the Captain had been fond of the slight, washed-out woman whom Sal Boyd scarcely knew; but her end could hardly have come as a surprise, for she'd been dying by inches for days: weeks ago he must have braced himself against the shock. Yet he could be taking his grief out on the sentries. He could be throwing himself furiously into the work, so as not to *feel*, so as, for a little while anyway, to remain *numb*.

Sal Boyd believed that there was an additional reason.

Standish was every ounce the military man. To him war and the preparation for war were everything. What his religious beliefs might have been, if he had any at all, nobody knew; but in any case he must have been made angry by the preponderance of religion and of religious thought in this queer company, where the Book was all. Hadn't Elder Brewster himself justified Captain Standish's presence and his occasional drills by means of quotations from Isaiah, from Hosea, and Zechariah? They had hired Standish as a soldier, and they sought to use him whenever a soldier's services were needed; but they were much more interested in conquering his indifference, horrible to them, and in justifying before him their action in breaking away from the Church of England.

"Didn't St. Paul urge it in his second epistle to the Corinthians?" John Carver would cry. "Didn't he write: 'Wherefore come out from among them, and separate your selves, sayeth the Lord, and touch none uncleane thing, and I will receive you'?"

"Did he?"

Now it was different. No drills had been held since Mayflower dropped anchor—there had been too much else to do—but now they wouldn't deny him scouts or men to haul the cannons to the top of the hill. "Pillars in war, caterpillars in peace," the soldiers used to say of themselves; but here it had become war, here in New England, and Captain Standish had the whole settlement hopping when he spoke.

There was more to it than that, as Miles Standish himself must have seen. In this curious company of zealots, which operated on no known rules save those that it made up as it went along, and in which there were virtually no distinctions of rank, any man who wished to get something done would have to seek his authority from most of the others. They could be made accustomed to granting this authority only if the man in question had his own little clique, his personal following. When Standish had first spoken dulcetly to him, on Cape Cod, Sal supposed that this was prompted by no more than the respect that one fighting man instinctively would have for another. He still believed that this had something to do with their relationship. But he also believed that he was being used. Already here in camp he was thought of as Miles Standish's "man." Well, that was all right. Sal did not mind being somebody's "man," provided that too much pressure wasn't brought to bear. Everybody had to answer to somebody just above him: that was the way this world worked, even here in New Plymouth, where the settlers essayed to govern themselves. Right up to the King. True, the King had to answer only to God, but he *did* have to answer.

By the same token, a man should protect those beneath him, those who owed him obedience. This was why Captain Standish, without even having heard the details of the case, had plumped for Sal and his story of forty-three savages. His adjutant *must* be right, especially when a state of alarm existed. If the missing tools had not been vouched for by Francis Cooke—a hardheaded man of good eyesight, good hearing, and impeccable honesty, one who couldn't be doubted—Sal wouldn't have put it past Captain Standish to hide the things himself. This colony needed a good jolt, a scare. But Cooke's confirmation made the Indians' presence certain. There would be no snoozing on sentry go tonight.

At sunset the fires were lighted, four big ones, but none near the burial place, and when after dark they brought Rose Standish's body ashore they buried it by the light of a single pine-knot torch. Afterward they shoveled and raked away the mound. It was not much of a mound, for she had been a slight, short woman.

Sal, being busy with inspection, did not attend this ceremony. He was told, though, that Miles Standish had evinced no emotion whatever, simply standing there, his back straight, his heels together, helmet held over breastplate; and immediately afterward he had returned to work.

Sal got very little sleep that night, and he questioned whether the Captain got any. Standish's order was that one or the other of them should be on duty all the time, pacing from fire to fire, checking the sentries, and keeping an eye peeled in the direction of Strawberry Hill and indeed all the other places on the far side of Town Brook. The off-duty officer could avail himself of the blankets and brazier of the Common House for an hour or so, but Sal doubted that Miles Standish ever did so: there were other men in there all the while, and his was a shy heart.

Despite the intensely small type and all the small squiggly marks he had complained of when he had taken lessons in reading—lessons, alas, put off and not resumed since the coming of The Sickness—Sal Boyd had known no trouble with his eyes. But then he had studied *something*. Staring at nothing was a different matter, and much harder. It made his eyes throb. He could scarcely see the cornfield, and couldn't see the forest at all, and when soon after midnight a fine, dusty, languid snow started to fall it was all he could do to see the very brook. Nevertheless he always kept to the outside of the usual line the sentry paced, near the brook, nearer to the forest. It gave him a creepy feeling to think that if those savages sneaked up under cover of the darkness and snow, he, Salathiel Boyd, would probably be the first killed. It was an unpleasant reflection. Yet he kept the outside course, for he reckoned that that was what was expected of an officer.

When a veil of gray was drawn across the eastern sky—not dawn but the false dawn, what soldiers call first light—Sal jumped the brook and strode back and forth a little while in the cornfield. He did this more to reassure the sentries than for any other reason. It made him nervous, himself.

Captain Standish was to take over at this hour, so he went down to the Common House. He passed around to the back of this, the only complete building in New Plymouth, for he meant to relieve himself before lying down. There still were no women in the settlement, but it is part of any man's training to get behind something on an occasion like this.

He stumbled from tiredness, and was not trying to be quiet, but the snow must have muffled his footsteps. At any rate, Miles Standish did not hear him approach.

The Captain was on his knees behind the Common House. His head was lifted, ignoring the swirl of snow, for his face already was as wet as it could well be—wet with the tears that coursed down his cheeks. He was holding high before him a small silver crucifix, something Sal had not seen since the last time he helped to sack a Spaniard. Twice, with fervor, he kissed this. His eyes were shut. His lips moved. Pauselessly the tears streamed down.

Sal Boyd backed away, and this time he *was* trying to be quiet.

He never told anybody about that scene.

Chapter Thirty-five

In the middle of the morning a military conference was called, when, quite as gravely as though there had been some choice in the matter, Miles Standish was elected captain of the separatist "army," with Salathiel Boyd as sergeant. Why there was need for a vote Sal could not understand. Moreover, they talked and talked about it. Before the show of hands, and though there wasn't a touch of opposition, saint after saint rose to deliver a sermon to these two, admonishing them to preserve better walking, to be ever conscious of their responsibilities, to shun the Devil and all his works, and so on, until Sal, writhing on a hard seat, might have cried, with Habakkuk, "Oh, Lord, how long?" —and almost did. Some time before the vote was taken—it was unanimous—Miles Standish himself had slipped out of the Common House, leaving Sal to bear it alone. When at last the inevitable decision had been reached, the saints were dismayed to learn that their commander no longer was present. Where was he?

"Gone out to make sure nobody's fallen asleep, I guess," Sal said.

Oh, he must be summoned! so that he and Brother Boyd together could be blessed and prayed for. At a time of such significance this certainly should be done.

"Might be better if we got those guns up the hill first," said Sal; but he said it to himself. He was tired, edgy, and—he admitted this—worried about Priscilla Mullins, whom he somehow felt, illogically, to be in peril.

A moment later he heard shouts outside.

It was two of the sentries. They had quit their posts and were running down the settlement's only street.

"Indians! Indians!"

Everybody grabbed a weapon and ran out.

There were only two of the savages on the crest of Strawberry Hill, but from the low general jabbering that rose from the other side, the settlers assumed that there were many others just out of sight.

If the two on the hill did not cringe, neither did they wave their bows, yelling defiance. They seemed not so much frightened as unsure of themselves. Perhaps they were daunted as much by the jeers and goading of those behind as by the firmness, the impassivity of those before. They did not put out a foot to start down the hill. Instead, after a few uncertain moments, they beckoned the settlers to come to them.

"Don't move, anybody," Captain Standish cried.

He handed Sal his musket, and stepped forward. From behind he looked slightly ridiculous, with his arched back, his red neck; but no doubt the face he turned upon the Indians was sufficiently stern, and when he raised his arms the gesture had majesty.

He signaled for them to come down the hill. He did this once, twice, a third time.

The savages did not confer, but it was several moments before they made answer. They shook their heads. They made their original gesture again—come. The settlers should climb the hill.

"If we all go there might be a fight," Standish decided, "and if I go alone they might get my gun. I'll take one man."

"All right," Sal said, and stepped to his captain's side.

"No."

Standish looked around. This is getting to be a pattern, Sal reflected.

Standish crooked a finger at Stephen Hopkins.

"You."

He took his snaphance from Sal Boyd and waded across the brook—with his stumpy legs he would not risk a jump—and after only an instant of hesitation Stephen Hopkins followed.

Hopkins did not have a musket. Like Francis Cooke of the day before, he must have been near forty, a portly self-important man. He could be spared, he was expendable; but whereas Cooke was a saint, Hopkins here—the Captain was maintaining a balance—was a stranger.

They paused on the far bank. Then the Captain very slowly raised his musket. He did not point this at the Indians, nor did he put the stock against his chest or his shoulder, but rather he raised it as though in salutation. Then he placed the musket on the ground, and he and Stephen Hopkins began to walk up the hill.

They went very slowly, and at first the savages, fascinated, watched them. But suddenly the savages broke, and as though in a panic whirled around and disappeared beyond the brow of the hill.

Hopkins and Standish continued their climb, not changing pace, as though nothing had happened. When they reached the top they stood there a little while, fists on hips, their heads moving back and forth.

Soon afterward they reported that there was nothing in sight, not so much as a footprint.

Sal immediately requested and was granted permission to return to the ship for a few hours.

Chapter Thirty-six

A death these days was hardly cause for amazement, and Sal was not astonished when, as soon as he boarded the Mayflower, he was told that Alice Mullins had died a few hours ago. What did astound him was the news that Johnny Mullins too had come down with the disease they called The Sickness. Johnny was only seven, and until this time The Sickness had spared children.

It was noteworthy that three persons had given Sal this bit of information before he even reached the waist, while he still was climbing. Clearly, they considered him to have a special interest in the Mullins family. They were right; but he wondered how they divined it. He thought that he had been extremely careful to keep his feeling about Priscilla to himself.

He nodded in acknowledgment, said something fitting if vague, and looked around.

This was the first time in two weeks that he had been aboard, and he remarked in his mind that the mariners in sight were fewer, and more sour in their treatment of the settlers. For this latter he could not blame them. After a six weeks' crossing, they had been cramped in this wild, unresponsive place for two months and the ship still was crowded with passengers, its hold heaped with supplies. The Sickness, the season, the need to post sentries, the awkwardness of getting from ship to shore, irked them. It might be a month or more yet before everything could be put ashore, if these bloody Brownists didn't get down to work instead of wasting so much time in argument and prayer. The mariners' own food supplies were perilously low. When at last they were able to start the long haul back it would be with weakened bodies on half or even quarter rations, and they would be short-handed, so that they'd be even more than usually overworked. In the circumstances it was little wonder that the mariners had no love for these damned pilgrims, as they contemptuously called the passengers.

Now Hicksom, the bosun, rolled up to Sal.

Hicksom was an arrogant young man who had gone out of his way to harrass the strangers and saints, breaking up their meetings with a cloud of curses, placing all sorts of restrictions upon them, literally pushing them around.

"Captain said he wanted to see you next time you came aboard."

"All right."

There was no one watching, so Hicksom did not feel called upon to bluster and strut. He was eying Sal Boyd with what was, for him, respect.

"Matthews back there, he tells us that you used to sail with Oosterlinck."

"Well . . ."

Sawn Matthews, for all his saturnine appearance, was an incorrigible gossip. It would have been strange indeed if the forecastle had not long ago learned all about Salathiel Boyd's profession. The wonder was that Hicksom troubled himself to bring it up now.

"That must be a wonderful life. You get rich."

"I didn't."

"You go everywhere."

"Aye. Including the harmans. And the gaol. And maybe after a while the gallows."

"Now, hold still a minute. The Old Man can wait."

"Maybe I can't?"

"Listen, Boyd. I'm a hard case, I am."

"Oh?"

"I'm nimble and I've got a cast-iron stomach. Maybe Oosterlinck could use somebody like me, when we get back to London? I mean, if you was to speak to him about the way I feel."

"Maybe. If I get back."

"Christ, man! You ain't thinking of *staying* in this ice-box, are you?"

"We'll see," said Sal, stepping around him.

"But Jesus, man! You can't really—"

"I said we'll see."

Crossing the waist, which as usual was cluttered with gear, he heaved a small sigh. It was all so familiar. The smell of tar and of bilge, the creak of timbers, the clatter of holystones: he could not say that he had ever loved these, or ever would, but he had lived among them and they made him feel at home—as much as he ever did, he guessed. He had forgotten how comforting they were.

He had intended to go directly to the poop cabin to give his condolences to Priscilla and to William Mullins, but a skipper is a skipper. He made for the Captain's quarters instead.

The scene was somewhat different from what it had been on his previous visit. For one thing, Sal's head was clearer this time. For another, the skipper was worn out. Christopher Jones did not fawn upon Sal, but the earlier truculence was gone.

This man was as tough as hickory, a seafarer since boyhood, for many years a whaler in the Arctic; but everyone has his limit of endurance. Captain Jones had more men in sick bay than he had on duty, and there was still an immense amount of work to be done. On the one hand he was faced with what might turn into a mutiny, for his able-bodied mariners were openly resentful of their lot and three of his four mates had been carried away by The Sickness. On the other hand, if he hustled all of these poor, simple, misguided, earnest lubbers ashore, sick and well alike, and left them, to learn long afterward that the colony had been wiped out, his conscience—for he had a conscience—might trouble him for the rest of his life, spoiling his sleep. He was one-quarter owner of this vessel, and ready to retire. This was to be his last voyage. He'd be shut of the sea. Understandably he was eager to get home, to rejoin his family.

He studied Sal, nodding a begrudged approval.

"You look well."

"Thank you, sir."

"Psalm-singing must agree with you?"

Sal said nothing to this, and Christopher Jones wasted no further time.

"You heard that Webster's dead?"

"Yes."

"Will you sign on in his place? He had no relatives, and I can see to it that you'll get his wages both ways. I can promise that. It might help, if they nap you for that connection with Oosterlinck. Oosterlinck was having trouble when we left, you know."

"Yes, I know."

"It was nip and tuck then. But if you had a little money in your purse when you stepped ashore, and if I was to testify that you'd come back on your own accord—"

"Sir, that would mean leaving these fools without any gunner. Isn't a one of them can handle anything bigger than a blunderbuss. And those Indians are coming back, that's sure."

"Tell me about the Indians, Boyd. What happened today? There was a lot of running around over there."

When Sal had finished, the skipper sighed.

"And yet you'd stay here, with things in that shape—and getting worse?"

"I guess they need me, sir. Hell, I *know* they do."

"Leave out the profanity, Boyd. This is a respectable ship. Now—even if the heathen never got over this superstition or whatever it is that's holding them back, and even if you managed to struggle through the winter, then what happens if your seeds won't sprout?"

"Well, I suppose we'd starve."

"I suppose you would. And have you even got any beer left?"

"No. No beer. But we can drink water. It isn't bad, really. And there's plenty of it."

"Rot your stomachs," the skipper growled.

He tried another tack.

"And what about the Frenchies? They claim all this coast, you know. And have, for years."

"I know."

"D'ye think they're going to just forget it when they hear there's been a colony planted here? Oho, no! They'll come with a ship of war and blast the whole place to pieces—yes, and hang everybody they find. Because to them you're as bad as—as—pirates. Well, I didn't exactly mean—"

"That's all right," Sal said. "Sure, we've taken the French into consideration. There isn't a one of us that don't look out here twenty times a day. We're afraid of seeing a French sail, naturally. What we'd do if they did come I don't know. We'll just have to keep hoping they won't, I reckon. We'll just keep up our trust."

"Trust in what? Your ability to run?"

"Well, I guess trust in God."

The skipper snorted. Then he sighed.

"Which means that you're saying no, you won't sign on?"

"I'm afraid so, sir."

Christopher Jones picked up a list he had been checking. Clearly, he had expected this answer.

"All right. Close the door when you go out."

Chapter Thirty-seven

It was a shock when he saw Priscilla. Instead of being con-
vulsed by sobs she was seated, as plump and lovely as ever,
making him reproach himself yet again for the fact that the
first thing he had admired about her was her behind. She was
reading the Bible to her father and perhaps to some others.
Sal did see when she looked up that her eyes were red, though
they were not puffed, nor were there any tear channels on her
cheek. She tried to smile, and almost succeeded. She was, truly,
pale. She looked as if she needed an airing.

"You come at a good time."

"Any time's a good time to see you," he replied, taken aback
even as he did so by his own gallantry.

She ignored this. She put the Book on the edge of the bunk,
open, and got up, smoothing her petticoat, patting back her hair.
Sal made the customary expressions of sorrow, and she thanked
him. Just for a wee while they were most proper.

The poop cabin was a small sick bay itself. There was the
empty bunk, carefully made up, out of which Mrs. Mullins'
body so lately had been lifted. There was little Johnny, by the
side of his father, both motionless. There were the Mullins'
servants, John and Alice Rigdale, who also suffered from The
Sickness. There were three or four others, all women, indistinct

figures in the semidarkness. Excepting Priscilla, everybody was either asleep or feverish, at best less than half conscious. It was close in there, and the air was acrid with smoke from the brazier: it rasped Sal's throat and prickled his eyes.

"I don't like to leave them, even for a few minutes, but I just have to go to the jakes." She picked up the Bible, and pointed to a place. "Here, here's where I was. Thank you—Salathiel."

It was some time after she had gone before he was able to get into the swing of the reading. Except when he had perused the Mayflower compact, this was the only occasion on which he even had tried to read outside of her presence, and it gave him a slight feeling of embarrassment, as though he was doing something dirty. Also, there was that "Salathiel" to think about. It reverberated through the cabin. Sal wondered if any of the others had heard it. He doubted that.

" 'When thou shalt goe forth to warre against thine enemies, and shalt see horses and charets, and people moe than thou, be not afraid of them: for the Lord thy God is with thee, which brought thee out of the land of Egypt.' "

It came easily after all. Some of the words he was not sure how to pronounce, and he would pause, looking around, but nobody made complaint and probably nobody had even heard.

" 'And when ye are come neare unto the battell, then the Priest shall come forth to speake unto the people,

" 'And shall say unto them, Heare, O Israel, ye are come this day unto battell against your enemies: let not your heart faint, neither feare, nor be amazed, nor adread of them.' "

He paused, proud of himself. There was no moan of protest at the suspension, so he sat for some time with the Book on his knees, studying William Mullins' sunken, ashes-pale face.

Sal Boyd knew something about scurvy, something too, at least as much as anybody else, about The Sickness. Red-hot irons could not have forced him to tell Priscilla this, but he thought that William Mullins here was as good as dead. Nay, he was sure of it. Johnny too, perhaps. The lad was sickly enough. And the Rigdales. But of William Mullins there wasn't the slightest doubt. They would be burying him on Corn Hill any night now.

Then Priscilla would be alone in the world, he told himself.

He straightened when he heard her coming back. He made himself look upon the Book, his forefinger marking a place while his lips moved. She must not see him staring at her father like that.

"Thank you so much. It was kind of you."

She took the Book from him, but she saw that all the sick were asleep, so she did not even make a show of reading it, only sitting there with it across her knees. She gave Sal a wan but fond smile.

"Why don't you go out and walk on deck a while? Do you good."

"No. It wouldn't be right. One of them might wake up."

"I've got two hands, and a voice. And I'm not exactly a half-wit."

"It wouldn't be right," she said again.

So they sat there for some time, in the semidarkness, seldom saying anything, since even a whisper might disturb some of the sick. And when at last he left her she thanked him yet again and gave his hand a small squeeze—or so, at least, he believed.

In a little while, he was telling himself over and over again, in a little while she would be alone in the world—with nobody to protect her.

Chapter Thirty-eight

Sal Boyd was not, properly, a mariner—he was a seagoing gunner—but he had sailed enough to pick up certain techniques and to form a standard of judgment. He rated the Mayflower seamen high. They did their work adroitly, swiftly, and with no more than the conventional cursing. The mates too, and the bosun, though he personally disliked Clarke and Hicksom, Sal had marked in his mind as efficient, like poor put-upon Christopher Jones, the skipper. Canvas was well handled, the course well kept. Stowage, that all-important matter, was something else again.

How the ship's own stores were stowed Sal had no way of learning; but the stowage of the greater part of the supplies belonging to the settlers-to-be was the most lubberly job he ever had seen.

This had been done in Southampton, long before Sal ever heard of Mayflower, and it had been done very badly indeed. Sal did not know what the local circumstances had been at that time, but he could not understand why some experienced member of the crew had not been assigned to supervise the loading of the passengers' gear and supplies. Except for the barrels, which presumably had been rolled into position under the eyes of young John Alden, everything was in the worst possible places. Nor had the articles been regularly inspected, and some, because of the shifting, had been damaged or spoiled. Sal blamed Clarke for this.

"They just can't do *anything* right, the fools," Sal cried to Sawn Matthews.

"Except sermonize."

Traditionally the first mate of a vessel is in charge of stowage, and Sal blamed Clarke for the bungling here. True it was that the saints and strangers were responsible for their own provisions and supplies, just as though their part of the ship was a separate ship entirely; but Clarke surely had been *there*, and he could have seen for himself what an appalling mess was being made, so that his very pride as a mariner—regardless of how he felt about these passengers—ought to have prompted him to intervene.

The whole business, from beginning to end, had been marked by mishandling and delay, a contrast to the ship itself, which was well run. Because of the financial arrangements with certain merchant adventurers of London, Speedwell had been late in sailing from Leyden. Because of a squabble over the contract, the passengers' provisioning of both vessels, Speedwell and Mayflower, which had joined them in Southampton, had taken an unconscionably long time. Because Speedwell, the smaller vessel, recently rerigged, had been heavily overmasted, oversparred, she had twice sprung leaks, making it necessary to put back first into Dartmouth, then into Plymouth, from which port Mayflower at last had issued alone, several months late, just in time to hit the equinoctial gales head on. Because they had not been sure of their landfall or even of the place where they meant to go, more days—when every day was precious before the full coming of winter—were spent in feeling out the coast; and even after the anchor had been let go, the assembling and rigging of the shallop had taken seventeen days, instead of the six allowed for this— largely due to the fact that the needed tools and replacement parts had been stowed in obscure, far, deep, and all but inaccessible places.

After the cooperage, the armory was the least disorganized of the stores departments; and for this no doubt they could thank Miles Standish, a man who stood for no nonsense. Perhaps unavoidably, because of their weight, the cannons had been nested very deep, so that the settlers were not able to have them out and get them ashore until March 3, several days after the Indian scare on Strawberry Hill. That was almost four months after they had first sighted the New World.

To Salathiel Boyd, the artillerist, this was an unmixed madness. It hurt him, like a low blow.

"If they were psalters they'd've been fetched up fast enough," he grumbled.

The cannons had not been cleaned properly before being stowed away, and they were flaked, though lightly, with rust. There were no recoil pads, no recoil cables, no blocks or timbers for the building of firing platforms. It would take weeks for Sal to get the things into operation. He sighed.

On the other hand, the small arms were plentiful and in fair condition. There was enough armor, and there were almost enough swords. The only snaphance was the Captain's, privately owned, and there were no wheel locks at all—these would have been too expensive—but there was plenty of ball and powder, extra ramrods, wadding; and of the muskets only four were blunderbusses.

The blunderbuss was well avoided here, Sal thought. It was a good enough weapon to carry on a boarding party, where the fight would be at close range. It was good enough for a householder who wished protection against marauders, since a close look at it would terrify the boldest. A coachman who feared knights of the pad would do well to drive with a blunderbuss across his knees. But it would be of small value in battle, and not practical for fowling or any other kind of hunting. It threw a staggering load—nails, rocks, chunks of tin—but, like a pistol, it simply could not be fired far enough. The four blunderbusses might have been brought along because of a lack of real muskets, or they might have been meant to frighten the savages of America with their wide muzzles, their cannon-like roar.

The fishing equipment was woefully inadequate. It saddened Sal Boyd to reflect on how the sick might have been revived if only fresh fish could be caught. All reports from previous travelers in these parts, and particularly that of Captain John Smith, had extolled the New England fisheries; yet such nets and hooks and lines and poles as the settlers did bring appeared to have been an afterthought: they had no connection with one another. It was clear to Sal, no angler himself, that these inland men, these city men, knew nothing about fishing.

Again he sighed.

They were poor, and their backers had not been bountiful. There were biscuit and oatmeal in barrels, butter (though not much of it) in firkins, rye meal in hogsheads, cheese in boxes, pickled eggs in tubs, and smoked herring, salted cod, salt beef, canvas sacks of smoked hams, and many barrels and bags of beans. But their chief reason for hoping for a continued existence lay in their seeds—parsnip, turnip, pease, cabbage, and the Indian corn they had taken from Cape Cod. These could not be planted until spring.

It was to be primarily an agricultural venture. They had brought plows and harrows and other such instruments, though many of these had been badly damaged on the voyage. Their most flagrant failing, as Sal saw it, lay in the lack of wooden shafts. Hoes, rakes, axes, shovels, spades—not one was fitted with a handle. A few chunks of timber, easily obtained in Southampton, Dartmouth, or Plymouth, would have been enough: the work could have been done in the course of the long voyage. No such arrangements had been made. Before a tree could be felled, a foundation dug, or any other work begun at New Plymouth, it was necessary to cut and shape and fit handles for all the tools.

This was one of the reasons why it had taken them so long to build enough structures to accommodate that tragically cut-down company. Not until March 21, almost three weeks after William Mullins died, a week after they had buried Hicksom the bosun—who died despite the most assiduous nursing on the part of the saints he had reviled and persecuted—did the last of the passengers leave Mayflower.

It was the loss of the handles as much as that of the metal tools themselves that had made the Indians' theft so grievous a crime.

They were to get those tools back, however, in a most extraordinary way.

Chapter Thirty-nine

It was March 26, Friday, a bright clear day, even balmy, as the earth was beginning to stir with spring, and there was much muttering—there was so much work to be done—when Miles Standish at last succeeded in calling a military conference.

New Plymouth had by this time something of the aspect of a village, albeit a disheveled one, littered with chips and shavings, strewn with scraps of wood. There was only one street, extending from the boulder on the beach to the foot of the hill that they had named Fort Hill, but this street now was lined with no fewer than five houses, most of them, admittedly, not yet finished. They were all about the same, those houses: made of upright logs peaked at the top, the walls wattle-and-daub, the roofs thatch. There was plenty of grass for thatch, as there was good sticky clay and light, clean sand: these had been considerations in the selection of the site. The wattle-and-daub house with a thatched roof had been thought ancient in England for as long as the oldest could remember, and surely it was not comfortable, as it was exceedingly susceptible to fire, but nobody seemed to have thought of trying to design something more modern, more suited to the surroundings. There wasn't time. Sal Boyd did suggest, tentatively, that since they had so many trees to get rid of, to clear the land for planting, why not use logs for the walls of houses? Not just upright, as corner posts, he pointed out, but horizontal. Just how these logs could be notched together at the ends he didn't profess to know; but it should not be hard to devise a system. Such a house would be more solid, more enduring, and it would really keep out the wind as well as the rain. The logs themselves might be chinked together with mud made for this purpose. Nobody listened to this plan, though Captain Standish did say something about having seen such houses in Sweden; and Sal himself wasn't sure enough of it—for he knew next to nothing about working with wood—to push it.

Sal shared a house with Miles Standish and three young men, one of them, unexpectedly, John Alden. This house was the farthest from the shore, at the very foot of Fort Hill, so that Standish and his adjutant could man the guns at a moment's notice—once the guns had been hauled up the hill and mounted. It was mean, a hut, merely a bed of hemlock boughs sufficiently wide for five men, fenced in by saplings and sticks, and roofed, very low, with thatch. They did not loaf there, for the place held no amenities. For this reason, among others, Sal and Alden, though thrown into such close quarters, did little snarling. There simply wasn't time. They were too tired, when they trudged home, to do more than scowl.

Priscilla Mullins—her brother Johnny had died too, as well as both of the Rigdales—was taken in by the Brewsters, whose house was near the Common House.

The Common House itself, the first to be built, the largest, the strongest, was at all times the most important building in town, being at once their church, their storeroom, their hospital, forum, and court. It was in the Common House, of course, that the military conference was held.

This had barely begun—the Captain had not even had a chance to lose his temper—when there came an Indian alarm from the sentries, and the conferees, snatching up their weapons, rushed outside.

"No muskets pointed, no swords drawn," Standish cried. "If there's to be a war, let *them* start it."

There was nothing belligerent about the savage who approached New Plymouth, and certainly nothing bashful, nothing furtive. He came with long, swinging strides around the shoulder of Fort Hill, and across the empty cornfield toward Town Brook.

He was tall, handsome, virtually naked. His face was not painted. He had a bow slung across his back and held a pair of arrows in his hand, but he made no move to use them.

The women had retreated like well-trained servants into the shelters, taking the children with them. The sentries fell back, to join the men who stood before the Common House. Motionless, these men watched the savage draw near.

He jumped the brook. He waved to them. So far from scowling, he grinned.

"Greetings," he cried. "I speak English. You give me some beer, eh?"

Chapter Forty

It was humiliating. The last of their beer had been drunk more than a month ago, and they had been subsisting, and even thriving, on spring water. They could hardly believe this themselves, and they could not explain it to the visitor, who clearly expected more cheer from Englishmen.

"My name Samoset," he said again and again, thudding his forefinger against his chest. "Me. Samoset."

"Yes, we understand that, Mr. Samoset, but—"

"You English. Give me beer, eh?"

They might have sent the boat out to Mayflower and begged Captain Jones for some of the brew they knew he had left; but that was little enough, and what there was was turning sour, and Christopher Jones, near the end of his patience, might refuse. They stopgapped by producing a flask of geneva water, meant only for emergencies.

Samoset accepted this graciously. They could gather that he never had tasted spirits. He knew that it wasn't beer, but he must have supposed it was something similar, something of about the same strength. He took a huge swallow and made a face that caused them to fear he might scream, summoning others who lurked in the forest. Samoset, however, once he had caught his breath, only grinned. He was a singularly good-natured brute.

"Samoset," he pronounced. "You give me food, eh?"

They did this, it could be with unbecoming eagerness. They brought biscuit, butter, cheese, even a pudding, even a piece of duck, which he wolfed, beaming. Afterward Samoset tried the geneva water again.

The women, naturally, prepared these things, but they were not admitted into the Common House while the savage was there. Instead, the men took the food from them at the doorway, serving it themselves. Even after John Carver had sent for a long scarlet riding cloak and had draped this over the savage's sinewy shoulders, they feared to expose the women to this barbarian, who might at any moment shrug the cloak off.

Samoset, it would seem, never had seen a stool or bench. To eat, he simply squatted. It looked uncomfortable, even painful, but he didn't seem to mind. He grinned and talked all through the meal. It would have been hard to understand him even in the most favorable circumstances; but when his mouth was full it was all but impossible, and they had to ask him to repeat much of what he had said.

When you stopped to think of it, reflected Salathiel Boyd, probably half the people in the world, maybe a heap more than that, never sit on anything but their own heels. It's just a matter of getting used to it.

When he had finished eating, Samoset, obviously relishing the stir he had caused, took another swig from the flask, and rose easily, gracefully. He walked back and forth, delighted with the cloak. He might well have been, for it was meant for a king. Some time ago the settlers had decided that they would trim it with froggery and drape it across the shoulders of the first monarch they should meet among the American savages, as an opening move of conciliation. This trimming, this decoration, was yet another of the tasks that they had intended to do during the voyage, and that it was not done was due to the same reason of stowage: the coat had been in one place, the braid in another, where until well after the anchoring nobody could find it. Since then there had been no chance to work on the cloak, which remained bare.

Samoset didn't mind. He loved it as it was. He strutted in it, back and forth across the Common House floor. Now that he had finished eating, they plied him with questions.

Amiable as always, he tried to answer, and the result was bedlam. It was hard enough to make out what Samoset meant to say at any time.

At length—but not at *great* length—an interrogator was elected from among them. This was Governor Carver. Instead of all the white men talking at once, the Governor alone should talk for them.

The first question was, tactfully: How had Samoset learned to speak such impeccable English?

He flushed with pleasure and explained in very bad, halting, ungrammatical, sometimes sheerly stupid English; but it *was* English. He was a stranger around here himself, for he came from Pemaquid, far up the coast to the north—somewhere in Sir Ferdinando Gorges's grant, as well as they could make out, up near the French claims—where he was a sagamore or subchief of a sept known as the Abnaki, which he said meant "people of the dawn." He was down here to visit friends and relations, and when he had learned of the appearance at Patuxet of white men he decided to try out his English, rusty right now, and also to get some beer. Where was the beer? He looked around.

Governor Carver diverted him by repeating the question about language.

Why, Samoset had learned English from fishermen who often put in, in the summer, at Pemaquid, and he was enormously pleased when the settlers congratulated him on his command of the tongue.

He could not grasp the truth that there was no beer. He appeared to think that they were belittling or harassing him. Englishmen and beer must have been inextricably fastened together in his mind, and even as he talked he might have been having doubts that these really *were* Englishmen after all.

They hastily asked him, through John Carver, what was it he had called this place. Patux-something?

"Patuxet. Home of the Pokanokets. Many, many Pokanokets. Fierce warriors. Not here now."

"They—went away?"

"No."

"But—where are they then?"

"Dead."

"*All* of them?"

"All dead. Every one. All Pokanokets dead."

Chapter Forty-one

The details came slowly, not because of any unwillingness on the part of Samoset, but because his English words were few.

There had been a plague, four years ago, since Smith's visit to these shores. It might have been smallpox, with which the settlers were acquainted. They could not be sure of this from Samoset's description, but certainly it had not been their own waning Sickness, being much more virulent. Up and down the coast and far inland as well it had struck, and tribe after tribe had been decimated, quartered, halved—even, like the Pokanokets, wiped out.

It had been worst of all here, at Patuxet, Samoset told them. Even the murderous Mohawks, who used to roam through this part of New England at will, no longer ventured so far east. It wasn't worth while to plunder a desolated land, and the Mohawks saw no reason to raid when there was no chance of tribute.

Many of the tribes or subtribes, weakened to the point of helplessness, had combined with others, making free of one another's territory in an agonizing attempt to stay alive; but nobody would come here to Patuxet, to occupy the land that the Pokanokets had left, for they were afraid even to set foot upon it. The colonists believed that Samoset was trying to tell them that the surrounding savages thought this was the place where

Death was buried. But lightly buried! The grave was not deep, and Death might rise from it at any time and ravage the land yet again. The settlers believed that this was what Samoset was trying to tell them: it was something like that, anyway.

And who were these surrounding Indians?

They were of many septs—he rattled off names meaningless to those who listened—but all of them were loosely under the suzerainty of Samoset's friend Ousamequin, or Yellow Feather, more often called Massasoit, the Big Chief of the Wampanoags, who lived about forty miles to the southwest of New Plymouth (as nearly as they could make it out) on the shores of Narragansett Bay.

Yes, Samoset would go to Massasoit for them. He would take a message of peace from the white men. Were they *sure* that they had no beer?

They were.

They described in detail the "huggery" on Cape Cod, and asked the reason for this. Samoset countered by asking for a description of the place, and when this was supplied he nodded knowingly.

"The Nauset. Many braves. Hate white men."

"Why?"

Samoset went on to explain that the Nauset were the fiercest of the several Cape Cod tribes, also the one least hurt by the plague. They were all generally under the overlordship of Massasoit, but the Nauset could be perversely independent. The reason for the huggery was plain to Samoset. Some years earlier, before the plague had hit, an Englishman—Samoset apparently supposed that all white men were Englishmen—had visited these waters and by means of held-up trinkets had lured a dozen or more natives aboard of his vessel. That was the last seen of him, or them. A few of the victims had been Pokanokets, Samoset said, but most of them had been Nausets, and the Nausets, an unforgiving lot, had vowed to make war on all white men they should ever see. The Pokanokets would have done the same, Samoset said, had any of them survived, for in their day they had been a numerous and powerful people. A few years ago these white men would not have been permitted to land here.

"It was the will of the Lord," more than one settler said aloud, "that brought about such a plague."

Was it the will of the Lord, Sal Boyd wondered, that had sent here an adventurer in search of slaves for the markets of North Africa?

They told Samoset about the theft of the tools, and he nodded, unimpressed. Yes, he had known about that, he said. Indeed, it had been the sight of those same tools that caused him to learn that white men were near, and to make inquiries. Would he get them back, please? All right—casually—he'd get them back.

They decided to exhibit Samoset. The females should be given a chance to see him. Making sure first that the cape was well fastened in front, they led him to the door, which they threw open.

The women, the children too, though until now they had only glimpsed this magnificent specimen of the American race, behaved with more dignity and reserve in his presence than ever had the men. They showed, in fact, somewhat less eagerness to study the lineaments of Sagamore Samoset than to see for themselves that their fathers and husbands had not been hurt. Eyes sought out faces, and there was a long, audible exhalation of relief. Sal caught sight of Priscilla Mullins, and laughed as he realized that she thought he might have been in peril; he grinned and wriggled his fingers at her, and she smiled back, dewy-eyed.

So far from being flattered by this attention, Samoset, a sensitive savage now, was indignant. He trembled, and fairly snorted. He withdrew.

The man was waxing cantankerous, possibly as a result of the geneva water: he had never relinquished that flask. They tried to persuade him to go back into the forest today, now, for they were frankly afraid to have him here, but he refused. Yes, he would bring some friends to see them, along with the stolen tools, and he would ask those friends to bring whatever they had that they might want to sell. But not today—no, tomorrow.

As abruptly as a man who dives into a pond, he fell asleep.

They kept him in the Common House the rest of that afternoon and all the night, with a discreetly posted guard; but though he snored gustily he did not twitch or turn.

On the morrow, without demur but after a hearty breakfast, he went back into the forest.

The day after that—unfortunately it was a Sunday—he emerged in the company of five friends. These were large naked men like himself, and there weren't cloaks for all of them. Their faces, unlike Samoset's, were painted in repulsive colors, seemingly with some kind of mud. Of course they spoke no English, but they did bring with them three beaver pelts in fair condition, *and* they brought the tools.

They were fed as a matter of form, and they ate ravenously, while the settlers, less well filled, teetered in anxiety, watching each precious morsel disappear.

Afterward, no doubt in gratitude, the Indians shuffled to their feet and proceeded to give an exhibition dance. Salathiel Boyd thought it mighty awkward, with no agility, no spirit, no real music, only discordant grunts and squawks; but the separatists were horrified. Any dance at any time would have been bad enough, dancing being so clearly a sin, but on the Lord's Day—

At least, when they saw the pelts and heard through Samoset that more could be brought, the settlers resolutely refused to truck with them on such a day. They urged the braves to come back later in the week. Business might be conducted then.

This was difficult to explain, even to Samoset, while the five others, it had to be assumed, never did comprehend. But at last they agreed to depart, promising to come back soon—with many pelts.

Thus it was that the tools were recovered and trade with the aborigines opened.

Chapter Forty-two

The ship Mayflower, out of London, riding at anchor off New Plymouth, was higher in the water every day. Passengers and passengers' provisions had been carried ashore, and the ship was lighter too from the removal of many another load. For instance, all of Elder Brewster's books had been landed. No shelves had been built for these, but Master Brewster had unpacked them nevertheless, for he declared that he was happier when he could see them. Sal Boyd gasped when he saw them the first time he went to the Brewster house to resume his reading lessons. Books would not ordinarily be thought of as weighing much, but in this case there were so many that they massed heavy. Though Elder Brewster said that these represented only about half of his library, there must have been two hundred of them, more books than Sal had supposed to exist. He could read many titles: *History of Florence* by Guicciardini, Peter Martyr's *Decades of the New World*, Bodin's *Republic, The Advancement of Learning* by Francis Bacon, Raleigh's *Prorogative of Parliaments, The Prince* by Niccolo Machiavelli.

"You've read every one of these?"

"Some of them two and three times."

"Go to! I'd think it would take most of your life."

"You read faster when you get used to it."

Sal was picking up books, blinking at them as if they were crown jewels.

"D'ye suppose I could ever get to read one of these, myself?"

"I don't know why not. With Mistress Mullins to instruct you. Here she is now."

And she was, and she showed so dink that Sal made a muttered excuse to turn away from both her and Elder Brewster, so that they should not see how he felt.

In his aerie on Fort Hill, where he spent most of his time these days, Sal was surrounded by five additional reasons for the lightening of the Mayflower. These comprised the separatists' artillery. There were two bases, weapons that would throw a half-pound ball, though not far; a falcon, a two-pounder; a three-inch minion that weighed half a ton; and their star, a ten-foot, 1,800-pound saker with a four-inch bore. This last must surely have been the largest weapon ever seen in this part of the world.

The New Plymouthites were inordinately fond of these pieces, and proud of them, and they often used to climb the hill just to look at them. The Indians too—for the settlement was filled with Indians once Samoset had broken the ice—were encouraged to gaze upon such splendors, which they were told could kill men by the score. Sal Boyd didn't agree. These were poor pieces. They might be made to carry a couple of hundred yards, or they might burst. To place them on top of a hill was bravado, nothing more. Anyone who could skip inside of their line of fire—which should be easy for any reasonably nimble man, so long did it take to reload these cannons—was perfectly safe. He could run right up the slope without fear of a ball, unless it was a ball fired from a musket. For the cannons could not be depressed. Yet they did have horrific muzzles, and they were black.

Sal knew many troubles up there on Fort Hill, which wasn't a fort at all but only a gun platform. Even after he got the cannons mounted, a job he had to do alone since there was nobody else who knew anything about it, he was plagued by the problem of powder and ball. The iron balls they had were not many, and they were of all sizes and shapes. No gunner had bought these; none fitted the saker. Sal searched for stones, in vain. Stones in these parts appeared to be either pebbles or else boulders like the one near their landing place, and each was useless. Sal thought of loading the biggest gun with chunks of metal, as though it had been a huge blunderbuss; but any metal, large or small, was hard to come by. He at last laid in a supply of small smooth hard round stones that he had garnered from the Town Brook. These would serve as wadding, to hold the charge in place. They would probably be blown to smithereens and shower the enemy with nothing more destructive than sand; but they *would* make a noise like thunder.

The powder posed another problem. He was allotted only two barrels, not much for such a battery. But—where should he put these? Any good gunner knew that powder should be stored about forty or fifty yards from the gun for which it was destined. Farther away would be inconvenient, nearer would be dangerous. But forty or fifty yards from the guns atop of Fort Hill would be on the hillside itself, and even if it had been practical to build a magazine on a slope like this, it would have been an exposed position, so that the men or boys who ran the scoops might be killed by arrows or, if the French came, bullets. Also, the powder must be protected against snow, sleet, rain, yet the one known roof was thatch, which Sal thought too touchy for a magazine.

"The bulk of the powder's down in the Common House, and *it*'s got a thatch roof," Isaac Allerton insisted.

"Yes, but there's no guns mounted there. You don't have to think of a flareback. Ever see one of those when the wind's the wrong way? Why, they can leap clear across this whole platform. And *then* if the roof caught we'd have no guns *or* powder left. It'd take off the whole top of this hill. You'd like that?"

So he dug, right into the middle of the fort itself, a hole exactly large enough to contain the two gunpowder barrels. This hole was covered, as it was lined, with tarpaulin. It was likewise covered with a thin layer of earth. Two old musket barrels thrust through earth and tarpaulin alike served as ventilators—for it would have been courting disaster to leave such a store without air—but at the same time, since this would admit moisture as well, Sal wedged in on either side of the powder barrels small hole-poked boxes of charcoal and of chloride of lime, calculated to absorb the wetness of the air. Every third or fourth day—and it was a chore that he refused to delegate—he had to unlid this hole and turn the barrels upside down. Otherwise the heavy saltpeter would have found its way to the bottom and the mix might not explode.

Despite these and similar duties, Sal allowed himself to cease work from time to time, and stretch his limbs, and arch his back, and lean against the rough log parapet, and look down upon the bleak, huddled, small village and upon the Mayflower far beyond, the vessel that had been their home for almost half a year. Even at that distance he could see that Mayflower was rising, and lately he had been able to discern antlike activity.

"They're fixing to go out, all right," he said late one afternoon when he stopped at Elder Brewster's house for his lesson. He looked around. "How's it happen you're not getting your things together?"

Priscilla smiled a little. The grief of losing father, mother, brother, all within a month—it might have driven some persons mad. It had not even sullied her beauty. She was a shade less plump than she had been on shipboard, but this was no more than what might be expected in view of the work she had to do now and the scantiness of their rations; she was still a fine figure of a woman. She would some day be fat, Sal reflected, but she was not fat now.

Priscilla was not stolid; she must have had her bad times, but she kept these to herself. Without ever being playful, roguish, coy, she could now and then muster a smile; and this one caused Sal's heart to leap.

"Everybody seems to think I'm going back."

"Of course."

"Why should I?"

"*Eh?*"

"What would I do at home?"

"Why, if—"

"What *is* my home, coming to think of it? My father's shop was sold before we left. All he had was his adventure in this company, which I suppose is my share now. Elder Brewster here has offered to keep me warm. And I'm entitled to my part of the common fund anyway."

"But—the men!"

"What's the matter with the men?"

Sal was not shocked that she had forced him to speak bluntly in the presence of Elder Brewster. They had never been mealy-mouthed, any of them. But Sal was impatient. She had no right to ask that the obvious be set forth like goods for sale on a table.

"What's the matter with the men?" he echoed. "Why, what always has been the matter with men, mistress! There's a might of widowers been made here lately, remember that. And look at the indentured lads. They'll be getting ruttish, see if they don't. They'll be slobbering around you."

"I think I can cope with that, Master Boyd."

They were careful to call one another "master" and "mistress," except when they were alone, which was seldom and never for a long time. Privacy was a rare commodity in Plymouth. You ate with others, slept with others, and of course prayed in company. Not because of moral objections, nor yet any longer because of the Indian scare, but simply because there wasn't *time* for pleasure; you were not even supposed to take a walk. This was one of the reasons—though only one—why the reading lessons were precious to Salathiel Boyd. Almost always there was somebody near at hand, if not in the very room with them then just outside; nevertheless, concentration upon the same page, the very same words, somehow brought them together. They were physically close at those times too, which made Sal feel good.

"Slobbering? It might be rather—pleasant," she added, as though this thought had just occurred to her.

Sal snorted. He waggled his hands.

"But it'd be as hard on you as on them, when you can't get married," he pointed out.

"And why shouldn't I get married?"

"Out here? By who? This Reverend Robinson of yours that you're always talking about, I hear he's coming over from England some time—but *when?* And right now there's no priest."

Elder Brewster cut in, kindly as always.

"Master Boyd, in this persuasion a marriage is a secular affair, a civic contract. Our pastors do not join men and women. They would as soon think of blessing a bill of sale."

"They don't? Then who does?"

"The properly constituted government official. In this colony, John Carver."

"But he's not a real governor."

"Why not?"

"Why not? Because he wasn't appointed by the King. He's nothing but a man you set up among yourselves. If he did anything like performing a marriage it wouldn't be— Well, it wouldn't be *right.*"

"It would be right in the eyes of God, Master Boyd."

"What about the laws of England?"

"We are not living in England."

"Well, we're sure not living in Heaven, either!"

He was fairly raving now, yammering, and he strode back and forth, hands clasped behind him. He knew an all but overpower-

ing urge to kick something, something hard enough to hurt his
foot. Such meekness, and yet such arrogance at the same time!
It was getting too much for him. They were setting up a whole
new world, which could scarcely be called the act of men with
watery milk in their veins, and at the same time, as bland as that
many kings, they made laws for themselves.

Sal pulled himself up short, frowning, mumbling some manner of apology. Elder Brewster was staring at him in genuine
amazement. No more than he could understand them did these
men ever seem able to understand Salathiel.

"Master Boyd, please," he remonstrated. "You must learn to
take us the way we are, as indeed you have. Let your mind be at
rest."

"It—it'd be illegal!"

"There is not a single solitary word in the Good Book that
commands or even authorizes marriage by an ordained person.
Not one word."

Sal sighed, turning away. There they were again! No matter
what you brought up, they threw the Bible back at you.

"Speaking of the Good Book," said Priscilla, as she sat on the
bink and smoothed the skirt over her lap, "here's where you
were, Master Boyd—"

Side by side, his thigh against hers:

" 'These also are they that came to David to Zigklag, while
he was yet kept close, because of Saul the sonne of Kish: and
they were among the valiant and helpers of the battell.' "

Sal did not do well in that lesson.

Chapter Forty-three

Mayflower sailed April 1, a clear, bright day, indeed a radiant day; and as they watched it from the shore, having ceased to work for this little while, they did not move, though by instinct they huddled closer together than was their wont.

"Stupidest thing you ever did, Sal," Sawn Matthews had pronounced from behind an oar as the last boatload was about to start back for the ship. "These people ain't for you."

"Suppose you let me decide that," curtly.

Whatever their individual feelings might have been, none of the company either wept or gave a cheer. Though fewer than sixty were left, so wide a swath had Death's scythe cut in their ranks, nobody even said anything about going back. They needed no calendar to tell them that spring had come, and spring by tradition and naturally is a time of uplift, yet they had but to look around to remind themselves that they still teetered on the edge of a precipice. If they were resupplied from home before the next winter set in, if the Mohawks stayed in the west and the Pequots in the south—for these fierce and numerous tribes had been untouched by the plague—and most of all, if the seed that they had planted grew into healthy grain and vegetables, then conceivably they might survive; though even then they might perish.

When the sail had slipped out of sight they held a praying and preaching there on the beach beside the boulder, and after that they went back to work.

The Governor of New Plymouth, small, meek, amiable John Carver, carried no wand of office, nor was he preceded by a mace, or announced by a fanfare. He toiled with the others, and never made complaint. One week after the Mayflower had sailed he quietly put aside his mattock, said that he thought he should lie down a little, and went to his hut. Almost everybody else in the colony went to the same place, asking questions, offering help. Priscilla came from the Brewster hut to comfort and assist Catherine Carver, who herself had been ailing. Sal Boyd came down from the fort.

It seemed impossible that the Lord would allow such a sweet man to die at such a time, but die he did, two days later. His wife never spoke again; and she followed John Carver by less than a week.

That reduced their numbers to just half of what they originally had been. One hundred and two had been aboard of Mayflower when she dropped anchor. There were fifty-one now.

Oddly—because of this exact half? because nothing short of annihilation could have been a heavier blow than the death of John Carver?—from that time they began to take heart, working harder than ever. William Bradford, a younger man, more energetic, was elected governor, and Bradford, perhaps in an effort to forget Dorothy, drove himself furiously. The days were longer as summer came, the ground softer. Snow they had never greatly minded, but it was a relief no longer to have to buck that knife-edged wind and rain. Nor did they now need to bury their dead after dark, breaking the frozen earth with axes: the last to go, the Carvers, had been decently interred, their graves marked with a cross.

Freed from fear of attack by the near-in Indians, and reassured by Massasoit, with whom they had struck a treaty—a strictly illegitimate treaty, as Sal believed, but Massasoit didn't know this—they could and did venture farther afield for game. Venison was not uncommon these days, and the savages had taught them how to catch eels by walking barefooted in the bay and trapping them with their toes. There were no oysters, but clams they had in plenty. Though they had no sheep or cows, and hence no mutton, veal, or fresh beef, they had brought some chickens, pigs, and goats, to supply them with "white food," and these were multiplying, so that not all of their fare was salty.

Sal's glum guess that the unmarried men would cluster around Priscilla proved sound. She was seldom unattended. As the weather became mild she would sometimes move her Saxony wheel outside the door of the Brewster home, so that while she spun she could chat with those who paused or who passed. She was a friendly person, and liked company. How many of these casual callers she found "pleasant" Sal had no way of knowing, but he particularly resented John Alden, who since the landing had blossomed forth in a pair of Irish stockings, bright red in color—red was fashionable—that were the envy of every other man in the place.

"Disgusting," Sal muttered.

"I don't see what's disgusting about it. Why shouldn't they stop and visit, just like any folks? *You* come here often enough, Salathiel Boyd."

"Don't you want me to come?"

"I didn't say that."

"I come here to learn to read."

"Elder Brewster could teach you that, and I'm sure he'd be glad to. Or Master Bradford."

"Well . . ."

"Besides, there's Desire Minter and Mary Chilton. Why can't the men bumblebee about *them?*"

"They ain't pretty."

Though the lessons were shorter, for Sal's duties often took him away from the settlement, and he had to spend a lot of time on Fort Hill, they were more numerous. He used to drop in on her whenever he found a chance, and he would read aloud from the Book while she spun.

He had never ceased to marvel at her reading skill. She displayed no scintilla of interest in the other books that Elder Brewster had unpacked, but she sure knew her Bible. Never missing a thread, her foot busy, she would help him whenever he hesitated and infallibly correct him when he erred.

"You act as if you know this whole big thing by heart," he cried one day.

"I do know a heap of it by heart. Especially the early Old Testament, where we are now. Though not the begats, of course. And other parts come back to me as you read. Now—how did you spell that last name?"

They were only up to Deuteronomy, for Sal was slow, but Priscilla did not appear to fret. It was as though the Word, in any form, from out of any mouth, was as music to her. Yet she kept working as she listened.

One afternoon she did take the volume from him.

"Let's just skip a little, for today. Let's see if we can't find where Salathiel comes in."

"Oh, am *I* in the Bible?"

It astounded Sal, who had always taken his name for granted. Now that he thought of it, he never had met another Salathiel.

"Somewhere in Chronicles, I think. Let's see . . ."

She skimmed, flipping the pages expertly. She was very fast. She did not move her lips as she read to herself, and neither did she point her place with forefinger.

"Ah, here it is! 'And the sonnes of Jeconiah, Assir, Salathiel his sonne—' "

"Oh."

"So, you see?"

He was silent a little, pondering this.

"That means that I was—that this man Salathiel was the son of Assir and the grandson of Jeconiah?"

"That's right."

"And who was this gaffer, this Jeconiah?"

"Why, he was a king of Judea."

"Oh, a king, eh?" It gave Sal an odd feeling. "That would make me a kind of prince, then?"

"Well, the man you were *named after* was a prince, yes."

"Like Prince Charles now?"

"Yes, more or less like that."

"Did this Salathiel ever get to be king?"

"I don't know. It doesn't say. Now, here we are. Deuteronomy again. Twenty-five, fourth verse. 'Thou shalt not mousell the oxe that treadeth out the corne.' "

Sal took it up doggedly: " 'If brethren dwell together, and one of them die and have no sonne—' " but he was even slower than usual, for his mind was on that ancient Jew, grandson of a king. What did he look like, the original Salathiel? Did he wear a coronet? Did everybody call him Your Highness?

Chapter Forty-four

Sir Walter Raleigh (so Sal Boyd was told) had reported that when he visited the New World he saw or heard of ivory palaces, oysters that grew in trees, men with only one eye and that in the middle of the chest, men who sprayed themselves each day with gold dust, and a ferocious fair race of female warriors, the Amazons. To be sure, that had been Guiana. Sal saw nothing like it in New England; and yet the place was not entirely without its wonders.

There was the beaver. No country man, Sal had known little about beavers at home, though he believed that there were not many left. It was otherwise near New Plymouth. Even after winter had gone you seldom glimpsed a beaver, for they were shy and worked only at night, but there were evidences of them aplenty. They *chewed down* trees and trimmed these with their teeth, and built dams that were everywhere, some of them thirty-five or forty feet across. They made the dams so strong from constant repair that they lasted for years, and the lashed- and plastered-together trunks, usually willow, poplar, or birch, would put down roots and send up branches: Sal had seen them so tall that birds built nests in them.

Never to be discouraged; to mind your own business; to do so much while being seen so little; and even in death to be useful—this seemed to Sal a fine thing.

The savages—or so Sal had been told—ate these scaley-tailed beasts. He could believe it. An American Indian, from all he could see, would eat almost anything. Some of them even ate their own lice.

The three dried-out pelts Samoset's friends brought when they returned the tools were not acceptable in New Plymouth because the day was the Lord's Day, but the savages were urged to bring more, at an appropriate time; and this they had done. Once they learned that they would not be fed indiscriminately, along with their wives and children, whenever they chose to come crying friend—though it was made clear to the Big Chief that *he* would always be welcome at mealtimes, as would any of his personal friends—they began to bring out these beaver skins by the score, by the hundred, so that trucking began, the settlers offering trinkets and in exceptional cases knives, of which they had brought a goodly supply.

It answered a pressing question for them, this trade. The adventurers in London were not in the least interested in the Holy Discipline, but they were very much interested in getting their money back, and more besides. If the settlers hoped to keep this colony, if they even hoped to stay alive, they must send something to England whenever a ship put in. They had cut a great deal of sassafras, which, being famous for its medicinal qualities, would help to reduce the crushing debt: it was worth three shillings a pound in London. They had cut sundry planks and staves, though they could ill afford these, which would not bring a good price anyway. The pelt of the beaver was surer, more valuable, and easier to get.

It was the more welcome in New Plymouth because, being unexpected, unlooked for, it inevitably was attributed to Divine Providence. Humble in many ways, these practitioners of the Holy Discipline nevertheless had the Chosen People conviction firmly driven into their minds. Most of them, like Sal, had scarcely heard of beavers before this, and had not given the

beasts a thought until now, so that this made one more proof—
if one more was needed—that God Himself personally exercised
His gracious goodness and His ingenuity to see that the colonists
were provided for. Surely the beaver was a sign of this. Bless,
then, the beaver!

"Mind you, Boyd, *these*'re what will save us, if it pleases the
Lord that we be saved at all," cried Isaac Allerton one afternoon, waggling a handful of beaver pelts at Sal. The Lieutenant
Governor, an ex-tailor from London, a saint, small, shrewd,
sharp as a crab apple, Allerton by common consent was the
settlement's business manager, its figure man. *"These* things,
not codfish!"

Yet they could not snare the beaver itself, for they didn't
know how. They were obliged to depend upon the savages, who
kept the secret. Not even Squanto would tell them this.

Squanto was another of the wonders of the New World, something that approached a miracle, a living, moving, often laughing evidence of the Creator's forethought.

He was, literally, the last of the Pokanokets. When Samoset
told the settlers that the entire tribe at Patuxet had been wiped
out, he forgot Squanto, that exception to all rules, who some
time before had joined the Wampanoags.

Squanto was short. He was darker than most, stumpy, quick
with a smile. He was eager, in some ways boyish, shamelessly
ingratiating. His actual age was uncertain, but he could hardly
have been more than a child when in 1605 an early explorer in
these parts, Captain George Weymouth, had picked him up and
carried him—quite of his own free will—to England.

Just what Squanto had done in England in the nine years
before he returned to New England with Captain John Smith,
in 1614, was never established. The savage was shifty about this,
his narrative made up of unconnected fragments.

It would seem that he had been shunted from place to place,
being exhibited like some misshapen animal, some freak of

nature, now in a nobleman's house, again on a street corner. It could be gathered at least that he had not often been whipped, and that by his own standards he had not suffered.

He picked up a great deal of English—perhaps too much, for at times he would come forth with some unfortunate words.

Smith had left him among his own people again, and there, the following year, Captain Thomas Hunt had picked him up, along with nineteen other men from Patuxet and seven from Nauset, all lured aboard of his vessel by lies. Hunt had taken these poor wretches to Spain, to sell them in the slave market at Malaga.

What happened to the others nobody knew. Imaginably they had ended in the galleys or made into eunuchs for some Moorish harem. They would of course be valuable as curiosities. Even the Spaniards had not yet grown accustomed to the sight of American savages.

Squanto himself had been rescued by a priest, who worried about his soul, and successfully converted him. Though Squanto thus had satisfied the Holy Office, at least sufficiently to save his life, he was not happy in Spain; so at the first opportunity he had smuggled aboard a vessel bound for London, where he knew he still had friends. Through them he met Captain Thomas Dermer, who in 1619 took him back to New England. Thus Squanto already had seen more of the world than anybody else at New Plymouth, always excepting the rover, Salathiel Boyd.

At Monhegan on the Maine coast Samoset had come aboard to practice his English, and a little later, just half a year before the arrival of the strangers and saints, these two friends had come to Patuxet, which they found deserted, blasted by the plague. They learned from neighboring savages that every last Pokanoket in residence had succumbed, and that Squanto was a man without a tribe. Samoset, after visiting with some friends —he was an exceedingly sociable heathen—had returned to

Monhegan, near Pemaquid, and his "people of the dawn." Squanto had joined Massasoit's men at Sowans.

A tragic figure? He was anything but that. His was a cheery disposition, for he was one who, like a cat, would always land on his feet, always make himself at home. No one ever saw him mourn for his departed tribesmen, nor did he romanticize himself as the last of a none too meritorious line. He liked the English, his friends, and often said so. He vowed that he would never leave them. Though he could hardly have comprehended it, for all the excellence of his English, almost at once he embraced the Holy Discipline, becoming a member of the saints' church or chapel or congregation, whatever they called it. He was among the first to cry "Amen" at the end of every prayer, and his voice was loudly raised when they sang the psalms. Every Thursday—Thursday was Lecture Day, a sort of midweek Lord's Day—he would stand impassive, a statue, on the men's side of the Common House, listening by the hour.

Squanto was puzzled, also dismayed, when they asked him to seek out the owners of the corn they'd unearthed on Cape Cod, so that they could pay for this. He simply couldn't make sense of the request, and he was loth to leave the settlement even for a little while. The corn itself, however, he knew well. He could give no instructions concerning the planting of the seeds they had brought from home, but with Indian grain he was familiar.

"You put it in ground when the oak leaves get as big as a mouse's ear," he told them. "This earth worn out. The alewife will come soon, and you catch them and plant them three to a hillock, the heads in."

The alewife, it developed, was somewhat like a herring. In the spring, at a date not foretellable, these creatures would swarm out of salt water and up the streams to lay their eggs. Squanto could not tell how he knew when the run would start; but he did know, and he was right.

If preparations were made—and Squanto demonstrated how

to build nets—these fish could be caught by the hundreds. They were edible, if scarcely flavorsome, and it was only with a wrench that the settlers parted with most of the haul for planting; but they trusted Squanto, who must have been sent by God.

Unexpectedly this added to Sal's duties, already multitudinous. The fish were buried only a few inches deep—Squanto made sure of it—and while this blotted their smell for the settlers it did not do so for the wolves. Night and day the fields had to be guarded—and the guards checked—lest those beasts dig up all the work.

It was Squanto too who first showed them how to seize eels with their bare toes, a process the squeamish abhored, though it did bring them fresh food.

Chapter Forty-five

Squanto, in short, was a mountain of strength to them. If only he would mind his tongue! Though he was propriety itself at prayer meetings, out-of-doors he chattered like a jackdaw, and some of the expressions that crossed his lips reddened ears and lowered heads. Nor could he be made to see why they were wicked.

Sal, who didn't like the man, at least could feel with Squanto in this. On shipboard, where everyone was so cramped, it had not been hard to guard his speech; but here in the open air, where the endless forest stretched behind him, a man found that his vocabulary as well as his lungs and limbs tended to expand.

"God's own meeting house!" cried one of the saints in an unaccustomed outburst one afternoon. He had been working in the fields, and he dropped his hoe and poetically spread arms in the direction of the forest. *"His* temple! *His* tabernacle!"

Sal Boyd could not agree. Among the trees, or high in the fort overlooking them, he felt no touch of the chest-tightening, the slight choking, that by habit afflicted him at Holy Discipline prayer meetings. He did not feel confined when he was out-of-doors, but free; and this feeling extended to his tongue.

The Spaniards have a saying that Spanish is the language for lovers, Italian the language for singers, French for diplomats, German for horses, English for geese. Not all but many of the saints had lived for some years in Leyden, in the Low Countries, the place from whence the expedition had started, and these could speak Dutch. The others, including all of the strangers, were monoglots. The Dutchers, however, were active, including as they did the most influential families—the Brewsters, the Carvers, the Allertons, William Bradford—and it would be as well, Sal reckoned, for him to mind his language while in their company, to preserve, as it were, better linguistic walking. Yet in moments of stress or sudden keen disappointment, foreign expletives leapt to his mouth, exploding there like squibs. The separatists, though scarcely likely to applaud these, did not object to scatological or just plain bawdy expressions. Sal without tremor could rip out a *"porco cane!"* a *"putero!"* a *"baizzez mon cul!"* and even, on request, translate these; but if he ventured upon a *"Gott,"* a *"Dios,"* a *"mon dieu,"* he would be looked at askance; and his old favorite, *"God verdomme,"* they would scowl at, all but snarl at. Any flippant reference to the Deity was a sin.

"Merde!" he cried once, impulsively, in the presence of Priscilla Mullins.

"What's that?"

"It— Well, it's a French word."

"What does it mean?"

He floundered, turning his head away, feeling his cheeks go hot; but he recovered.

"It means 'good Heavens.'"

This was an awkward lie. If he had told the truth the girl probably would not have felt any notable embarrassment, for she was anything but mealymouthed, and they had all been living in close quarters. As it was, she was profoundly shocked. She feared for her friend's very soul.

"You shouldn't say that, Salathiel. Would the Lord take it lightly that the mansions of the elect were made a cry of vexation?"

"No, I suppose not," Sal muttered.

"You must always remember the Fifth Commandment. We read that together."

"Yes, I know."

"Please—I mean this, Salathiel—please promise me that you won't use that word again—what was it?—"

"*Merde.*"

"*Merde.* You mustn't ever say it again in anger."

"Oh, I won't," earnestly. "I promise you."

Another astonishing thing, another wonder, occurred when on May 22 Susanna White, a sister of Deacon Sam Fuller, was wed to Edward Winslow. Her first husband, a north-country wool carder, had been carried away at the very height of The Sickness, three months ago; but Winslow's first wife had been in her grave for less than two. Both of these were saints, and Sal esteemed it scandalous—unless, of course, the woman was carrying Winslow's baby, which was unthinkable if only for the reason that there was no *room* for adultery in this place. Moreover, and this was the worst part of it, they were married merely by William Bradford, who wasn't even a deacon, much less a pastor, minister, prior, or priest.

Triumphantly: "But you have read Ruth, by this time?"

"Oh, aye. We're in Second Samuel already."

"Do you remember one word in the book of Ruth that even hinted that any ecclesiastical personage was present when Boaz took the fair Moabite to wife?"

"Well, maybe not, but still—"

"So you see!"

There was no arguing with them.

It was a queer sort of wedding. Nobody got drunk. Nobody hurrahed, or thwacked the bride's behind. Yet married they apparently were, for they went to bed together that night, seemingly with the approval of everybody in the settlement save only Sal, who retired to the foot-of-the-hill hut shaking his head.

They did strange things in this part of the world, he reflected. Yet if it could happen once . . .

And it was just barely conceivable that these separatists really were the chosen of God, so that they could violate the laws of decency.

The Captain was not in the hut. He had not slept well since the death of his wife, and no doubt he was out making the rounds yet again.

Because of the enlarged facilities elsewhere, the two young male servants first assigned to this shack had been moved in with their masters, and now Miles Standish and Sal Boyd shared it only with a savage, Hobomok, and the cooper John Alden. These two already were lying on the platform strewn with pine needles and deerskins, a bed that occupied virtually all the ground space.

Hobomok was a pinese of the Wampanoags. That is, he was a pledged brave, a warrior among warriors, stern, dedicated, like a knight in the early days of chivalry. He was Massasoit's un-official, unacknowledged ambassador here in New Plymouth, and it had seemed politic to station him in the Hill House, near the fort. He was tall, taciturn, contemptuous. He did not con-ceal his dislike of the eager-to-please Squanto. He pretended that he could not make out a word of English, but he was no fool and doubtless learned fast, keeping his eyes open. Sal rather admired Hobomok, who was clean for a savage and didn't stink much. Just now he was sound asleep, snoring.

John Alden was awake; but though his eyes were open, his hands clasped behind his head as he lay on his back, in truth he was entoiled in a dream. He too had attended the wedding, and it had set him thinking. He had removed only hat, collar, and shoes, as Sal proceeded to do, but he had changed from his hand-some red Irish stockings into a simple black knitted pair to preserve the red ones as long as possible. Staring at the conical ceiling, he did not stir, and didn't even seem to be aware of Sal.

"Well, are you going to shift that rump of yours," Sal asked, "or am I going to have to kick it over?"

Alden, startled, gave him a sour look and shoved Hobomok nearer to the wall. The savage never ceased to snore. John Alden turned his back on Sal.

Sal lay for a long time, thinking.

If it could happen once . . .

Chapter Forty-six

The thought of Ed Winslow and Susy White living together, as man and wife eating and praying and sleeping together, was pushing against his mind when he went for his lesson next day.

Despite a nip in the air, she sat outside. The Brewsters would hardly be using firewood in the hearth at this time of afternoon, and anyway Priscilla liked to nod and smile at the folks who passed.

As always, she had a sweet, grave smile for him; but there was a slightly wanton look about her today, perhaps because her shipboard pallor had been replaced by a healthy glow, perhaps because a few rebellious wisps of hair had escaped from under her cap and were fluttering back and forth across her cheek.

She had regained the weight she lost while nursing in The Sickness, he noted. Nobody could call her fat, but the buttocks she shifted to make room for him on the bench were not the pinched stingy meagre things they had been a little while ago, while her forearms were as he had first seen them, deliciously round.

She kept spinning.

"You are early," she said. "That's good."

"Um . . ."

He sat. The Book was on the bench between them, and he picked it up, but he didn't open it, just let it lie there in his lap, his hands folded over it.

He started to clear his throat, then paused, fearful that this might sound portentous.

"I—I was wondering about Winslow and that White girl," he said at last.

" 'That White girl'? It sounds as if you thought her a slut."

"I didn't exactly mean that. But—"

"Oh, I'm sure they're happy. It should be a union blessed by the Lord."

"Isn't every union blessed by the Lord?"

"Well, it's supposed to be, yes."

"But you don't think that they all necessarily are?"

"I don't know much about—marriage."

The Street at this moment was empty, and for a little while the only sound was the whirr of the wheel. Sal sighed. He cocked his eyes toward her, but she had not moved. He knew that she must be wondering what he was getting at. Or—perhaps she wasn't? Perhaps she had already guessed?

"Well . . ." he started; and then he was still for another spell. She helped him.

"I hear you don't approve of marriage without a minister?"

"It's not up to me to approve or not approve. I just think it looks—well, strange."

"How?"

"It don't seem legal, that's all. But I suppose I'm wrong. If you think it's all right, then it is." He turned to her. "You *do* think so, don't you?"

"Oh, yes."

"That people that get married here are really married, I mean in the eyes of God?"

"Oh, yes," she said again; but she said it swiftly, and there was a small catch in her voice.

He shifted a little. He put the Book aside.

"That's good," he said. "Because I want to talk to you about marriage."

The color leapt to her face and neck, and she closed her eyes, not coyly but by instinct, as a defense; such was her confusion. When she replied it was in a low, even voice.

"Good," she said. "I was wondering when you would."

"*Eh?*"

"Well, why shouldn't we get married, when you stop to think of it—and I'm sure you have. After all, I need a husband. And not only just to help the colony to go on either, though there's that too."

It jolted him.

"I—I don't think you ought to talk of such things," he muttered, looking away.

Elsewhere, in a different society, in different circumstances, many a woman might have bridled, or simpered, or affected great astonishment and indignation. Priscilla Mullins was not like that. There was no guile in her. She never beat about the bush.

Sal didn't dare to look at her again, just now. His joints used to turn to jelly whenever he watched her cross a room or just lean over her spinning wheel. And if he felt that way, so did many another man. She was a prized resident, this girl. She could have her pick.

"Did I hurt your feelings?" she asked after a while, smiling a little but still not looking at him. She had her spinning for an excuse.

"Oh, no. It isn't that."

"I think if you hadn't proposed to me, just now, I would have proposed to you, Sal. But don't think it'd be easy!"

"I—I can see that."

He shifted his feet.

"It's just that there's a few things I ought to point out first. For instance, you, uh, you have a share in the enterprise."

Her eyes were opened very wide.

"What in the world's that got to do with it?"

"It might have a heap."

"Salathiel, are you turning me down?"

"Why, no! No, I didn't mean that. But—think it over. *I* haven't got anything. Not a groat."

She shook an impatient head. Such stupidity!

"You have a position. You have rank. And hear me: *You have the respect of your fellow men.*"

This was true; but it never failed to startle him. He looked about. Several persons were passing on the Street—they called it only that, the Street—and they nodded and smiled encouragement. All the world, it was said, loves a lover. Sal was beginning to believe that. Priscilla, who had labored without stint through The Sickness, even after her own family was taken away, was beloved by all, naturally; but he himself, Salathiel Boyd, was well liked too, and if this gratified him it flustered him at the same time, for he wasn't used to it.

"You can't eat your neighbors' good regard," tartly, heavily. "And it won't keep you warm on winter nights to know that you've striven."

"It might help."

"Huh!"

"You certainly feel better than you did when I first met you, Salathiel. Anybody could tell that."

"*Huh!*"

"But—you *are* fond of these folks, ain't you, Salathiel?"

He swallowed, wincing as though the air hurt his throat.

"Oh, I've gotten used to them."

She made no immediate comment. Neither did she cease to work, the wheel whirring. But she was a forthright person who would not be put off; she returned to the original subject.

"All right. I'll marry you." She paused, moistening her lips. Then: "You *did* ask me, didn't you?"

"Oh, sure. Sure I did. But I don't think you ought to accept all that fast."

"Why?"

"Well, you ought to kind of think it over."

"I have. A good many times. But—what about you?"

"You have a share," he said again. "You're part of the company. As things go out here you're as good as rich, with your lay. And I'm a pirate."

Now she looked at him in amazement, for "pirate" was a word he never before had used, preferring to call himself a privateer.

Sal, for his part, in a wild instant was wishing that he had her out in the forest, where there was nobody else around. He had better arguments than just talk, if he was given a chance to use them. But such a stroll would be unthinkable in New Plymouth; and you don't hug and kiss a girl and pluck at her skirts in broad daylight with people passing.

Besides, that might be the worst thing he could have done.

So he sat silent for a while, staring out over Thievish Harbor toward the open bay, an easterly direction, the direction of Home.

"Sooner or later a sail's going to put in," he said at last. "They won't go on forgetting us. We're an investment, and men like that watch their investments."

She finished the roving and changed spindles, her foot motionless only for a moment.

Yet her hand had trembled the least little bit, which was extraordinary for Priscilla Mullins. Was she having wild sudden doubts? Did she wish she hadn't spoken?

"So?" she whispered.

"So when that vessel does come we may find out what happened to my captain, Jan Oosterlinck. What if I'm a fugitive? What if I'm wanted for piracy? That wouldn't speak well for New Plymouth, now would it?"

"N-no."

"And this colony needs all the credit it can get, I tell you!"

"Would anybody have to—"

"Oh, my name could be struck off the roster, I suppose. I mean, assuming that it's ever *been* there. Officially I guess I'm not alive any longer. But they'd learn, in London. It would get out. A man can't hide in a wilderness like this. It's not like Morocco or the Barbary Coast."

"And you think we should—wait? Oh, I didn't mean that!"

"It's all right."

"Well, I guess I did mean it, then."

"It's all right," he said again. "Yes, I think that we should wait. If I'm going to be your husband I ought at least to be a real husband, not a man that might be snatched away to stand trial before you half got to know him."

"You—you don't think—"

"I don't know what to think. But I do know that Captain Oosterlinck was in some sort of briars back there at home, and I do know that the laws about piracy are mighty strange—and mighty strict too. So it'd be just as well for us to see what that ship brings in the way of news."

"Very well." She pointed to the Book, though her bobbin wheel kept going all the while. "Now, here's where we were: " 'And David said, This is the house of the Lord God, and this is the altar for the burnt-offering of Israel.' "

Hands on knees, he regarded the passers, those amiable ants, all toil, no sense or feeling. He felt a mite dizzy, and very weak.

At last he did clear his throat.

"And in the meanwhile," abruptly. "Has John Alden proposed to you?"

She did not need to lower her gaze, for already it was on the Book, but once again blood tingled at her ears and cheekbones as she bent over.

"Don't you think, Salathiel," she whispered, "that that's my own affair?"

"Aye," he said, for his question had been answered.

Chapter Forty-seven

The summer passed swiftly, one bright day sliding into the next. A spirit of confidence tingled through New Plymouth as the settlers saw their Indian corn sprout and yellow, and knew that they would have a goodly crop. The seven-odd acres they had planted with the seeds brought from England were not doing well, but the grains stolen from the Cape—already generously paid for in hatchets and knives and beads—were doing very well indeed. Also, there were berries and nuts. And they were getting many fish. And a few deer.

They were piling up the beaver skins and otter skins as well. These were bigger than the ones in England, an important consideration since they were priced by the pound.

Since the accession of William Bradford to the governorship there had been a new air of activity in the small New Plymouth army. The drills were braver, if noisier. The men stepped with snap.

Massasoit, chief of barely 300 persons as compared with the 30,000 he'd commanded before the plague, nevertheless might have stamped these settlers out any night, despite their new log palisade; but he had made a treaty of amity with them and clung to his word, so that they were not molested by the savages excepting those in search of food, who prowled like mangy mongrels in a castle hall.

Squanto, that great friend, seemed doomed to trouble. A minor sachem, one of Massasoit's, a fierce personage named Corbitant, had seized upon Squanto, whom he cursed as the mouthpiece of the white men and whom he swore to kill. Notified of this, the settlers dispatched fourteen men under Captain Standish—Sal, to his chagrin, was left behind as military commander of the settlement—with orders to bring back Squanto alive or Corbitant dead. Corbitant escaped, badly scared, and later through Massasoit he sued for peace, making many pacific promises. Squanto, fortunately, was unhurt.

But soon after this he was denounced to Massasoit by the alert Hobomok for *not* having, as he'd claimed he had, the secret of where the white men had buried the plague. Massasoit flew into a rage, and demanded that Squanto be turned over to him for trial, in accordance with the terms of the treaty. To comply would mean Squanto's death; and while Squanto undoubtedly had played the fool—probably he had been moved by jealousy of Hobomok, whom he sought to outshine—he remained a very valuable aide. The matter at last was settled, though not without hard feeling.

In August one of the Billington boys—a limb of Satan if ever there was one, the same lad who had all but blown the Mayflower skyhigh when she was anchored off Cape Cod by playing with firecrackers near some broached barrels of gunpowder—got himself lost from New Plymouth, and there was a week of frenzied search. The boy at last was located out on the Cape, and the savages there, those same Nausets who had such good reason to hate Englishmen, returned him without demur. This was good.

Thus it was that when autumn was pressing and the leaves became crisp at the edges—in fact in October—the suggestion was made that they have a feast of thanksgiving to the Lord for their deliverance.

Salathiel Boyd was opposed to this plan, and said so.

He pointed out that they were not delivered yet. This coming winter might be even worse than the first one. True, the meagre weekly ration of one peck of meal from the Mayflower to each adult person recently had been doubled by the addition of one peck of maize, or Indian corn, but this too Salathiel thought extravagant. He was not heeded.

He never could understand these strangers and saints. He was aghast when they not only ignored his warning but decided that the savages should be invited to the feast, which would last three days.

"*Ask* an Indian to eat?"

"Are they not the children of God, as much as we are?"

"Well, I suppose so. But they've got the appetite of a school of underfed sharks."

Yet it was done. Massasoit appeared in all his dignity, all his glory, a fine solemn figure of a man, slightly stout, his face painted mulberry, a deerskin slung across his shoulders, around his middle a skimpy fringed strip of leather; and he was followed by no fewer than *ninety* braves.

If the settlers were taken aback, they quickly rallied. The women were the busiest. They had been preparing for this feast for almost a week. The men had built long rough-hewn wooden tables and benches underneath the trees behind the Common House, no great distance from the field at the foot of the hill where so many of their sisters and brothers, wives and fathers and mothers and husbands slept.

"*Into* the mouths of babes," muttered Sal Boyd.

They had hasty pudding made of Indian corn, also some made of rye. They had venison and roast duck and roast goose, and they had fried chicken. They had omelets. They had a great deal of fish, clams too, and eels. They had waterfowl: the season was just beginning. They had leeks and watercress and berries. There were no turk-turks, for this curious bird remained extremely hard to kill, but there was an abundance of everything else.

As a feast it didn't bubble, it didn't seethe. It was not Salathiel Boyd's idea of an orgy. For one thing, the women, what with cooking and clearing and serving, never had a chance to join in. For another, most of the men, being Indians, couldn't talk any known language.

No, that party did not remind Sal of one of the taverns in which he had rioted in the past; though he did not suppose, changed man that he was, that he would have liked it if it had.

He could snatch but the briefest of talks with Priscilla, who worked from dawn to sundown, so their reading lessons had to be suspended.

He couldn't even get drunk. There was a vast amount of wine, both red and white, made from wild grapes, but though strong it was excessively sweet. It would make you sick before it would make you feel like singing, and then you had to start all over again.

Sal's heart never was in that prolonged feast. He felt lost, alone. He attended such prayer meetings as he couldn't get out of, and surely he ate his share of the food, but a good part of those three days, when he was not parading the men on the far side of Town Brook, he was up at his post on Fort Hill. There was much military display, for the edification of the unclothed guests. There was a great deal of tramping about, the beating of drums. Again and again Sal Boyd showed the five cannons to gaping aborigines whom he would have preferred to kick downhill, and on the third day he was persuaded against his better judgment to discharge the saker.

"I'd rather board an Indiaman," he said. "But I'll do it."

Shaking his head and clucking his tongue at the waste of powder, he cleared the hill. If the thing burst he meant to be the only one killed. Nobody could see him, from below; and after he had charged the piece and rammed charge and stones and wadding home and goosed some of the powder out of the touchhole, he attached a very long strip of match. He lit this. He ran across the gun platform and vaulted the parapet on the far side, the forest side, where he sat with his back against the fort, his eyes squinched shut, his fingers in his ears.

He had just begun to fear that the match had gone out, though he was not prepared to thrust his head above the parapet and see for himself, when the thing went off.

The earth seemed seized and shaken by that roar. The parapet pressed against Sal's back as though it would push him, seated, down the hill, and the very ground beneath him gulped convulsively, while the tops of the trees the far side of the field rocked. The limber scraped and thudded, the recoil cables screeched like some poor overstretched wretch on the rack. Through the echoes Sal heard a pitter of stones fall upon field and wood. The air was crowded with smoke.

He climbed over the parapet and dropped to the platform, which felt as though it still rocked from the blast. He crossed to the other side, and waved to the men below, laughing, at the same time coughing because of the smoke, his eyes bitten by tears.

The settlers waved back to him, cheering him. Some of the savages had thrown themselves flat on the ground beneath the tables, though a few, more valiant, had vaulted Town Brook and were running pell-mell for the shelter of the forest, no doubt convinced that the end of the world had come.

"I'd hate to have to do that again," Master Gunner Boyd said to himself as he turned back to clean the cannon.

It was the high point of the feast, and he was much congratulated.

Three days later the village fathers rechecked their store of food and made a dismaying discovery. Not only had consumption at the feast of thanksgiving been much greater than their estimate, but there had been a serious miscalculation in the first optimistic report that inspired them to proclaim that feast in the first place. The truth is, they remained perilously close to the edge of starvation.

The weekly ration for each person was cut in half, as they waited for winter to set in.

Chapter Forty-eight

He rested his elbows on the parapet, as he had done a hundred times before, and looked down at New Plymouth.

Not long ago, when first he was helping to mount the guns, the village had been a muddle of tarpaulin tents, conical huts, booths made of branches, bark, turf, and clay, a mere rickle of sticks and thatch that any sinewy wind might flatten, any rain wash away. Even now it was no Cadiz, no Marseilles, or Bristol. Yet in addition to lean-tos and tents there were seven substantial structures, four of them private, the others the property of all. The public ones included, besides the first Common House, a depot slowly filling with sassafras and pelts, and a small and rather pert chapel.

Unexpectedly, the chapel was surmounted by a sort of steeple made of planks; and this amazed Sal, who would have supposed that the saints esteemed such things as steeples pagan or Roman or both. That steeple, crude though it was, and stumpy, and unpainted, slightly awry too, lent a homely touch to the view from the fort.

Gazing at it from above, Sal blinked a bit. These fools! These blundering, bumbling, good-hearted fools! They were almost unbelievably clumsy, as they were almost unbelievably kind, and Salathiel Boyd could not help but think tenderly of them—

not like a father, for that would have been presumptuous, but rather like a case-hardened, worldly-wise returned traveler who looks upon the enthusiasm and preposterous plans of his younger brothers and sisters with indulgence, pity, and perhaps sometimes fright. They couldn't do anything right, yet they never *meant* anything wrong. It was so like them to fashion that steeple down there, when with the skimpy materials they had in hand they should have been building benches, stools, tables, shelves, chests. But—a finger pointing toward God meant more.

Sal could hear them in that chapel right now, for this was a Thursday, Lecture Day, early in November of 1621. Doubtless the congregation, standing to sing, wail rather, had been "dignified," as they called it—that is, the men were on one side, the women on the other, while the children, lest they fidget, were in front, under the watchful eyes of their elders. Now they were chanting their own version of the Old Hundredth:

> "Shout ye to Jehovah, all the earth;
> Serve ye Jehovah with gladness—"

A mite godlike himself as he leaned there, Salathiel Boyd smiled lazily down, musing.

"You are fond of these folks, ain't you?" Priscilla had said.

Well, he was. He was more than fond of them. He guessed he loved them. He might laugh at them, and he did; but it was true that he had never before felt so warm as when he was among them. He almost wished, wildly, as he loafed there, that no ship ever would come from the outside, and that these people, these queer, kind, unpredictable zealots, would go on living here forever, making their own civilization, their own peculiar world.

> "Before Him come with singing mirth.
> Know that Jehovah he God is."

The air nipped. The sky showed low and gray, glowering. This was not a time for revery. There was work to be done. Sal was supposed to be checking the cannons.

There was a step to his right, a martial step, heavy, though in fact it was made by a small man; and Captain Standish entered the fort.

He tossed Sal no more than a noncommittal nod. Before any of the men these two would have saluted stiffly, but now they had the fort to themselves. Sal never knew how Miles Standish would act in private. Standish was a shy man, and as an officer, *the* officer of this pathetic small wilderness force, he was at all times afraid to let his real feeling show.

Now he walked around the platform, nodding, studying the landscape, studying the bay, inspecting the cannons. He was no artillerist, and was glad to leave such matters to his second in command, but today, as so often, he displayed the busyness of a man who does not dare to seem idle.

At last he came over to the parapet and ranged himself alongside of Sal. He said nothing, didn't even grunt.

Sal waited.

The start of the conversation, when it did come, was abrupt.

"Are you going to marry that Mullins girl, Boyd?"

Lying was for women. Lying was something the weak needed to do, something that you yourself did only when you were in a corner and were unable or afraid to put up your fists. Sal did not like to lie. Besides, he had a poor memory.

"That's something I can't rightly say now, sir," he replied slowly. "Why do you ask?"

He swiveled his eyes to risk a sidelong glance. The Captain undoubtedly had colored. On the parade ground, when he was shaken with rage and impatience, this often happened, and it helped to account for his nickname of Captain Shrimp; but neither impatience nor rage was the cause of it now.

The Captain was painfully embarrassed.

Sal pretended that he hadn't looked.

"Well, she *should* be married, of course."

"Of course," Sal agreed.

"And no doubt she's been proposed to."

"Shouldn't wonder."

"But d'ye think she's been bespoken, Boyd? I—I wouldn't want to make myself ridiculous . . . at my age . . ."

"I see."

"Rose and I were very close and very happy, for years. But still—"

"I see."

Sal gulped, carefully. He would not now even move his eyes in the direction of his superior officer.

"I think that you could say that she was bespoken, sir. Yes. In fact, I'm sure you could."

"Well, uh, maybe I shouldn't have mentioned it. But I knew you'd know."

"Yes, sir."

"Well, thank you, Boyd."

He started away, then paused. Plainly he thought to beg Sal not to tell anybody about this, but it was quite as plain that he changed his mind. He went out.

The gate clicked quietly behind him.

Chapter Forty-nine

No leaves fell upon Sal as he stood there surveying the village, nor did any fly past his face, for he was too high; but they came down pauselessly in the forest behind him, one somewhere every smitch of the time. He could hear them strike their fellows already on the ground, making a click-click, very soft, dry, brittle.

Sal never had known an autumn like it. Never had he seen such a blaze of color, even in the tropics. Well, the color climax had passed now, and the world was waxing dun again. Sal clucked his tongue. He heaved himself away from the parapet.

Was he getting maudlin? Those falling leaves down there—whenever he paused in his walk around the fort he could hear that steady yet doleful click-click-click—were they making him mawkish, causing him to go all soft inside?

He shook his head, as though to scold himself, while he strode from one to another of his iron monsters in a show of inspection. He couldn't find anything wrong with them. It was different with himself. More and more often these days—did the nearing chill have something to do with this? the riot of colors that had lately subsided?—he was asking himself if perhaps Sawn Matthews hadn't been right after all.

Perhaps these people *weren't* for him. Or, to put it another way, perhaps *he* wasn't for *them*. He could trust them, he could love them, but would he ever be able to understand them?

266

Just now his feeling was, as it had been for some time, that he dare not leave them, for fear they'd starve or blow themselves to pieces, something like that. They were after all only children, even though they did happen to be playing a grownup's game and wearing grownups' clothes. They even called themselves and thought of themselves as that—the Children of the Lord. Well, should they be left to the Lord, then? Yet this feeling wobbled. Much, he knew, would hang upon the first vessel to put in from England, and what she carried in the way of provisions, settlers, news.

Priscilla? He didn't know there, either. Her proposal had jolted him, so that his mind raced.

It was a hell of a long while since he'd had a woman, and he hoped that he was not just slavering, the way he had seen mariners do, going ashore after a long voyage and heading bee-like for the nearest brothel. Undeniably Priscilla Mullins was well rounded; and Sal reckoned that no man need be ashamed of himself for feeling that way about her; but the peril lay in letting such lecherous thoughts steer a man into misalliance. He sighed. Priscilla was a part of these naïve people, while he, Salathiel Boyd, was not—and never really could be. If he found himself free, if he married her, there could be no question about his future. He would have to stay here in New Plymouth, at least as long as the colony lasted.

On the other hand, if he *didn't* marry her—well, he thought he knew what would happen then. He had told Miles Standish, just now, that the girl was bespoken, for he knew that the Captain's correct sense of honor would not tolerate courtship in those circumstances. And in a sense, that was right anyway. She *was* bespoken. For the moment, at least, she was his—if he wanted to take her. Did he?

It was a tremendous temptation. Lonesomeness always had plagued Sal Boyd, and it still did. There were times, here, when his heart was lifted by some sign that showed that he was valued, appreciated, even liked, for he had not been inured to such signs. All the same, he remained alone, for every practical purpose. Marriage might change that. Or—it might not. It might make him even more lonesome.

It was not good for a man to be alone, they said. But Sal was used to it by this time.

He sighed again, distantly hearing the click of leaves behind, the caterwauling from the chapel before.

"I'm glad I found you here."

John Alden came through the gate. He was not panting, as most men who came through that gate were, having just climbed the hill. He had been careful, saving his wind. Now he moved slowly toward Sal, his chin low, his head outthrust in the truculent way that he had.

Sal waited, feet spread, thumbs hooked into his sword belt.

"Well, what do you want?"

Alden took off his cloak. He took off his tunic.

"You know damn' well what I want," he said.

Chapter Fifty

Sal, noting the turkey-red stockings, and knowing that this lad had been sparking Priscilla, felt a little sick. He had sensed for a long while that this was coming. As winter would follow the fall of the leaves it was inevitable. He didn't like it any the more for that reason.

"Has she said no?" he asked.

It was a stupid question. Where was his soft answer for the turning away of wrath? Had he become a mite giddy, up here all alone for so long at a stretch?

"You keep away from her!"

A year ago Sal Boyd would have laughed; and indeed, a year ago in similar circumstances he *had* laughed. It was different now. Now he felt sorry for John Alden, a boy who was uncertain of himself, and just now torn with love and desire. Alden was afraid of him, Sal knew; but this would only cause him to fight more ferociously. There would be little profit in trying to reason with him. Alden was no intellectual genius, and for many months he had been convinced, despite all evidence to the contrary, that Salathiel Boyd the pirate was in all truth one of Lucifer's lieutenants. Thus, fear and lust and religious zeal all raged within him; and these made up an explosive combination.

Sal should have temporized. He should have tut-tutted. He

didn't. No more than ever was he pleased, out here in America, by being told what he might or might not do. Oh, he should keep away from Priscilla Mullins, should he? He bristled.

"And what if I don't?" he said.

Alden jerked his head back.

"You won't go through that gate again until you promise you will."

Sal studied the situation, not liking it.

Once before, soon after the original landing, there had been a duel in the colony of New Plymouth. Edward Dotey and Edward Leister, indentured servants both of them, young men, fools, the property of Stephen Hopkins, had met on the beach, each with a cutlass in his right fist, a dagger in his left. But in a company so small and so cramped secrets were not possible, and even such an informal, improvised *rencontre* called for some preparation. Leister and Dotey had been seized before a blow could be struck, and tied by necks and ankles, back to back, until they were glad to give a solemn promise never to break the peace again.

There had been something comic about the Dotey–Leister meeting, though the results might have been tragic enough if the saints had not acted quickly and with a commendable firmness. There was nothing comic about John Alden here this afternoon. He meant what he said. He had been thinking about this for a long while, and he'd picked his time well.

"Now look here," Sal started, "there's other ways of settling a matter like this."

"Not to me there isn't."

Again Sal sighed. He turned away.

"All right. Lock the gate. You're closest there."

He heard the balk thud into place and fall as he took off his hat and shrugged off his cloak—Dorothy Bradford's cloak. He took off his shoes too, and wriggled his toes, ruefully regarding them.

When he turned back he was startled to see that John Alden had removed doublet as well. Alden wore no shirt, and his chest and shoulders and arms were bunchy with muscle.

"You must be cold, like that."

It did not work. The cooper was deliberate in his manner, and made no response. Sal had hoped to taunt him into making the first rush. An infuriated foe was the easiest to handle in single combat, especially with fists, Sal believed. But Alden did not even flush, and perhaps he did not hear. He nodded at Sal Boyd's dagger. Sal had already put aside his sword.

"You've got that. I haven't."

"All right. I won't touch it."

"How do I know?"

"Don't you believe me?"

"No."

Once again Sal had to hold himself, muttering inwardly. Once again he resisted the old Salathiel Boyd as he might have resisted Satan, and with as great an effort. He shuddered. But he snicked out the dagger and tossed it to the other side of the platform, where it clattered tinnily on the boards.

Alden, standing with feet widespread, his head down, in a notably bullish position, did not seem to see or hear this; but in a moment he went unhesitatingly to the dagger, and picked it up.

Was the man mad? He moved slowly enough.

Sal eyed the gate, the heavy balk, and decided against that. He might be stabbed in the back while he scrabbled to get the thing open. He'd faced men with drawn dagger before, and himself with empty hands, and he reckoned he could do it again. But he didn't like this.

John Alden picked up the knife by its point, gingerly, with thumb and forefinger, as though handling some odious reptile. He tossed it over the parapet. He turned back toward Sal, his arms slowly swinging at his sides, fists clenched.

"Now," he said.

There was a babble of voices down in the village, and the report of a sentry's musket, a signal for attention from the fort.

"A sail! A sail!"

They could hear men running up the hill.

"Boyd, fire one of those pieces! There's a vessel in sight!"

Sal crossed to the gate and threw back the balk. Then he went to his least touchy cannon.

"I guess we'll have to finish this some other time," he said, as he started for the cellar in which he had stored the powder. "I've got work to do now. Excuse me."

Chapter Fifty-one

Robert Cushman was large, florid, forty-odd, canonical in his manner, with white hair that framed the face of a petulant cherub. He might have been trailing robes. He would have caused heads to turn in any corner of the world, and had but to clear his throat to make any occasion a portentous one.

Deacon Cushman was in the very first boat that came ashore, and he stood in the bow of that boat, arms upraised, like some tritonless sea god who had only just surfaced.

"Praise be to the Lord," he shouted, "I have found you!"

Not *we* have found you, *I* have.

Sal Boyd, down from the fort, regarded this man with a great deal of interest. Sal still was out of breath, there had been so much to do. The sight of canvas—and this though there was not one of them who hadn't been in the habit of scanning the entrance of Thievish Harbor a dozen times a day in the hope of just such a sight—had given rise to a panic-scraping rumor that here were the French come down from their northern provinces to blot out a settlement on coastland they called their own. All defenses, therefore, had to be put in order. New Plymouth prepared to resist.

Even when the arrival ran up a large white flag with the red cross of St. George upon it, announcing herself, there was much to be done. This was a momentous event. New Plymouth should look impressive. Helmets had to be polished, also breast- and backplates; muskets had to be checked, boots cleaned, the drum dusted; the men themselves had to be persuaded to back away from the parapet on the bay side, so that Sal could fire a signal shot—from one of the bases, not from the minion or the saker—in such a way that its cough could be clearly heard and its smoke clearly seen from the vessel that approached. Nevertheless Sal had his cannon cleaned again and was down on the beach by the time the first boat was beached.

Deacon Cushman, he knew, would have all the official as well as unofficial news from London. For better or for worse, he had Sal's future in his wallet.

Sal glanced sideways at Priscilla. No saint, not one of the basic Leyden group, she refrained from pushing forward to greet Robert Cushman; but she was eager to hear what he had to report, and for the same reason that Sal was.

For here was one of the first of the separatists, a man who, with the late John Carver, had made all arrangements in London for the financing of this expedition, who had been in charge of the passengers aboard Speedwell until that leaky vessel was forced to put back into Plymouth, and who since then had been the sole representative of the saints among the moneymen. It was Cushman who without authorization from Leyden had accepted a change in the articles of agreement between the saints and the merchant adventurers—a change the saints at Southampton refused to sanction. Now he himself had come to the New World. This could mean that all was well, or it could mean that the merchants repudiated them and would leave them to their own devices. The settlers had done all that they could do, here. Lacking support from London, they would die.

First, of course, they had a long prayer, a series of prayers rather, right there on the shore, while the longboat went back for a second load. Everybody said "Amen," many times. However, there was no sermon.

Deacon Cushman wept unabashed when he heard that his beloved colleague, John Carver, was dead. Ceremoniously he handed over to William Bradford, as governor of the colony, a letter addressed to Carver in that capacity. *What was in the letter?* Deacon Cushman announced that it was from Thomas Weston, leader of the moneymen and their spokesman. Without breaking the seal, Governor Bradford tucked the letter into his tunic and offered his arm to Cushman; they would go up the slope to Elder Brewster's house. Priscilla, intent upon the preparation of food, after a last swift glance at Sal scuttled off ahead of them.

But Robert Cushman paused a moment, looking around. He whispered something to William Bradford, whose eyes instinctively flicked toward Sal. Then the governor shook an impatient head, and hurried the newcomer along.

By this time the second boatload was being landed. The vessel was Fortune, 55 tons, out of London, and she carried only thirty-five passengers, twelve of them saints, the rest strangers. She carried no supplies of any sort for New Plymouth—only new mouths to feed.

A few of the strangers were women—one, Goodwife Ford, barely got ashore in time to give birth to a baby—but most of them were callow young men, all unequipped, grumbling about the accommodations aboard of Fortune, and demanding to know where they should sleep and who would assign them bedclothes and when they would be given breakfast.

They had another question, those puling newcomers. Every third one, as he splashed ashore, was heard to ask: "Where's the pirate? We hear you have a pirate here?" Sal pursed grim lips. His name might not be on the records, but it was well known; the Mayflower mariners had seen no need for silence, and Sawn Matthews's babbling alone would have been enough.

Yet this question embarrassed Sal less than it did some of the others. "Boyd's no pirate," a few growled. "He's a privateer—or he used to be." Sal smiled to himself.

There was one indignant lad who fairly stamped his foot in vexation when he learned the size of the ration he would thereafter receive and the skimpiness of the slop chest upon which he might occasionally draw.

"What *have* these people got, then?" he squealed.

Sal swung about, and grasped the front of the boy's doublet with both hands, all but lifting him from the ground.

"Listen, Pimples, I'll tell you what they've got," Sal said. "*Courage!*"

As he strode away, Sal heard a long, wobbling, sibilant exhalation; and he was later to learn that Pimples, when he had been told that his accoster was Salathiel Boyd the notorious pirate, almost fainted.

Sal decided to leave all present military tasks to his captain, the already overworked Miles Standish. There would be loquacious seamen aboard of Fortune as well; and it was bad enough for the report to get back that one of Oosterlinck's men was being harbored in New Plymouth just like a human being, without the additional information that the same sea thief actually was a sergeant, second in command of the colony's "army."

He wouldn't be missed right now, he reckoned. Everybody was busy.

Indeed, there was so much bustle up and down the Street that he felt pushed aside, and to get out of the way he leapt Town Brook and struck out across the stubble of a cornfield to where the forest rose as a black wall—but a wall farther from the settlement than it had been a year ago, and much less terrible to behold.

It was cool in there, and quiet, soothing. The slithery small sounds that he loved were all around him again. He walked a long time, aimlessly. Oak leaves and dry acorns crinkled under his feet. A hare skittered away, popeyed, and he waved to it. A partridge rose with a clatter of wings and a thin screechy throat-sound. On the trunk of a tree to his left a woodpecker went rat-a-tat-tat-tat, then paused to cock its head and beady eye at Sal, who thumbed his nose, grinning.

Sal could have run. He knew enough about the forest so that even in this season he could subsist for several days, and from the description Squanto had given him he was sure that he could reach Sowans, where he might throw himself on the mercy of Massasoit, the big chief Yellow Feather, offering his services as a liaison man, a sort of ambassador, a white Hobomok. Doubt-less the fathers of New Plymouth would be glad to attest, with clear consciences, that Salathiel Boyd was out of their hands and could not be forced from the protection of Massasoit without danger of a war that might obliterate the colony. Sal was sure of this, and it amused him. Humming, he wandered on. The New World, he reflected, was very fair.

When he returned to the cornfield, and was seen emerging from the forest, near sundown, sundry men ran out to tell him that Governor Bradford and others requested his presence in the Common House.

He nodded amiably. He had expected this.

"I'll be right there," he said.

Chapter Fifty-two

First, and before there was a word of explanation, or even introduction, Deacon Cushman had to recite a long tearful prayer over Salathiel, as though Sal had been a fallen woman. Sal, who a year ago would have snarled, took this meekly, standing with his head lowered, his feet together, hands clasped before him; and when it was ended at last he said "Amen" as loudly as the most pious of them.

They took him into their confidence, which pleased him. They read him the whole of Thomas Weston's letter: they even offered to permit him to read it himself, but he declined, pleading that he was slow.

It was a long disagreeable letter, a scolding letter, irate. Weston appeared to be much more concerned with his own and his friends' money than he was with the health and well-being of the colonists. He insisted that his terms for altering the contract—terms turned down in Southampton, but he said that he had not dared to tell his associates of that refusal—be met immediately. Otherwise, he pursued, shrilly, he could promise no kind of support. He was furious because they had kept Mayflower so long, and allowed her to return empty.

" 'That you sent no lading in the ship is wonderful,' " he wrote, as William Bradford read it aloud, " 'and worthily distated. I know your weakness was the cause of it, and I believe more weakness of judgments than weakness of hands. A quarter of ye time you spent in discoursing, arguing, and consulting' " —Sal, who smelled letters from the strangers here, could not suppress a smile, but he didn't think that anybody saw it— " 'would have done much more, but that is past.' "

William Bradford folded the letter and put it down. He must have read it many times, like a medieval monk who scourges himself.

"What do you say to this, Boyd?"

"I'm not a man of business, Governor. I'd just say that it must be much more comfortable there than it is here."

"Yes . . ."

"And that you made a very bad bargain with a very nasty person."

"That may be so, but we *did* make it. And without supplies— Well, if he wishes to forswear us we'll starve. Legally, I mean. With no laws broken."

"Excepting the laws of common decency," said Sal.

"And those of God," amended Deacon Cushman.

"Well then," said Sal, "if I was you I'd do whatever he said. I might feel like knocking his teeth down his throat, where they belong, but I'd do what he said—as long as I had to."

"We have other things to consider besides our personal feelings, of course."

"Of course," cried Sal, mildly annoyed. He spread his hands. "But you didn't call me in here to read letters to me. What else did this—this *putra madre* want?"

"Who?"

"Well, this man Weston."

There was some silence, and they studiously refrained from looking at one another—or at him.

"Oh, come, come," cried Sal. "He said—he said it privately, I suppose—he said you must send me back, didn't he?"

"Well, he did."

"He said," Deacon Cushman took it up, "that one pirate in a colony would be like one rotten apple in a barrel—it would spoil all the others."

"He did, did he?" muttered Sal. "What does he know about pirates? Have I spoiled anybody here?"

"He said that once your presence in New Plymouth became known it would be an invitation to others engaged in the same profession to try to make this their headquarters. Or even if they didn't, he said, the merchant adventurers would fear that they would—and they wouldn't invest another penny."

"So," said Sal, "you either ship me back or he washes his hands of you?"

"I'm afraid that that's about it."

Elder Brewster interposed.

"To lose Master Boyd, who has been so kind, would break our hearts, every one of us. If he went to join the Wampanoags couldn't we contend that he was out of our jurisdiction?"

He might have argued this further, for it was clear that the others, having had the same thought, wavered; but Sal shook a vigorous head.

"Live with those illiterates? No, thank you."

"But, Boyd, if you—"

"My masters, no more, pray. I'll go back. I am not accused of murder, I take it? Or piracy? There's no royal warrant out for my arrest?"

"Well, Oosterlinck and his men were cleared, at Plymouth. But they've not lingered there, of course. How it would be with you alone I don't know."

William Bradford had been staring hard at Sal. Possibly he was thinking that here was the man who all but lost his own life in an attempt to save that of Dorothy. Possibly it was a matter of abstract justice in his mind, or one of simple humanity. He was strangely moved when he cried out:

"Boyd, do you realize what this might mean, if you go back?"

Sal did not bow. You didn't bow to separatists: they might think it papistical. But he did go to the door, where he turned.

"My job's done anyway. I've trained a couple of lads enough so that they can do the work, and I'll lick 'em into shape while we're loading the Fortune. No, don't you worry about me."

With a tip of a forefinger he touched his Adam's apple.

"This is a neck that was meant for a knife, not a rope."

He opened the door.

"Now, if there's nothing else you want—"

Chapter Fifty-three

She came to his house that night. He did not hear her step, for she could be as quiet as any cat, but he heard with a start the scratch of her fingernail on the piece of canvas that served as a door, and he sat up, catching back his breath.

"I—I'll be right there," he whispered.

How he could tell that it was Priscilla Mullins he didn't know, but know it he did, and at the time he did not even wonder about this.

With hasty hands in the dark he put on his shoes.

Captain Standish and John Alden were down in the Common House exchanging snippets of gossip with the fresh arrivals, and Hobomok that very afternoon had started for Sowans with the news of the arrival of Fortune, so that Sal had the Hill House to himself. Doubtless she would not have dared to come, otherwise.

She wore that dress of light, bright French gray that he liked so much: it showed almost white in the moonshine, and her face too showed white, the eyes enormous.

"You're going away," she cried, even before he could greet her.

"It's best."

He heard a very small sob, which she tried to gulp. Her head was lowered. Though he did not touch her, he thought that he could feel the prickling of her skin all over.

"Is it because of—me?" she whispered.

"Partly. I sure couldn't go on seeing you every day unless I could have you. And if we got married it wouldn't be a real marriage."

"Why not?"

"Well, because even this man Cushman who came today isn't a minister of God."

"Maybe in my eyes he is."

"You'd only be half of us," he pointed out, "if we got married. And I'd fret. I know I would. I know myself."

She was silent a little while, her hands twisting and untwisting before her as though she would have reached out to touch Sal but lacked the courage. As for him, he wanted to put his hands on her shoulders, but he too was afraid.

"It's almost like I had a wife already. No, I haven't," he added hastily as he saw her head jerk, "but it's sort of the same, me being a pirate. It's something that'd always be with me, something I can't cut off any more'n I could cut off a wife. Only, a wife would die, sooner or later. My past never will. I—I can't fasten that past on you, Priscilla."

She said nothing, and with a great effort he did put his hands upon her shoulders, feeling her start as he did so. They were trembling—the shoulders, that is. But the hands weren't steady either.

"The reason I didn't go back on the Mayflower was because I still thought then that I could—well, get over you. Get used to you. I know better now. And these fools we're surrounded with here, they needed me then. They don't any more. Look what's come! Look at those beefwits! And have ye heard what the moneymen have to say about me? This is a different place from what I thought it was going to be, and it's getting more different every day. If this was Heaven I'd believe it, with you here. But it isn't. And I'd never be able to stand such a life, even if I was married to you."

He cleared a cautious throat. He had been lying, he knew; and he believed that he had done well; but it was an edge he stood on, a verge.

"Think of this, too: It isn't as if you was completely alone. Sure you've got to have a husband. But you will, soon enough. After all, there's nothing wrong with young Alden."

"He's a lout," listlessly.

"No, I don't think so. He's just not certain of himself, like he would be if you was his wife. He's the way I was about a year ago, so I know. Whenever he don't know what to do next he gets scared, and then he wants to hit somebody. But he'll grow up. *I* did, and there's no reason why he shouldn't."

He slid his left hand across her shoulders, and with his right hand he lifted her chin so that her face was uptilted to him. He kissed her for a long while.

"Good-by, Priscilla," he muttered.

She broke away, and stumbled down the slope to Elder Brewster's house. She was like a white shadow in the moonlight. She was like a ghost.

Chapter Fifty-four

What the boys in the forecastle of Meermin would have thought, had they watched this scene on the shore, Sal didn't dare to imagine.

Everybody prayed for him. Most of them were weeping. He himself wept, the tears tickling his cheeks.

This was something over a month after Fortune's arrival, and sundry things had happened at the colony of New Plymouth in that time, including a marriage.

To one side, above the boulder, those who had but lately come, the ones from Fortune, a ship that was about to start back, stood in a puzzled group, marveling that all this fuss should be made about a criminal, an outlaw; but they said nothing.

After prayers the first settlers came to Sal, as he stood ankle-deep in water, preparing to step into the longboat, and one by one, sobbing, they wrung his hand. Then they lined up along the shore, intoning the Twenty-third Psalm, which swelled as others joined them there.

"The Lord is my shepheard, I shall not want.
He maketh me to rest in green pasture, and leadeth me by
  the still waters.
He restoreth my soul—"

William Bradford, that bleak man, that painfully conscientious man, gaunt, slab-sided, earnest, held Sal's hand a little longer than most.

"Brother Boyd, you make me feel an ingrate. We could still sway them. You could remain. Let me call another meeting, and—"

"No, no. I've made my decision. It didn't take long."

"But after what you've done for us—"

"Governor, it's no use. A man can't hide. You know that."

"A man can't hide from the wrath of God, no. But the agents of the King might be different."

"Governor, I'm shocked. You, uh, you don't think much of the King, now do you?"

"No."

"Well, I do. I trust him."

They were silent a moment, Bradford still holding Sal's hand. At last:

"She—she did call out for help, didn't she, Boyd?"

Sal pretended to bristle.

"Sure she did! Listen, Governor, are you calling me a damn' liar?"

"No, no! And—thank you. God bless you."

He turned away, to join the others on the bank.

"—and leadeth me in the paths of righteousness for his
        Name's sake."

William Brewster's face was a spray of tiny white wrinkles, like a pane of glass that had been shivered but not smashed. His eyes were the blue of the sky on a happy day. He smiled, which was sunshine.

"You greeted me in anger, that first night, son. I pray that we don't part in any such spirit?"

"Before the Creator, Elder, I love you! I love you!"

"If you'd only stay. There isn't a man here who wouldn't—"

"Please! Let's talk sense when we have so little time left. Speak my farewells to your good wife, sir. And—take care of that girl."

"Girl?"

"Missus Alden."

"Oh, I will. I will. God go with you, son."

"Yea, though I should walk through the valley of the shadow of death, I will fear no evil—"

Miles Standish was bluff, as became a soldier.

"Good-by. You're an ass to go, but I wish I had more like you."

"Good-by, Captain. Say a prayer for me sometimes—but don't let anybody see that rosary."

"—for thou art with me: thy rod and thy staff, they comfort me."

Even John Alden pushed through the crowd and offered his hand, which Sal grasped joyfully.

"Good-by, Boyd. I'm glad we didn't fight, after all."

Sal grinned right into his face.

"Oh, I'm not so sure. It might have done us both good."

"Thou dost prepare a table before me in the sight of mine adversaries:

Thou dost annoit mine head with oil, and my cup runneth over."

And then there was Priscilla standing there. She too was weeping. The tears did not break but hung in her eyes, glittery, as she looked up at him.

"I brought you this," she said. "My father's Book. So that you can go on by yourself."

"Thanks. I'll go on. But it was better doing it with you." Reverently, even lovingly, he touched the Bible she had given him. "You've handed me heaps," he muttered. "A great deal more than I can ever tell you about." He wiped his mouth, for he was nervous. "Well, I—I wish it could have been different, with us."

"So do I."

Then she went away, her head held up, to join the others, standing by the side of her husband.

"Doubtless kindness and mercy shall follow me all the days
   of my life—"

Salathiel Boyd climbed into the boat. His feet from immersion in the water were so cold that he could hardly feel them, but his face was aflame.

"Well, come on, whoresons," he yelled to the oarsmen. "What the bloody hell are you waiting for—the second coming of Christ?"

He turned, standing, to catch the last of the psalm. Town Brook pittered importantly, flecks of ice along its edges. The shocks of stacked Indian corn, a dull yellow-brown, were iridescent now with frost. A few sere leaves stubbornly clung to the oaks, and the pines were so dark a green as to show black against a rat-gray scowling sky.

"—and I shall remain a long season in the house of the
   Lord."

Salathiel Boyd raised both hands, the palms out.

"Amen," he cried. "Amen."

www.ingramcontent.com/pod-product-compliance
Lightning Source LLC
Chambersburg PA
CBHW050355260626
47156CB00003B/733